Coast

matthew branton

BLOOMSBURY

BY THE SAME AUTHOR

The Love Parade
The House of Whacks

First published in Great Britain 2000
This paperback edition published 2001

Bloomsbury Publishing Plc, 38 Soho Square, London WID 3HB

A CIP catalogue record for this book
is available from the British Library

ISBN 0 7475 5217 7

10 9 8 7 6 5 4 3 2 1

Printed in Great Britain by Clays Ltd, St Ives plc

Volenti non fit injuria.
You play, you pay.

– legal maxim.

It started the day the Indian boys fell out of the sky.

I don't know if anyone saw them. Can you imagine? Drivetime, late July; you come out of the cleaners with a summer suit over your arm, thinking about closing your fist round a cold one the moment you hit home, thinking about the sundeck; you glance up to check the angle of the sun, see how long you've got; and suddenly there are two bodies coming at you like extreme-freefallers with boundary issues, whirling down out of the blue like outsize sycamore pods, dark shadows against the sky. But maybe I'm imagining too much; they would've gone foetal as they froze to death, so they probably just fell like cartoon anvils. Either way, they punched a hole in the High Street big enough to lose a Ka in.

Summer in that town, you couldn't forget you lived on a flightpath. I can't picture a blue August sky there that isn't strafed with aerosol vapour trails: shining jets dopplering overhead, stacked at layered altitudes for Gatwick, Heathrow, Stansted. My town is the one you fly over, as you climb or descend, the one that makes you turn to your seatmate and say, 'I can't believe so many people have pools.' That's us; there wasn't much else to the place, which is why what happened that day was so freaky.

The boys fell out of the sky, they hit the ground . . . and then nothing happened. No cops, no fire trucks, no move-along-ma'ams. It was one of those towns that are too loaded to have much in the way of civic machinery. The JobCentre, for example, had shut down fifteen years before (so my father once told me, with not a little pride) to be replaced by a pinboard in the rarely open library. The local police knocked off at five o'clock, since their burglary and car-crime work was handled by security companies hired by residents' associations. That summer, one gang of enterprising chavs liberated twenty barrels of Caffrey's from the coldroom of a newly bankrupt café-bar, rolling them down the High Street in the secure knowledge that it would take twelve minutes for a cop car to get there from the nearest open station, even if someone could be arsed to notify them.

So when the boys came out of the blue there were no heliographing sirens, no crime-scene tape, no diverted traffic. Not for the first half-hour or so anyway. Someone must've called the cable news, because there was a camera crew in position twenty minutes before the police; but mostly they just called each other. However much you think no one talks to anyone else in that kind of town, it swiftly became obvious that there were functioning networks of one kind or another at work here – golf buddies, crèche mums, twelve-steppers – because more and more people came to gawp, until by half past seven it seemed like the whole town was there, me included. Everywhere I looked there were faces that seemed familiar – from primary school fêtes, from firework displays – but that I hadn't seen mob-handed like this for ten years. I remember remarking to myself, in that smartmouth way you can excuse when you're a kid, that it took bodies falling out of the sky to get people out of their houses and onto the streets of a town like they lived there.

The day it started was not a day like any other; this I can be sure of because I remember it. I can tell you everything that happened, because it was one of those days you wish weeks away waiting for. I didn't get up until well into the breakfast shows, but that was more to make the morning shorter than anything else. On school days I had to be out of the house by seven if I was going to catch an hour at the gym before registration; but this was summer holidays, and an extra hour in bed meant that I'd miss the commuter rush between six and eight, and that by the time I came out there'd only be a few hours left to get rid of before I found out whether we were on for that afternoon.

That was all I cared about. It was a brilliant morning, the roads almost clear in the lull between drivetime and the ferrying of kids to daycare or Kumon, but I was too preoccupied to enjoy it much. By the time I got back from the gym my dad had gone, but it was still way too early; I put his breakfast stuff in the dishwasher, then got myself some juice, tried to watch some kids' programming but couldn't concentrate. The cleaner came on Mondays and Fridays, so I checked to see if there was enough in the laundry bin to constitute a load; there was, and I filled the machine, emptied the lint tray in the dryer, then put it on an economy program. This barely advanced the clock at all, so I went out to do the lawn while I waited for the delivery from the superstore. I was actually getting a bit hacked off by now – it wasn't difficult to appreciate the irony that this was my last school summer holiday ever and here I was wishing the hours away – so I took it out on the Flymo, but even when I was finished there was still an hour to go.

The superstore van never came before twelve, was the problem; during term-time the guy would leave it in the garage and my dad would drop back whenever he was free, but in the holidays it was my job. Ordinarily I wouldn't have minded; I quite enjoyed sifting through all the crap my father ate, and there was a time when I'd even look through his *FHM* or *GQ* or whatever was new that week, check out the flesh; but that day I was anxious to get round to Alita's and find out whether it was going to happen that afternoon or not. Obviously the best thing would have been to go to the superstore and do the shopping myself, but you have to give them forty-eight hours' notice if you want to cancel your delivery. I hadn't known there was a chance of a session until the night before, when Alita had called to say the candyman had come and that there was a good chance Talya's mother was going to be out for most of the next day. So I hung around, rewatched some Jerry, replayed some *Silent Hill*, with one eye on the window. When he finally did show I let him leave it in the garage as though I was out, so as not to have to get stuck talking to him – this particular delivery guy was a redundant cab driver and he missed having a captive audience – then, when the coast was clear, I swiftly whacked the salad in the fridge and my dad's stuff in the freezer.

As soon as I was done, I ran up to Alita's. Technically she lived next door, but since her house was up on the road and ours was set back seventy metres or so, at the end of a driveway that ran down the side of her house, it wasn't as convenient as you'd think. There was a short cut, pioneered when we were kids, through the hedge that lined our drive and over her back lawn, and this was the route I took, letting myself into the kitchen. I stuck my head out into the hall and hollered upstairs for her; on the third shout, her face appeared over the top of the balcony and winked.

'We're on,' she said.

Alita and me learned the facts of life from my parents' pornography; we'd thought, until we were ten or so, that you needed one man at each end of a woman in order to accomplish sex. If you could have seen us an hour later in Talya's lounge, you could've been forgiven for thinking we hadn't moved on at all.

Take your pick: imported video montage or late-night cable softcore. Overbright lights, shiny-slick flesh looking rubbery and unreal in close-up; or the action off-camera, principals' heads (where do they get these people?) filling the screen instead, kissing *myong-myong-myong*, jaws working on automatic, camera drifting off to focus on a window or mirror instead, like the guy was a retard on Ritalin.

Either way, I need you to work with me here. My reception is a little fuzzy, and I can't help it. It was an unavoidable side effect. You had to do the drugs to be up for it, but the drugs stopped you remembering too much. It was like, all the big moments of my life so far – when Shana sat in my birthday cake, when Goofy put his arms around me, when my dad let go of the saddle and I was riding, no stabilisers, gathering speed down the grassy bank – all of those, someone was catching with a camcorder; and now, when I try to remember the moment, it's the video I see, not the view that I had from behind my eyes. It's the same with those sessions of ours that summer. We had to do crystal meth to be up for it – it was both the facilitator and the point, since we wouldn't have been getting it on in front of each other without it – but when you've got a meth swerve on, it wipes the game off your memory card as you come down.

Which complicated things. Part of the justification for doing it was that you knew there were thirty years coming to you, at the other end of your life, where you weren't going to be able to do, only remember. So what do you do? The answer seemed obvious: you store up memories against that day. You do everything you possibly can, so you won't think, when it's too late, *if only*. When you're seventeen, you can use this to justify most things that you do. The trouble is, if you do them on crystal meth, it's like flipping an Etch-A-Sketch; you can still see vague outlines, but mostly it's generals, not specifics. I could see the irony of this at the time, but being a smart-arse doesn't get you off: I went ahead and did it anyway.

So what can I say? Spin the wheel and get: Asia – seventeen, tan, developed – on her hands and knees, dirty-blonde braids splayed over her dancer's back, breasts swaying beneath her. Me on my knees behind her, my buddy Jojo lying face-up underneath. Euan – buff, six-one, buzzcut – kneeling in front of her, Talya on her side, craning her neck to fit her head between my and Jojo's legs; Alita pushing her face – the sexy kind that would look either geeky or beautiful on a boy – into the gap at the top of Talya's thighs. All of us so corn-fed and long-term aerobicised that every muscle was like pulled caramel under the skin. Spin the wheel again and rearrange us; do it once more for luck, and then a dozen times more, and the picture will probably start to emerge. Beyond that, I'm winging it. I can't remember.

The one thing I can be sure I did was to glance over at Alita every now and then, to see if anything anyone else was doing to her seemed to be something she specially liked; who made her come hardest, whether it was person- or context-dependent. Euan was bigger than me or Jojo, and I'd been sure he'd be the man with the girls; but it turned out that, after the first few times he'd knocked their ovaries, which they said was as painful as getting kneed in the balls, they made him go easy on them. He always had to keep some control, whereas I never did. Pornography can lie to you, it just goes to show.

The part that stays with me is the part before we tweaked up; knowing that now we might just be a bunch of dorky teens sitting around someone's lounge while their mum was at work, but in five minutes' time we'd be doing what people who've done everything else dream about. That was the best part. The worst was the next morning, especially after the first few times; when your meth head was gone and you had to face each other and try to be normal again, knowing that we'd done what we'd done all the while; I remember thinking once, I don't have the people skills for this. That and the guilt, on the in-between days, when it seemed beyond crazy that we were doing this; that it was the kind of thing you ought to save for when you were tired of normal sex, and like, we were seventeen.

At the same time, being so young made us want to do it. If we felt bad about it, it only made another part of us feel defiantly good about it, like you do with your first really effective pornography. I was a seventeen-year-old bloke and, for all my gym and UV work, that's something most women cross the street from; yet this was sex, mad sex, wilder than I ever dreamed of; I wasn't going to turn it down. Once I knew about crystal meth, I couldn't forget it was there. I couldn't pretend it didn't exist; and on the days I wasn't doing it, I was prepared to do almost anything to make sure that everyone else was as up for the next time as I was.

This was a lot of the time, since we had a far from regular supply. The candyman was Alita's little brother, who cooked it up in their loft conversion with his science-geek sidekick Harper. They'd been making it all summer, but, in the same way they used to give LSD to soldiers, it had taken a while to find out what it was for. When they made their first batch, from a recipe picked up in a chatroom from some guy in Sydney, they tweaked up on a sample bowl and then spent the next eight hours methodically labelling everything in their den. When they were done it looked like it had snowed Post-it notes; and then they did another bowl, and put every Post-it onto a spreadsheet, then cross-referenced the entire contents of the room for resale value, country of origin, chewability, and possible relation to the space programme: golfballs scored ten for their aerodynamic pimpling; golf shoes scored nada, unless they had velcro fastenings.

The point was, they correctly deduced (prompted along by antipodean e-mails), that this wasn't the only application for the shit; it wasn't like, if you took it at a party, you'd start sticking Post-its onto the dancers. What it really did was give you a kind of mental magnifying glass, so that whatever jumped out at you from your immediate environment became the sole purpose of your existence for the next eight hours or so. If there was loud music where you were tweaking, then you'd dance; if there were other horny teens tweaking with you, then you'd all go to it like bunnies with commitment issues. Bonus, it gave you almost superhuman powers to keep doing what you'd zoomed in on. For us, this meant guys could repeat, keep going almost indefinitely. An early experiment of Jamie's, featuring a stack of pornography and a bowl of Billy (the codeword they gave to crystal, after the versatile movie star of the nineties), resulted in him practically needing skin grafts, after he'd whipped his dingus for nigh on nine hours. He was walking bow-legged for a month.

So we all made sure to take precautions. We were careful

to change position fairly often, because if you didn't you'd just hump and hump till you strained your muscles practically off the bone. We'd warm up with some yoga stretches while the meth kicked in; we made sure to use lots of lube also, and tweaking sessions were inevitably prefaced by one of the girls going to the superstore for a trolleyful of K-Y, or the knock-off own-brand equivalent. Alita had got so many points on her reward card from buying tubes of lube that she was going to give her mum a flight to Barbados for Christmas. I bet that screwed up their market research ('Willya look at these readings? Quick! Turn over all of aisle six to sex grease!').

It's not even like we were druggies. We were the exception in our town. We made a point of it, of being wholemeal teens. It was our parents who were the hash-heads, still on an E-spree ten years after it was cool, still feeding the needs – clothes, parties, skeletons of Rizla packets down the back of the sofa – picking up where they'd left off, once they figured that the having-kids thing needn't interfere with their extended adolescence. Us first-time teens, meanwhile, had to find something else; until meth, we chose dishwasher-squeaky. If any of us had got onto a game show, our question categories would've had to focus around PlayStation, inept pulling strategies and the product ranges of the KFC or the 24-7 if we were going to score any points at all. We got our highs from life, and PepsiMax/Häagen-Dazs floats. I swear, if there'd been a phone poll for the kids most likely to turn into drug fiends, we would've figured in the lowest percentile. This was our rebellion. You ask yourself, do you really want to do what your parents do? Apart from making a heap of money? And you answer with whatever, in your case, is going to get you through.

It was like when they catch a serial killer and the neighbours all say, 'He was such a quiet man, a polite man.' If you're the least likely, you're the most susceptible. Until crystal meth, drugs were a joke to us. We used to rent from the Britflick section at Blockbuster and FF through the bits where they went to skin or shoot up, because you knew that was all that was going to happen till the next scene – like, wow, they're sticking cigarette papers together, how gritty and explicit! It was all a bit lame. Drugs were everywhere in our town – lots of money, lots of drugs – but because they weren't some rare commodity, some prize peccadillo, they were just another choice, and one you looked cool to turn down. Naturally we'd done this and that when we were fourteen or so, but (as Alita had said at the time) E and draw make you hornier than you really want to be when you're that age; don't do them, and you won't get so worked up. That'd been all right for a while, but then we were of an age where things were on the verge of getting complicated. And suddenly meth was there, taking the strain, keeping it just sex, and us just friends.

I can't tell you the relief. Already we should've been drifting apart, and we knew it. We were hitting the time when the reasons-to-go pile starts to teeter over the reasons to stay. We'd buddied up, like kids do, from way back: Alita lived at the top of our drive, Jojo was next to me on the register at kid school, Euan was on a football team with Jojo, Shana used to baby-sit Asia, Asia's parents were tight with Talya's. So we fell into renting videotapes and popping microwave corn together when our parents were out on weekend nights (which was most of them), holding sleepovers when they weren't, hanging out at the superstore café after homework, hitting each other's dads' home offices (more RAM than in our own rooms) for mammoth *Civ II* sessions. We'd all been out with each other – holding hands and hickies, nothing more – but had managed not to let it lousy up the group dynamic; but by that summer we were as ripe for going our separate ways as crisp twenties in a cash-machine feed stack.

We were at the age when everything conspires towards it. My sister Shana had counselled me, at length and with relish, that this was going to be the case.

'Your little losers' club has got six months, tops,' she'd notified me on my seventeenth birthday, six months before. 'You start driving, you say sayonara to the support group. Horizons widen, bro. Mobility feeds frustration.'

She'd been totally wrong, but then she couldn't have known about crystal meth, which was being synthesised by Alita's brother even as she spoke. It turned the trajectory of late-teendom off-track for us. Not only was it Welcome to the Wonderful World of Non-Solitary Sex, but hey bonus, here's something that makes it a thousand times better than it is for everyone else. We tweaked for the first time in the Easter holidays that year. Alita had walked in on her brother and Harper when they were having a meth-fuelled stroke session, and had blackmailed them into giving her some, whereupon she'd found herself in on the five-finger fiesta almost without realising what she was doing. She'd laid a bowl on the rest of us (after, Jojo and I suspected, a few girls-only sessions round at her place) when we all went out to the country to skinnydip one weekend around Easter; we'd ended up going at it so long that we got sunburn, despite the factor 20.

As spring turned to summer, body fluids had turned out to be thicker than petrol, whatever Shana said. They were flying thick and fast in Talya's lounge that afternoon, I can safely say. Within a couple of hours of tweaking we'd all have come three or four times and, given the parameters of the possible, would've been in danger of getting both repetitive and sore. Besides, we'd had to spread the meth more thinly than usual, and it was starting to wear off. I remember that we were taking a brief rehydration break, passing round the Evian while still locked together when, out of the corner of my eye, I saw Asia, on her way to the kitchen for more water, flash one finger, two fingers, one finger again at Euan – one-to-one, from the pager code. He heaved out of Talya and made for the kitchen too.

'Hey, no fair,' said Talya, who'd clearly seen the signal also. 'Beside, Four of Clubs is going to be back in a minute. There isn't time.'

Four of Clubs was Talya's mother. We all called her it behind her back. When she was young, and even more credulous than she was when dealing with Talya these days, she'd been shopping for clothes in London when she was discovered in the street by a guy who ran a model agency. For a minimal investment of a few hundred quid, he offered to help her put together the portfolio she needed to get assignments; he even suggested he take the pictures himself, to maintain the kind of artistic control he insisted on for his most promising discoveries. So, for the cost of a few glib lines, a couple of rolls of film and the Café Rouge lunch he bought her, he got three hundred quid from her ATM, a shag and a few dozen pictures of her in the buff. He sold the latter to a maker of novelty tits-out playing cards, and that's what she ended up as – four of clubs. I think the most embarrassing thing for her wasn't losing the money, or even having to face up to everyone after mouthing off about becoming a model. I think it was her position in the pecking order; not the frilly white-nylon heights of the picture cards, nor even the soft-focus frolic with long-stemmed rose or garden hose; the poor cow was right down in the low numbers, shouldering up to the other proprietors of two fried eggs and a face like a welder's thumb against a background of greasy, raw brick. Of course, we'd all passed round a pack and knocked one out over her nonetheless; it's not often you see someone you know.

'She was showing four houses after lunch, but she oughta be through by now,' said Talya. 'Can't we go to your place, Euan?'

Euan had the best pool.

'Sure,' he said, 'but my brother's there', and we all groaned; his brother was a total pain.

'Whatever. I'm getting sore anyway,' Talya said, but I was pretty sure the only thing she was sore at was Asia trying to go off with Euan. It was a major ground rule that one-on-ones were not part of the deal. At least, they weren't as far as I was concerned. I was pretty sure that if I'd asked one of the girls to pair off with me they would've told me to fuck off. Jojo told me he was with Talya once and had tried to get it on with her when all they were narcoticised with was Banoffee pie. 'Duh,' she'd said. 'I only do it to make the drugs work.'

On the way over to Euan's we stopped by the 24-7 to pick up a few litres of Sunny D to chug by the pool. None of us had much idea of what the long-term effects of meth might be (attention-deficit disorder? arthritis?) but it seemed unquestionable that vitamin-enriched citrus-style beverages were the antidote. Euan's younger brother, a creepy little piece of shit named Declan, troughed everything that wasn't locked up in that house, so we picked up some Pringles and Doritos too. Declan didn't look up from *Tomb Raider 4* as we trooped through the playroom – honing his skills in the belief it was going to help him pull someday ('You can do all of the Catacombs just using pistols? Ooh baby baby') – and we'd been out by the pool for maybe twenty minutes before he sauntered out and proclaimed to us that some weird shit was going down in the middle of town.

'What shit?' said Euan.

'It's on the news,' Declan said, licking his prepubescent eyes over the girls' halter tops. 'They're showing by the Blockbuster.' He sauntered back in to the darkness beyond the patio doors. Euan frowned but got up and followed him; a moment later he stuck his head back outside.

'No shit!' he said. 'Who wants to be on TV?'

Ten minutes later we were there. It took so long, despite Euan decking it, because the road from the south side was screwed; about half a kilometre before the High Street started there were cars parked all over the road, literally just stopped and abandoned, like there was a convention for blind drivers with attention-span problems going on. We had to walk, which was a little difficult for us guys because we still had hard-ons from the crystal meth. The girls scampered on ahead, and we followed grimly, tucking ourselves vertically into our waistbands.

Finally we were there, working our way to the front of the crowd, then looking at the hole in the High Street with the same faces that had seen pre-Christian palaces in Mexico and sauntering Transvaal giraffes before we were even ten – wide eyes, chin down, too much lower lip. We were still pretty spun on the meth, but it would've freaked anyone out. The surface of the High Street had been pocked, hugely, as though it wasn't made of metalled tar at all, but that dry, green, squishy stuff you push flower stems into at cemeteries. Inside, along with the fascinating laid-bare infrastructure of cables and road strata, was a colourless, viscous matter spattered around. The word was that this was a flush from thirty thousand feet, but it didn't look like a dump to me. It looked like Godzilla had got a bad headcold and evacuated his snout, brickie-style, into some monster roadwork.

Asia turned to Jojo and said something I didn't catch. I looked around at the milling masses: men in sports sandals and cargo shorts like it was a uniform, women in top-whack sunglasses, crop-tops and sarongs, babies plonked fatly on their hips. There were camcorders clamped to a few faces – no doubt most people'd had cash registers ker-chinging in their ears on the way, visions of flogging the footage to cable dancing through their heads – but most had given up on the idea when they saw that not only had everyone else brought their Digicam, but there was very little to document for posterity anyway; once you'd panned over the hole a few times, let's face it, that was pretty much it. They let them dangle by their sides, lens caps tweedling at the ends of their cords. Talya sat down on the kerb and asked me if I'd get her a Diet Coke.

'I don't think they sell it here,' I pointed out. This was, after all, the High Street – the only shops were Cancer Researches, Sue Ryders, estate agents. 'Got some gum, though?' She took a stick, and I sat down next to her to chew companionably while we took in the crowd.

There wasn't much going down. People just shuffled their feet on the heat-tacky blacktop, not knowing what to say to each other beyond 'What happened?' and 'Search me.' The few who'd got their cars this far were scrolling their AutoSeeks with the doors open, looking for an FM-station newsflash that would tell us what the proper take on this was. Until it came, there wasn't much else to do. People looked vaguely for solace in shop windows, but the High Street was a no-show, a nowhere, a drive-through strip of service outlets (dry-cleaners, cash machines, copy shops) whose pull over, pick up and go dynamic was broken only by the odd sorry-looking charity shop or Irish pub conversion of one of the old banks. But after a little while I gradually became aware that people were talking, after a fashion; picking out faces in the crowd and collaring them, drifting into little knots and eddies like at barbecues.

That was when it happened. Maybe it was seeing so many people wandering around where they shouldn't be, maybe it was being down at kid level on the pavement, maybe it was just the meth. But something went off in my head like a firework, and if I hadn't already been chilling, it would've knocked me flat with the force of it. As it was, I might as well have stopped breathing, broken out in hives and had to Heimlich up my Orbit. I remember trying to tell Talya about it and not being able to make any sense, and being angry that I couldn't.

What chilled me was realising that this wasn't because of the drugs. It was because it was the strongest thing I'd ever felt. I didn't have much experience at articulating that stuff. Girls can do it because they spend all their time talking. Boys can't because, though they'd like to when push comes to shove, in the meantime they'd rather go one on one at *Tekken*.

What's the use? *Tekken* was what I suggested to Jojo, it sounded good to him, and, since some fire trucks had finally arrived to cordon the area off, we broke it up there.

Next morning, I'd pretty much forgotten about it. At eight a.m. I was down off the meth and up on the Stairmaster at the gym, as usual.

I knew you shouldn't go every day – your muscles need downtime, to repair and rebuild – but I enjoyed the structure it gave to my mornings, and the fact that my goals in there, as opposed to in real life, were relatively clearly delineated and attainable. The only other people there were the last of the commuters, in their moustaches and skimpy slit-thigh sateen shorts left over from when they went jogging once in the eighties; either they were oblivious to the mirrors on all four walls, or they genuinely thought that what worked for Linford Christie worked also for paunchy, hairy, chicken-legged white gits.

The others were due later. The gym, that morning, was our first regroup after the meth session. We'd given the superstore coffeeshop a miss the night before; we went there most nights around nine, for comfort cappuccinos and homework postmortems, but with the meth still spinning our systems, and cranked up to eleven by the weirdness in the High Street, the consensus had been to bomb out and sleep it off, meeting up at the gym juice bar next morning.

I'd woken up pretty feelgood – perky, wholesome and horny as I rescreened disjointed highlights of the previous afternoon, somewhere between sleep and waking, in the platinum-edged blackout of my room. When I flipped the blinds the sky was like that Windows background, and I hit the shower and drove to the David Lloyd complex with the aircon off and the sunroof rolled back; it was another rare day, but reality kicked in as I drove, making me too hyped up to enjoy it.

The previous day had been too unfair. The contrast between our easy-going meth session and then that freaky shit in the High Street had been too much. I just knew it would prompt some reality-checking when we met in the juice bar after our workouts, and it was going to be a toughie. We'd never discussed what we did with the meth, the dozen or so times we'd done it, and that was fine with me as long as we kept on doing it. But now it was coming to a head. That stuff in the High Street when we were still strung out had brought the facts into focus: we were doing drugs like lowlifes, and someone was going to point out that the madness had gone on long enough. I'd known from the start that this day was going to come, and I'd assumed that when it did everyone else – Jojo and Euan at least – would band together with me to keep the dissenter sweet. Now that the time had come, however, I wasn't so sure.

It was just after nine when I finished my cardiovascular and started my weights. The commuters, having wound themselves up to a pitch of white-lipped territoriality, had left to hit the insanely overcrowded trains to Cannon Street, and the place was filling up with mothers fresh from dropping the kids off at daycare. Mixed in with them I could pick out Alita at the pec fly, Talya doing stretches on the mats, and Euan and Asia on adjacent treadmills. We were the only ones really working; the mums spent most of their time doing warm-up rather than exercise, faddy stretches they'd learned in some step class ten years before, so we didn't have to wait for any machines. When Asia and Talya climbed up on the steppers across from me and commenced pounding away like fugitives, I hit the pec fly: partly so they could gab without my being in earshot, but mostly so that I could check out their bubble-butts as they stepped.

After forty minutes or so I hit the showers and then the juice-and-bagel bar, taking one of the avocado MDF tables by the window with my breakfast-in-a-glass – muesli, banana, bio-yoghurt, kiwi, apple and semi-skimmed blended together in a 440-ml beaker – while I waited for the others.

It was pretty busy. Whatever time of day I hit the place, OJ's always seemed to be buzzing with women, talking over juice, over salads, over cups of herb tea. It was probably the kind of thing that they used to do in the High Street before all the shops went, stopping each other and chatting; today's topic, catching snatches from the tables around me, was what had gone down in that nowhere zone the day before. The room was smoking with it, as were we when everyone finally showed.

'That was so fucking freaky,' said Alita, tearing off a bite of peanut butter and banana bagel. 'I had the worst nightmares ever. I'm never doing meth again.'

Straight into it: this was just what I'd been scared of. If she stopped doing it, then we all did; I caught Jojo's and Euan's eyes briefly and registered the same dismay that I felt.

'I'm serious,' she went on. 'When we were standing around that hole I didn't know if I was upset or scared or sad, or whether it was just the meth. I think we're doing too much.' There was a moment's silence, and she slimmed the bagel down some more as she looked round the table.

'Oh, c'moff it,' said Euan finally, jumping in with both feet. 'You're the one whose room's plastered with heroin-chic shit.'

'Those wasters do look pretty good,' said Talya, trying to break it.

'Bitch cheekbones,' agreed Asia.

'I mean it,' Alita persisted, putting down the bagel. 'When we were there I didn't know if I was feeling something real or if it was just the meth. It's no way to live. Think of all the stuff we're missing out on.'

'Think of what people who don't do meth are missing out on,' said Euan, winking lasciviously at Asia, who giggled and wiped Florida-style juice pulp from her lips with an OJ's-logo serviette.

'C'mon,' said Alita.

I needed to say something. My problem was, I didn't want to let this get out of hand, but I couldn't just shout Alita down: for one thing it'd be counterproductive, and for another I'd had a thing for her since forever and wanted her for myself some day. I tried to avoid contradicting her wherever possible.

'It was pretty awful,' I said lamely, passing the baton.

'No, it wasn't,' said Talya. 'We don't know anything about it except some guy fell out of an aeroplane. And no one knew who it was at the time so what's the difference? Even the cable news was saying it was a toilet flush for the first hour or so. We don't know who it was who died so what's there to feel bad about?'

'I know who it was,' said Euan. Everyone turned to look at him. 'I mean, I saw it in the newspaper before I came out,' he continued sheepishly. 'It was two Indian guys, stowed away from Calcutta. They hid in the undercarriage but when the wheels came down for landing . . .'

He demonstrated the stowaways' progress with a halved kiwi. 'Splat.'

'Gross,' said Asia.

Alita was silently fuming. There was an opportunity for Brownie points with her and I had to take it.

'I can hear what Alita's saying,' I said. 'It freaked me out.'

'Yeah, what happened to you?' said Talya. 'You really lost it for a minute back there.'

'I don't know,' I said. I really didn't. I'd had this kind of event back in the High Street there. It might have been the meth, though it wasn't usually very visual. Maybe it'd had something to do with being hunkered down with Talya on the kerb, but I'd had this blast from the past and it had zoned me out. Looking around at the crowds milling all over the High Street, where you were usually more apt to see tumbleweeds than people, I caught a total flashback of being there with my mother, way back, when the High Street was a place with shops where you went shopping. On a sliding scale of revelations – finding out how to jerk off, realising that not everyone in the world has your own best interests at heart – it doesn't sound much, but believe me, if I hadn't already been sitting on it, it would've knocked me flat on my arse.

It was a flashback to ten, twelve years before – the same milling throng, the same skyline – and I'd remembered how it used to be: no one with trolleys, but gripping clutches of carrier bags instead, baguettes drooping over the tops, because not everybody could park next to the supermarket. There wasn't room there, and some people had to park in places where they couldn't just push the trolley to the car. They had to walk along the street, saying hi to people, carrying their shopping; and that was because they were shopping in the High Street, before the superstore was built. It was like being in a dream sequence, and I'd realised that the drugs were still in my system and I didn't have the control to deal with this. I jumped to my feet, eyes wide, adrenal system in fight-or-flight; and then the getting up too quickly caught up with me, the sudden demand for blood deprived my brain momentarily, and I went down. Smacked my head, choked on my gum and generally did most of the things (short of wetting my pants) that a seventeen-year-old really wants to do with most of the town looking on.

'I don't know what it was,' I said to the table in the juice bar, trying not to go red. I'd sort of hoped everyone else'd had too much of a swerve on to remember it. 'Everything got a bit intense.'

'Yeah, well, it happens,' said Talya, 'but it wasn't your fault. We didn't know when we did the meth that something bad was going to happen. You can't spend your whole life party-free just in case something solemn goes down, you know? It's like, censoring porno because one moron might think that's the way it goes in real life.'

'But that's precisely why it is censored,' said Alita.

Talya thought about it a moment. 'The girl has a point,' she said.

This was getting worrying. I exchanged glances with Jo, and I saw the same fear that I felt: if they suddenly got carried away on some dumb girl-power trip, then that would be the end of our little scene. My mother had taught me that women will break their necks to duck out of what they really want if there's peer pressure involved.

'But it shouldn't be,' I said. 'I mean, if that's why you're gonna censor porno then why not censor music too, y'know?

So that you can't buy any CDs except soothing ones, in case someone puts something loud on in their car and it goads them into driving aggressively.'

'Bay's right,' said Asia. 'Really. You gotta lighten up and hope shit doesn't happen. I mean, it did yesterday and what a fucking tragedy, but it was nothing to do with us. Now, who's coming over to mine for a swim?'

There was a momentary lack of take-up. Her father refused to employ a gardener out of territoriality, but never got round to doing much himself: consequently Asia's pool was dirtier than her mother's daydreams.

'It's clean,' she protested, defensive but seeing the joke. 'Jackson did it.' Jackson was her brother, back from uni for the summer and working nights at the 24-7 services on the M25, two junctions along. 'He got stoned after work and I caught him obsessively skimming the pool at six this morning.'

'I don't have my costume,' said Talya.

'You don't need one,' said Euan, licking his eyes over her aerobicised midriff, and somehow pulling it off. Euan was the kind of guy who, if he was getting it on with a girl and she didn't want to go all the way, would gesture at his crotch and say, 'You can't leave me like this'. He reminded me of my father.

'Duh, yes I do,' Talya pointed out. 'No way am I skinny-dipping round there again. That creepy little fuck next door jerks off at his bedroom window.'

'Relax,' said Asia. 'I fed their cat when they were on holiday at Easter, so I checked out the view from the little pervert's room. The conifers are high enough this year to block him.'

'Cool. Like an organic NetNanny,' Jojo said, but I was the only one who got it.

'I'll pass,' Alita said. 'I have to go and clean at my aunt's. Summer job,' she explained to our blank looks.

'Drag,' said Asia.

'Not really. Her regular cleaner still does the place every morning. All I have to do is mess it up a bit to show I've been.' She shouldered her Karrimor.

'Want a lift?' I asked her. She didn't have a car because her father had left, not her mother.

'No, I can get a cab,' she said.

'It's no problem,' I said, a little too quickly. 'I have to get back for the superstore delivery anyway.'

'Whatever,' she said, and made for the door. I raised my eyebrows to the others – like, what's biting her arse? – but only when I was sure she wouldn't see, and followed her out into the too bright morning.

I held back in the car to begin with, gave her some space, let the bass do the talking as I drove. I had to get my own head round what was at stake. Until things actually happen, you can kid yourself they're not going to, but after what she'd just said, there was no doubt about it. She was about to call time on our little sessions, and if I didn't handle this carefully, it could turn out to be the beginning of the end.

I couldn't let that happen. We were more than halfway home before I asked, right out, if she was serious about quitting meth. I was prompted by a gap between tunes at a red light and by the fact that I really needed to know. If she were to follow through and stop doing meth, then the day when I had sole access to her action was probably closer; and, true, I had designs on hastening its dawn. But if she stopped doing meth, then we'd all have to stop too, and meth was what was keeping us together, by keeping everything else on hold. It was a toss-up between maintaining the present or moving on into the future, and this was not a choice I felt ready to make.

'I don't know,' she said. She seemed to want to say more so I hit the fade on the factory-standard stereo. There was an awkward silence. Truth was, we never really talked about it among ourselves; we just did it. The potential for disaster was kind of like getting into an affair when you're married and don't want not to be: you've seen it so much on tapes or TV that you know it can't end well, but thousands of people every day go ahead and do it anyway. My mother, for example.

The silence persisted until I was pulling into our street, when finally she sighed out loud. 'No,' she said. 'Probably not. You want to come in?'

'Sure,' I said, nonchalant as if the subject had been dropped.

'I gotta go char myself up,' Alita said as she closed the front door behind us. 'Jamie's in the loft if you want to say hi.'

I could take a hint, so I headed up.

Jamie was another reason why it was hard to ignore meth. I had a pretty good feeling that he and his buddy Harper were the only people making it this side of Melbourne or Manhattan, and if this was true, it meant that me, Alita and the rest were in some kind of a unique experiment, a focus group of six. Like, you see on the news or *TW* that Swindon or Telford or some other armpit has been selected to take part in a unique trial for electric money or butane cars or transgalactic teleportation or whatever, and you think cool, how unfair, knowing that however successful the experiment is, you won't get to see it where you live for a couple of decades, if ever. But that's what Jamie and Harper were doing to us. We figured we were the only kids in the country doing crystal meth, and how many things does a seventeen-year-old get to be unique about?

I was pretty sure we were the only ones, because I'd never seen anything about it in magazines or on TV. It made sense:

when you did ecstasy you went to clubs and bought CDs and clothes; look at my father, with his wardrobe that ran from smiley T-shirts and bandannas at the crushed end, through Burberry crews and vintage Adidas in the middle, to Calvin vests and fatigues at the more recent end, switching abruptly to Ralph and Hugo at the point where my mother left him. There was a whole industry around E, to the extent that you could be forgiven for thinking that the only point of it had been to make people buy clothes in weird feely fabrics and twenty kinds of moisturiser. But what would people buy if they all switched to crystal meth? CK lube? DKNY muscle rub?

Admittedly, it was possible that my dad's magazines were keeping quiet about it because it was a cognoscenti kind of thing; but then that's what they were still pretending E was, more than a decade after they started with it. They must've been choking for a change, surely; if people really were doing meth up and down the country, they'd run stories on it just out of fear that someone else'd beat them to it. Shana's old room would be full of day-glo paperbacks with titles like *Tweaked* and *Spun* instead of *SortEd* and *W@sted*. I'd searched online a few times, and Clinton called meth 'the new crack' in the late nineties, but I couldn't find a single reference to it on any UK-originated sites. Jamie and Harper might've been the first ones.

They fitted the profile. However sharp blokes are at fifteen, generally they don't do anything about it; there's far too much other stuff to do, such as perfecting your skate tricks or *Tekken* technique, as if those will be the headhunters' prized skills when you leave school. But Jamie and Harper were the kind of kids who, if they'd been born a decade earlier, would've got beaten up the whole time for being pencil-necked geeks; now NASDAQ had made geeks bankable, they still got beaten up by the same sorry white trash, but now it was because they were going to be successful.

I'd spent most of my free time since I was a kid at Alita's, and had been able to observe the little freaks first-hand. When they were five they were having typing-proficiency tests on their pre-Windows PC, seeing who could punch in the alphabet in less than three seconds and therefore grow up to be the fastest programmer. When mouses and icons came along a couple of years later they'd carry out hand-eye contests, seeing who could click on specific preselected pixels in a JPEG with the greatest accuracy. Their future, it was obvious even then, would not involve hot or noisy jobs, or the kind that make you feel you've passed your sell-by date before lunch every day. I had a suspicion that one day I'd brag that I used to know them and no one would believe me.

They weren't just bright, they did stuff too. Soon I'd be filling out my PCAS form, ruefully reviewing the two crappy Saturday jobs I'd done for about ten minutes in the last year when I could've been doing something both original and rewarding, if only I'd got round to it at the time. But they'd been at it since they were so high. I'd been wandering up to the loft conversion that was their domain for almost a decade.

When they were ten:

ME: What's up?

JAMIE: See this guy on my pinboard? That's the kid who bought the rights to www.ibm.com for forty dollars and sold it back to them for sixty thousand.

HARPER: We're trying to figure out what the buzzwords

of five years away are gonna be so we can register the rights now and sell them on. We're gonna be stinking, man, I tell ya.

JAMIE: Like, imagine if you'd bought www.badhair-day.com five years ago.

HARPER: Mother*fucker*!

When they were twelve:

ME: What's up?

JAMIE: This is a poetry generator for local newspaper obituaries. You know the adverts people put in?

> The days we shared
> When the sun did shine
> I wish you were still here
> Mother of mine.

HARPER: We're having problems getting it to put 'did' or 'do' or 'does' before every verb, though.

JAMIE: Which the punters seem to be hot for. 'The rain does fall, my heart does ache.' But we've based the program on a grammar-checker that really doesn't like it, and we can't figure out how to disable it without ripping its guts out.

JAMIE: We will if we have to, though. No mercy.

HARPER: Kick ass!

When they were fourteen:

ME: What's up?

JAMIE: See this?

(He hands me a brochure full of colour photos of 2.4 children-type families on mountain bikes, businessmen giving each other high-fives, wind farms silhouetted against the sunset.)

It's called stock photography. Someone figures out what the feelgood images of the next couple of years are, takes pictures of them and then sells them to newspapers to pad out the pages.

HARPER: We mean to be the guys who decide what's feelgood.

ME: C'mon, then, what you got? Hit me.

JAMIE: Boating. We think boats will be big in the future.

HARPER: Yachts will be hot.

Okay, bad example. But say most kids use the net to look at porno. Most adults only use it for porno. The internet is primarily a breast-viewing device. But if Jamie and Harper went to porno sites, it was to check out the spec provided by the host as a come-on to punters shopping around not only for barely legal teens but for faster data-stream rates and download times also. If you climbed the ladder to their den when they were connected to the net and heard 'My God! Willya look at that?', they were far more likely to be admiring the SCI Origin 200 servers and 9.5 megabytes-per-second delivery promised by CyberJugs than the hooters on the girls therein. Their hero was a jailed Columbian chemist named Alvaro Badillo. There was a big picture of him on the wall, along with 3-D atomic diagrams of some of the compounds he'd synthesised; elegant scaffolds of chlorides and cyanides inside which he'd stashed the cocaine molecule. Until the cops caught up with his chemistry, he was exporting it, liquid or solid, in every colour of the rainbow and in formats from printer's ink to jeans dyed blue with a cocaine-bearing concoction.

As I climbed the ladder now I could hear them arguing about Nikes.

'Hey,' I said. 'What's up?'

'Jamie's new ped-performance system,' Harper snickered.

'Fuck you, my mum bought them,' said Jamie.

'They look pretty sharp to me,' I said, conciliatorily, as I stooped to examine them. They were top-whack, state-of-the-art, limited edition. I would've been proud to own them if I'd been their age.

'They suck,' said Harper. 'They're so well-cushioned that they give you osteoporosis. You need regular shocks to your foot to lay down new bone material. One of the astronauts on Mir wore an insert in one boot that delivered regular shocks to his foot, and nothing in the other. After six months in zero gravity, the foot with the insert was the same, but the one that hadn't had impact shocks had lost bone mass. This is an important principle. It's instinctive to embrace progress, but there's no reason why it's necessarily good for us.'

'You sound like the news,' said Jamie. 'This is bad for you! Now this is! And now this!'

'But that's totally my point,' Harper remonstrated. 'You'd think, if you'd been there at the start of it, that information – the news – would be good for you. But do you know anyone now who'd dispute the fact that regular exposure to news reports stops you caring?'

'You sound like the news,' Jamie grinned.

'Up your hole with a jelly roll, bro',' Harper said, and turned to me. 'What can we do for you today, my man?'

'Just outreach,' I said, sinking into a beanbag and picking up a copy of *PlayStation World*. 'Alita's getting changed. I'll be outta here in two so enjoy me while you can.'

'How was the last batch of meth?' said Jamie.

'Okay,' I said guardedly. It was a little embarrassing to talk about with Alita's younger brother, even if he was the one who was cooking it up.

'We thought it was a bit speedy,' he said.

'We get the ephedrine from boiling down cough mixture, but they started giving us weird looks in the chemist so we had to get the knock-off brand from the superstore,' Harper explained. 'It's a different concentration so the yield's different. We've done all the calculus now but we winged it a bit at the time.'

'Seemed the same to me,' I said, pretending to examine some *GTA* cheats. 'I didn't know you still tested it out yourselves.'

They exchanged a glance, then turned back to their PC. This should've tripped a switch, but I had other things on my mind as I flipped through the magazine. I wanted to talk to Alita about the project that had occurred to me, and when she called up, I bid the boys later and went down.

Her door was ajar.

'You decent?' I called, pushing it open into a blacked-out room.

'Like you haven't seen it before,' she said. She was sitting up in bed wearing a Gap sweat top with her hair in a high pony. The room was thick with sweet smoke, and she took a hit on the fat joint between her fingers as I stood there. Seeing Alita smoking dope was like seeing a man on the cover of a lad's magazine.

'Seen anything green?' she croaked, holding it deep.

'Christ's sake, Ali, what're you playing at?'

She exhaled a long column of depleted smoke. 'I get really buzzy the day after meth. This takes me off fast-forward.'

I couldn't believe this. 'What about your mum?'

'You can't smell it if you've smoked it yourself,' she said. 'And she always blazes up in the car the moment she's out of work. Ashtray in her car's full of roaches. Besides, she won't be back till six.' She took another hit.

'I thought you had to go clean at your aunt's,' I pointed out.

She shrugged, blew out smoke. 'When she gets home and nothing's broken or messed up she'll just think I've got more efficient. Anyway, what is it with you? You keep talking like a bitch, I'm gonna have to fuck you like one.'

'Yeah yeah, promises,' I said and sat down on the bed, but inside I was freaked. When Alita had said she was in two minds about crystal meth, I assumed that this was going to be some kind of born-again deal. My mother got that way since my father caught her on the sofa with her yoga teacher and she ran off to India: body-as-temple, you are what you swallow. Smoking dope – mixed with *tobacco*, for God's sake, Christ knew where Alita had got that from – was hardly detoxing.

And besides, draw was just not done any more. We'd all started out pinching from our parents' stashes, in the same way as old-tyme kids used to sneak drinks from their parents' wineboxes or whatever; which was okay for a while, but by the time you're fifteen that kind of thing is a little less than cool. I mean, if you're a child, copying what your parents do may make you feel adult, but when you're an adult there's nothing more childish.

Usually Alita's room was one of my most centring places, full of olfactory reminders that she'd slept, sweated and chilled in there for ten years; but that morning, with the Alita biosphere unbalanced, skunky with hash and tobacco, the thought of trying to get into any kind of deep stuff with her seemed as doomed an enterprise as trying to peel the bar-code label off one of those see-through four-for-a-quid lighters that my father favoured. I wanted to engage her, spin her, play on her sensitivities like a DJ with a thousand decks, and there she was Swiss-cheesing her cerebellum with hash and Old Holborn. I could remember what dope was like from when we were kids; how it got so that after an hour or two you were like, whoa! Back-to-back *When Pets Attack*! Cool! I almost got up and left. It was bad enough that she was smoking dope like a kid, but worse that she was getting wasted first thing in the morning, especially on a day when the sky was telling you to deck a vee-dub to Newquay and make with the Sex Wax. I mean, it wasn't even a school day.

'You want some?'

She flipped the joint round in her fingers so the roach was towards me. I made a face and declined; she shrugged, and put it down in the terracotta aromatherapy burner she was using as an ashtray. This was cool. Although I needed to go along with most things she said – I didn't want her wondering why we were never on the same wavelength – the occasional disagreement kept us zesty. But I couldn't play the high-from-life card too hard. I needed us to keep doing meth, at least to the point where I was sure that if the group was going to break up, then Alita would break away in the same direction as me.

But gear was something else. Draw was what other people did – fathers, chavs, wasters – and if she took up smoking full-time, these were the people she'd be taking peer pressure from pretty soon, and they might take her away for good in her gap year, take her away into squats, backpacking, road protests, god knew what. Yet if I pointed this out too harshly, it could trigger a face-off, a confrontation, which would make this impulse – to get baked in a dark room when the rest of the gang were rolling in bright water – escalate into something beyond appropriate.

So I picked up the joint and took a hit on it to show that I could party with her, that she needn't go looking for other people to blaze up with. I exhaled the smoke measuredly, so it wouldn't make me cough, then took another pull on it and handed it back to her.

'Whoa,' I said. 'You're right. I didn't know I even felt buzzy until now.'

'That's what I mean,' she said, totally serious. 'We don't think about what meth could be doing to us. I mean, we have no idea, long-term.'

I snickered. 'Apart from telling our future partners about it,' I said, putting on a comedy voice. '*Not many, honey; just a few teenage fumbles and a couple of one-night stands at uni. Uh, would you mind doing me from behind while someone else slips in in front?*'

She giggled. 'Yeah, but that's it. What if normal sex is boring to us now?'

'Want to find out?'

'I'm serious,' she said. 'People get into this kind of stuff when they've done everything else. We haven't even started yet. I mean, is this what you thought it would be like, being seventeen? Going on eighteen?'

'Yeah, kind of,' I said. 'Except I thought we'd be driving around in a van, solving mysteries.'

'Fuck you,' she said, batting me one on the arm. 'You know what I mean. It's like, you see year-five kids with boyfriends and mobiles – don't they just want to go play in the mud sometimes? You know? Think about where we are. We're never gonna be this sharp again in our lives. Our receptors are never gonna be so fine-tuned.'

So why are you getting baked off your butt first thing in the morning? I almost said, but I bit it back; this was starting to go where I wanted.

'When you're older your head gets scrambled. Like if you try to get teletext from the video channel,' she went on. 'We've got to do as much preparation for wherever we want to go in the future right now, while we can. I mean, it's great for us all to come together like that and, you know, sometimes it's almost spiritual, but every time we do some it blows out a couple of days. You can't function like you want to function until it's flushed out of your system, and I hate that. This is our last summer holiday before gap year, you know? We'll never have this kind of time again.'

I could work with this. And besides, since it was her brother who was manufacturing it, she controlled the supply. If she decided to cut it off, then it was pretty much over anyway; no one was going to go behind her back to Jamie, even if we did feel that we could still party without her. If that was the case, then I needed something else to bond with her over, to replace it. I took a breath.

'You remember our summer projects?'

She smiled – I saw the nostalgia kick in – and her eyes drifted off to the left as she pulled pictures up from deep memory. At the end of our garden my dad's contractors had dumped all the clay and rubble from when they dug the foundations for our house, so there was this kind of grassy knoll planted over with dwarf fruit trees down there. Every summer when we were kids we used to make it a project to turn it into a different kind of theme-park area: one summer it'd be the house of horror, with rotted-plank gravestones, stage blood daubed on the trunks and nooses dangling from the branches; the next it'd be Jurassic Village, with rubber pterodactyls suspended at eye level and an overturned Barbie Jeep of imperilled scientists. The big event of the summer would be our grand opening, when we'd haul the parents away from their barbecue and lead them round a path marked out by lines of Duluxed pebbles, snaking between the exhibits for maximum effect.

'You remember?' I said, and she smiled again. 'I got this idea yesterday,' I said. 'I want to do another project this summer. The last one, before we're grown up and leave.'

'Well, hey. There you go,' she said, leaning over to hug me. 'That's just what I meant. That's what you need.'

'Whoa,' I said into her shoulder, 'watch the coal on that thing.'

She pulled back and peered at it to check she hadn't stubbed it on me, then took a puff on it to make sure. I needed to bring this home before she zoned out on me.

'You know that time capsule?' I said. 'The one we did the project on in year seven?'

'Still got it somewhere,' she said. 'A+. Read it and weep, whiteboy. It was on the fridge for years.'

'You remember where they found it?'

'Huh,' she snorted. 'When they were excavating that new car park behind the High Street. Like yeah, people stopped going there because there wasn't enough parking, not because there weren't any shops. Dolts.'

'Do you remember when there were shops in the High Street?'

'Sure,' she said, 'don't you?'

I shook my head. 'I only ever remember going to the superstore.'

'You are weird,' she said, taking a hit on the roach. 'The superstore was built in what, '94, right?'

I did some sums. 'Yeah, I guess.'

'You and I must have got to the point where I'd shown you what was in my knickers by, what, year two? 1991. You don't remember our first trade-a-peek session?'

'Course I do,' I protested.

'Then you must remember other stuff.'

'Only vaguely.'

'Youth of today,' she said. 'No retention.'

'C'mon, help me out,' I complained. 'What would you've said if I remembered the superstore being built but forgot about our little peepshow?'

'This is true.' She grinned as she snubbed the joint out in the aromatherapy burner.

'But I tell you, I got this weird flashback yesterday,' I said. 'Seeing the High Street full of people? I remembered how it used to be, when we were kids. Or I kind of half remembered. I was sitting down on the pavement and I looked up and it was like, people carrying shopping and stuff. Then I did a double-take and it was just everyone standing around gawping again.'

'Freaky,' Alita agreed. 'You should talk to Talya. She gets the weirdest dreams after crystal meth. She told me this one where –'

'No, but this wasn't like a dream,' I said. 'It was more like, this place used to be so different, and I forgot about it. I never really paid any attention to it before. It's like, your room is a place that no one else sees the same way you do, because you see it a dozen times a day. I come in here and I'm like, jesus, the colourwash on that blanket box, y'know? I mean, no offence, but it's pretty gross. Hold on, hear me out,' I said, holding up a hand. I didn't want her to think I was riding her; I knew money had scarcely been cluttering the place up since her dad had got himself a loft in London and a girlfriend with a pierced navel. 'But you don't notice it because you see it every day. You stopped noticing a long time ago, and to you it's a nice place. Agreed?'

'I guess,' she said warily, only half kidding. 'But this had better be going somewhere.'

'It's the same with the town you grow up in. You stop noticing it really early, but at the same time it's your place, it's your hard drive. I mean, this place is like background to me, I never think about it. But seeing the whole town turned out in the High Street yesterday made me realise that we're going to be leaving it soon. And I won't know where I come from. It's like –' I was working myself onto a roll – 'you've always known what you wanted to do. I mean, you've always had direction. But I've always been like, duh, school, parents, future . . .' I ticked them off on my fingers and shrugged.

'But hey, c'mon, Bay, your mother walked out in the middle of GCSEs,' she cut in. 'That's going to throw a person. You were fine before then.'

'No, I wasn't,' I said quickly. I really didn't want to start trading separation anguish again. 'I never wanted to do anything at school. I always went for the window desks at the start of every year, even though it meant freezing my arse off all winter, just so I could see cars passing in the street outside the gates. I never really thought I'd need to do anything to get there, but now it feels like I do. I need to understand this place before I can leave it behind. Who I am is all about this place.'

'You think a place makes you, not the people in it?'

I took a deep breath. I shouldn't have tried to do this till she was straight again, but it was too late now. I could feel the conversation getting touchy-feely, a sure sign it was heading for dope-random, turning back in on itself. Monday mornings when I was a kid, I'd go to make my cereal and find teabags in the fridge and the milk in the cupboard from where my parents had been smoking the night before, coming down off all the Es they'd necked while me and Shana were parked at the grandparents'. I needed to take this home now.

'I was born here, y'know?' I said. 'I never told you that? I must have. I was on TV. I was the last kid born in the hospital before it closed down. I'm the last kid with this town on their birth certificate. I was born here and I was stamped here, and that makes it special to me.'

She put her head on one side, twisting some hair through her fingers. 'Why're you telling me this?'

That stung a bit. Since when did it stop being natural that I should tell her about my stuff?

'You only brought it up because you want me to argue against it,' she said, 'straighten it out in your mind.'

'No, I want you to help me,' I said. This was the plan. She'd been, like, top of the class in all the local-history-type projects you do in kid school, and you used to have to prise her away with a stick from the Discovery channel, from *Encarta* and those Dorling Kindersley books. She wanted to be an archaeologist, she'd told me once when we were about year eight. She loved all that Egyptians and Romans shit, she'd said, but there wasn't so much left to do on them. What was far more cutting-edge to her was an archaeology that was almost up to the minute.

'Duh,' I'd said, wondering what she'd plan to discover about the lost civilisation of like, ten years ago that wasn't already numbingly documented in videotape and magazines.

'But it's what wasn't on TV that's the most interesting stuff,' she'd said. 'Check it. We know all what Versace designed the year we were born, but do we know what they were selling in Tesco Home 'n' Wear? In Help the Aged? That's much more interesting to me.'

'But how would you archaeologise it? Whichever,' I said to her snigger.

'Imagine digging through a landfill where twenty years of a town's domestic refuse is piled up,' she said, sitting forward on her crossed legs. 'You'd be able to see what food fads there were that year – microwave Yorkshire puddings, French bread pizza – what packaging used to look like . . .'

'How could you tell one year from another?'

'There'd be a layer of Christmas giftwrap. And you could always reorient your position relative to the end of the eighties, which would be a layer where there was just organic mush – there was a fad for biodegradable packaging for a few years back then.'

I reminded her of this conversation now.

'C'mon, you're the man for this kind of stuff,' I said. This was my plan. She could teach me how to look scientifically at a place; it would add value to our hanging out, and give me excuses to go round hers even more than I did already. 'Come on, be a mate. Show me where to start with this.'

'How would I know?'

'Because you know everything. This is your turf. You used to spend all your time thinking about this kind of stuff, and I never did. Help me out here. Tell you what – the first time I'll let you help me for free. The next fix you pay for, but the first one is free.'

She snorted and shook her head, and I almost wept with relief. Finally she was maybe seeing the absurdity of getting a swerve on first thing in the morning. She stashed her Rizlas and draw under her mattress and stood up.

'Okay,' she said, palming her phone into her pocket. 'We start in your kitchen.'

Two minutes later we were there.

'Take your clothes off,' she said.

'You what?'

'You heard,' she said, 'shake your moneymaker. Drop your drawers. *Strip*.' She pulled her sweat top over her head and my stomach turned over: somehow it wasn't the same as when all the others were around. 'Your father won't be home for hours, will he?' she said, unbuttoning her Wranglers, then slipping them over her hips as she stood up, rolling her underwear inside them. 'Huh? So get 'em off.' She stepped out of the jeans and planted her fists on her hips as I tentatively unbuttoned my shirt. 'Are you trying to memorise my tits?' she said. 'Your tuition starts now. I am the master and you are the acolyte. You either get your keks off or I do it for you.'

I did it, with as minimal awkwardness as I could manage.

'Okay. Now follow,' she said. I tailed her out and towards the lounge, thinking too hard about car wrecks and school dinners – in order to control the obvious – to leave much space for what was going on. But she started to show me how, if you sat on top of file cabinets or stood on counters, then familiar rooms suddenly got weird; how, if you lay on your back on the floor, things looked much bigger, in the same way that you remember your infants' school towering over you but if you go and scope it out now it's a paltry little place. It was interesting. I even got used to the nakedness after a while, appreciating the way feeling the textures of walls, curtains, chairs against all of you could trigger a freshness to the familiar.

'Right, upstairs,' she said. 'On your belly. C'mon. Like this.'

She got on all fours on the stairs, and commenced to shimmy up them in a manner that didn't help at all. She stopped and looked up at me. 'Hmmm,' she snorted, eyeing my moneymaker on the half-lob. 'Well, that'll soon go. Come on, get down.'

'I'm not crawling on the floor. Like a cur,' I added.

'Yes, you are. Do you want me to help you? Then obey.'

I got down.

'Right,' she said. 'Feel the carpet along the length of you? Wriggle about a bit.' I wriggled. 'Now crawl.'

I followed her along the landing. This actually was weird. I did a lot of homework lying on the floor, but it was probably ten years since I'd crawled more than a couple of paces. I plodded gracelessly along behind her feline slink, the skin on my hands and knees complaining already as she went into my parents' old bedroom.

I hadn't been in here for a while either. When my mother moved out, my father retreated into the spare room downstairs, putting up scaffolding racks to hold his decks and amplifiers and WideScreen; ostensibly so me and Shana wouldn't be disturbed by his late-night a/v, but really so he could get women in and out of there without them having to run into us.

'Now down again,' Alita said, stretching herself out where their bed used to be. It certainly had got dusty in there; grey rolls of it lined the indentations in the carpet from the departed Slumberland Deluxe.

'You ever look at dust close up? Get your nose down next to it. See? It's whorled, latticed, complex, beautiful.'

'It's irritating my sinuses.'

'That's because you're not used to it. The cleaner Dysons every room in the house except this one, doesn't she? And bleaches the counters, and sprays anti-bac on everything you touch. You ever see anyone walking a dog round here? You ever see a cat slinking under a hedge? The only pets you can get at Pets R Us are flushable ones. We're allergic to everything else. All the millions of stuff they sell at the superstore has made these houses as sterile as an ICU. Your natural ecosystems of good bacteria are all shot to buggery. What allergies you got?'

'Hummus, tahini. Hayfever in summer.'

'That's just what you know about. Look at this.' She used her elbows to drag herself, SAS-style, to the wall; I crawled. 'See the crack between the skirting board and the plaster here? Leaking out of that is formaldehyde, from the cavity wall insulation. Plaster takes most of a year to dry, but I bet you moved in here as soon as your dad finished building it, yeah? So does everyone. They pre-sell places as they build them, the owners move in within months, they turn on the heating and the wall shrinks. Formaldehyde is a volatile organic compound. It gives you eye irritation and headaches; sleep in here a few decades and it'll Swiss-cheese your CNS.' She lay on her side, propped her head in one hand. The movement stretched her bosom in a way that was difficult to ignore.

'What's CNS?' I said.

'Duh. Central nervous system.'

I knew that. 'Then how come everyone's not Swiss-cheesed already?' I said.

'Cavity-wall hasn't been around very long,' she said. 'And people move – concentrations are hundreds of times less in older houses, and the kinds of people who'd get vocal about something that's wrecked their health tend to live in old places, not new. It's the affluent who complain, not the poor.'

We'd always lived in new houses: the last three were ones my father'd built. I'd never lived in a house where someone had died or been born, or where someone had stashed banknotes under the floorboards. There weren't even floorboards in this one – it was poured concrete downstairs, hardboard up. I knew because I used to stash porno under the carpet, before I found my parents'.

'You know it all, huh?' I was only half joking.

'No,' she said, fingering a green stain on the honey-coloured wall-to-wall under her breast, 'I don't know what this patch is.'

'Classic,' I said, snapping out of it. 'They were going to a wedding once, right? And my mother got this new dress, Nicole Farhi or somewhere, and the assistant must've been a bit dopey because somehow Mum managed to get it home with the security tag still on it. She only notices when she puts it on, the day of the wedding, and she goes ballistic on Dad to break the thing off. Well, he tries to do it with his hands but he can't, and she's giving him all this "you've got a grand's worth of Black & Decker in the garage" and "a man who can't use tools is not a man"; so he starts going at it with a power saw. Immediately it cracks open and there's green security dye spraying the walls, the carpet, both of them, and all over the dress. They repainted the walls, but they just put a yucca over the carpet stain.'

She snorted – she could imagine my mother – and I sniggered along.

'QED,' she said, looking at me oddly, when she stopped.

'What is?' I said. We were sitting cross-legged on the carpet, facing each other.

'What was the best part of this?' she said. 'Me telling you a bunch of crap about cavity-wall insulation, or you telling me a story about your parents?'

'It was interesting –' I began to protest.

'Jesus, Bay, you're such a boy sometimes,' she cut in. 'What was all that *I need to understand this place before I can leave it behind*? It's not this town you're talking about, it's your parents.'

'Oh, c'mon,' I said, 'my parents aren't –'

'Yes, they are. What triggered this to begin with? You had a flashback about going shopping with your mother.'

'Yeah, but –'

'It wasn't the place that made you feel weird, it was remembering doing normal stuff with your mum.'

I thought about this a moment.

'Can we get dressed now?' I said.

'In a minute. We've got mocks in six months, then A levels, and then we're out of here. Travel, uni, careers . . . and then the only time you'll see your folks is Christmas, if that.'

'They don't have Christmas where my mum is,' I pointed out.

'Exactly,' she said, 'and that's what's bothering you here. That's what freaked you out. You lost one parent already, and if you don't make an effort with your father now, you'll miss the boat with him too. Do you think I don't know this?'

The girl had a point. One of the things that had kept us so close was that her father'd walked out on her two years before my mother walked out on me. I hadn't known how to help her deal with her stuff, but she'd been there during mine. She'd already been through it, and even if it'd been hell for her, it hadn't been so bad for me because I could go to her. She kept me on the bubble because she could see through to what was really bothering me. Like, I was going on about how could she do it, my mum going with this ratty old yoga guy from the gym, and Alita said, 'What's really upsetting you is the thought of living alone with your father from now on.'

'I mean, look at this place,' she said now as we went back down to get dressed. 'You two live like a couple of teenage boys. You in your room, him in his –'

'That wasn't my choice,' I protested, though it was true I never complained.

'But it probably wasn't his either,' she said. 'He's scared of butting into your space, you're scared of butting into his.' She pulled her sweat top back over her head and fluffed her hair out of the back. 'If you don't make some contact now, you'll never have any. Do you want that?'

'I don't know –'

'Don't be such a boy. I'm serious, Bay.'

We were both dressed now, and held eye contact a moment, there in the kitchen. The cleaner hadn't been for a couple of days and it was starting to show. Me and my dad made a go of pretending we still lived in the real world, buying the latest sprays, keeping the laundry under control, eating fresh fruit and salad (or buying it, anyway), but our home life was always a razor's edge away from deteriorating into comedy flatshare squalor. My connection to Alita was a connection to life: drop it, and I'd become a men's magazine kind of guy, into sports, personal grooming, jerking off and stalking; maintain it, and I could enter the brightly lit world of adulthood, where there were women and products and a future. The way to get there wasn't in contradicting her.

'Okay,' I said. 'But you'll have to help me.'

'Good boy,' she said, and touched her hand to my cheek.

I heard him come in about nine that night and go straight to his room. The three-bean salad I'd left for him was still under clingfilm in the fridge when I checked, but this was par for the course – he often grabbed a kebab or something on his way home. I took a can of Red Stripe out instead and went along to his room, knocked on the door. There was no answer, just the faint murmur of golf commentary. I waited a moment and knocked again, switching the icy beer to my other hand.

'Yeah?' came from inside after a while.

'It's me,' I said, thinking, duh, who else would it be.

'S'matter?' came through the door.

'Nothing,' I said to the stripped pine. 'I just . . . brought you a beer.'

There was the creak of his futon base from inside, and the door opened. I held the beer out.

'Already got one on,' he said, raising a 440-ml to his lips. I waited for him to say, *Why don't you crack that open and join me?* but he didn't. Instead he said, 'Y'all right? Something wrong at school?'

'It's summer holidays,' I said. He was in his underwear, his belly protruding over the band of his Calvins.

'Oh, right,' he said, and looked at the beer in my hand. 'Well, another won't hurt,' he conceded, and took the can from me. 'You sure you're all right?'

'Yeah, no worries,' I said, feeling stupid. If everything was okay, then why did I come down here? 'You hear about that stuff in the High Street yesterday?'

'Did I,' he said, as though it had inconvenienced him personally; but he was already half turning his head as he said it, the better to hear his TV.

'All right then,' I said. 'See you later.'

'Okay,' he said, drained the open can and gave it to me. 'Cheers,' he said, and shut the door.

I would've given up there if it hadn't been for Alita. The way I saw it, maybe she did want to open up enough for us to take it to the next level, but she needed some proof of my ability to function first. So far there'd only been dysfunction: in her parents' split, in mine, and in the way my sister Shana had dropped out of uni a few months before, and gone to catch up with Mum in India. Alita had said, more than a few times, that she was getting closer to her mum since her dad left, and she seemed to find satisfaction in this; obviously she thought I ought to do the same with my dad while there was still time.

The trouble was, he was different with her than he was with me. He turned it on for her – she was a fit girl, after all – in a way he never bothered to with me. There was no way I could get her to swallow that we had such a hopeless relationship, him and me. We went out into the world, did our stuff, came back and went to our rooms. Even before Mum left, the most interest he'd taken in me had been that of a teenager anxious not to be seen with a dowdy relative.

DAD:	You gotta ditch those trainers.
ME *(age nine)*:	But I like them! They're my favourite.
DAD:	Huh. Air Jordans are so '91. Here – old skool Adidas. Get 'em on ya.

It was almost like being a povvo, forced to wear trainers that no one else did. The other kids used to rip it out of my Pumas, my Gazelles, my Vans and my shell-toe Adidas, until they all started wearing them a year or so later.

But this was him all over. He'd never grown out of the rave thing, because it was how he made his money. He grew up around here, same as me, itching to get out and get on; but then he started knocking around with my mother, got her up the duff, and Shana came along before they'd thought too much about what they wanted to do. They weren't much older than me. My granddad got him a job at some construction insurers in London and they played house for a while, him doing the commute, her hoovering the starter home. I was born before they woke up out of it, but that didn't stop them making up for lost time.

What snapped them out of it was the rave thing kicking off round the M25. Most of their friends were still around here, and they started going with them to these mad parties that were held in fields near motorway junctions, parking me and Shana at his parents', to give them some space. That's most of what I remember as a kid: round to Grandpa and Nana's Saturday teatime, Mum and Dad turning back up for Sunday lunch and falling asleep during it.

Anyway. I'd heard the story enough times on birthdays, his or Mum's, when we went out to the Harvester by the motorway and he was feeling expansive, a patriarch in a baseball cap that he wouldn't take off at the table. The people they met raving were brickies and sparks, trust-fund kids and city boys. It was the end of the eighties; property values were going through the roof, and he'd got a foothold in the business already, at his job in London. At the raves he met people with money, and people with the savvy to turn plots of scrapland into profit. The local council were drunk enough with the boom to believe that building endless office space would take the town into the twenty-first century. Augustus found Rome built of brick and left it in marble; my dad and his associates found this town built of brick and left it in breezeblock and MDF. Most of what they built was empty from the day the carpet tiles were glued down, but it kept him busy in the meantime.

It must have paid off somewhere, since they stuck together nonetheless; the people he used to go raving with were the same people he did business with now. They might have got into golf and bought Range Rovers, but they were still totally into it, getting buzzcuts to disguise the male-pattern baldness, buying the new workwear, the new DJ compilations, slipping up to the Ministry and Turnmill's of a weekend to pull backpackers. My dad was the only one who'd been married, as far as I knew; some of the rest of his crew had kids dotted here and there, but like him they hadn't let it slow them down. It wasn't surprising he found it hard to do the father-figure with me, particularly when I was getting towards the age he seemed more or less stuck at.

But, as Alita pointed out, the fact that I knew his story – the fact that he'd told it so often – showed that there was a time when he used to open up, when he used to like talking. He'd only started living like a troglodytic loser since Mum left. If I didn't want my relationship with him to end up like his with his own father's – i.e. none, since Grandpa and Nana had got tired of being a crèche for Shana and me every weekend and gone to Mallorca forever – then I needed to make the effort. And besides, it'd give me Brownie points with Alita.

'It's not working,' I complained to her a couple of weeks later.

'You just need to jump, flip, roll left and come up shooting,' she said, reaching for the PlayStation controller.

'No, my dad,' I said, letting her take the control. As she started to play I relayed my latest attempt to get him talking. Following her advice that I needed to create a setting, open up some space for it, I'd gone to the 24-7 Shell the previous Sunday and bought a disposable one-shot barbecue. We had a regular one, but it had rusted where it stood on the patio since Mum left, since Dad stopped having people over. I got pork steaks, ribs, hot wings, the works from the superstore, and blazed the whole thing up around two when he still hadn't emerged from his room. When I was on the verge of going in and dragging him away from his Sky Sports, he just came out, stoned, said 'Ribs, cool', filled a plate and went back to his TV.

'You know your problem?' she asked. 'You give up too easily. Look at this. Flip, roll, fire – ha! – and down he goes.'

'Okay,' I said, 'but what about my father?' It was her stupid idea.

'You give up too easily,' she repeated, eyes never leaving the screen. 'You know how they say that when the cops bust gangsters, they always find a shelf of *The Godfather* and *Goodfellas* and shit?'

'I can't find the tracking on the video,' Talya complained, sticking her head round the door.

'It's on the machine, not the remote,' Alita said, without looking up. 'We'll be with you in a minute. The point being,' she went on, as Talya disappeared, 'that even gangsters have to learn respect and honour and whatever else they're supposed to do from gangster tapes. It isn't something that comes naturally to people. You have to work at it.'

'I have been working at it,' I said, squinting at the screen. She was in a part of the level I hadn't got to before.

'Well, not hard enough,' she said. 'Don't expect him to drop what he's doing whenever you want. Go along with what he likes to do.' She busied herself at the controls for a moment, the tip of her tongue creeping out of the side of her mouth. 'He still plays golf, doesn't he?'

Everyone in our town played golf. You looked up at night, the stars were outshone by the floodlights from the driving ranges that ringed the town. If you saw the place from the air, you'd think the spare tyre of sculpted green around it was some kind of ancient fortification.

'Yeah, he plays golf,' I said.

'Then go caddy, boy. Whooh!' The end-of-scene jingle burbled from the TV as her statistics filled the screen. 'Eighteen kills, two hundred sixty-eight hits with two hundred eighty rounds. Read it and weep, whiteboy. Read it and weep.'

Mostly he played in the week. His office was his Range Rover, driving from one construction site to the next, and he kept his clubs in the back, handy for when he could wag a couple of hours. This was no good because, one, I never knew when he was going to do it, and two, school was back on before I knew it and I couldn't have got away in the day if I'd wanted to.

With the end of summer came that feeling you get from a dozen years of school – that autumn is the time to buy a pencil case and a geometry set, and get your head down.

Dad started saving the golf for Saturday mornings; whether this was because he genuinely had less time in the week or because Saturdays yielded better pickings from networking, I don't know. Either way, I started skipping the gym first thing on Saturday so I'd be around when he surfaced, ready to suggest, as I poured his coffee, that I could come too, learn to play from the master.

He wasn't as unreceptive to this as I thought. Having your teenage kid hump your clubs for you was something of a status symbol at the course, as I clocked from the other straight-A, square-jawed kids I saw there, so busy being stand-up guys with their fathers that it took them twice as long to go round as anyone else. Complaining about this to each other gave us a reference point, though what got on his wick most was the golfing umbrellas the other guys used, emblazoned with the corporate logos of City firms. I would've thought that his own Burberry one was the coolest, but there was a kind of one-upmanship going on, he explained; since the umbrellas were handed out on corporate jollies – salmon fishing, racing and so on – displaying your latest one at the golf course on a Saturday showed everyone else what a big shot you were.

'Bet that twat's been praying for rain,' he'd remark, watching a Nike'd stockbroker unfurl a spotless Deutsche Bank satellite-dish job that matched his spanking club covers.

I could see where he was coming from. I was so jealous, this one time after GCSEs when we all had to go to our parents' work for a school thing, and everyone else went up to London, to the City, but I had to go to some construction site out by the bypass. I felt like such a loser. Yet it was only because no one knew each other in that town any more that he didn't get more respect. If this had been fifty years ago,

I could've walked down the street and everyone would've known who I was – son and heir of the local entrepreneur, the man who made things happen in that town.

But if he was just some other chav out on the greens, then afterwards, in the club bar, everyone knew who he was. It was networking central in there. All kinds of guys – Daks or Diesel, tweeds or Ted Baker – would come over while I was trying to dredge up conversation with him, take his arm and shanghai him away. I caught the odd snippet: did he want a piece of the pie, and how sweet it was going to be. If I'd been any younger I might have thought he was getting into patisserie. It was almost like being a kid again, parked in the corner with a post-mix Pepsi while he did the grown-up stuff elsewhere.

This wasn't how I presented it to Alita, naturally. We were still all getting together for the odd meth session – Jamie and Harper were churning it out, having refined their process – but school was piling it on with the mocks coming up, and there just wasn't time to hang like we used to. We caught up in the superstore café a couple of nights a week, and drove to school together most mornings, but what little time we had was just fighting traffic of one sort or another. When she did ask me how it was going with him, I laid it on thick.

'Really cool. We're clearing up a load of stuff. You were right. I'm so glad I had a chance to do this.'

And so on, with fabricated examples ranging from his unresolved conflicts with his own father, to how his grief and loss at first my mother's, then Shana's desertion was being countered by the growing bond between us. I could scarcely tell her that I'd brought my own TV down to the living room after golf one time, to try and open it up again as common ground, but the one in his room was WideScreen, and he stayed in there when he was home at all. The only time I really saw him was out on the greens, where he wouldn't let me contribute anything, except to hump his clubs for him. Thinking I could start to phase myself out of the deal, I suggested he play against other people rather than just stump round in silence with me.

'I thought you wanted one-on-one time,' he said, standing back from his fourth-hole address, apparently unaware that, even if I had wanted quality time, it was hardly working out. Sweet that he'd twigged there was something more than the pursuit of golfing excellence on my mind, but even so.

'Yeah,' I said, taken aback. 'I mean, I'm learning a lot but it can't be helping your game much, just demonstrating for me. Why don't you set up something with Gavin? I see his van in the car park most Saturdays.'

I regretted it as soon as it was out. I'd stumbled into a minefield here without thinking. Gavin went way back with my parents: used to go on their weekenders, was on the A-list for barbecues when we were kids, as much Mum's mate as Dad's. Consequently, though Gavin was into landscaping, and probably still picked up some contracts on Dad's developments, they'd barely seen each other since the split, at least as far as I knew.

But having jumped in with both feet, I had to follow through. I talked it up all through the remaining holes, teasing stories out of him (though I'd heard them a dozen times as a kid) about japes he and Gavin used to pull when they were having it large, and pointed out Gavin's van in the car park as we left. He said he had plenty of people he could play with, but since I was on a roll with it I plucked one of his business cards from the handbrake well, had him write on the back '*Didn't know you played – let's sort one out*' and ran over, tucking it under Gavin's wiper. It turned out that he was only parked there because he was doing some work on the grounds; but he had a bag of clubs like everyone else, and they set up a game with him as Dad's guest the week after.

It seemed to go all right. They were guy-gruff the first few holes, maybe sizing each other up, but since it soon became pretty obvious they were as crap at golf as each other, they lightened up a bit. They started off winding each other up about the clothes they used to wear, and it was even relaxed enough for me to protest a bit: like shut up, the nineties may've been the decade taste forgot – men in sandals, women in leggings, everyone so busy looking for their third eye that they forgot to use the two on their face – but it was my time, y'know? It was all I had to go on. And then they started shooting the shit about the old days, before Mum left, though all of us were careful not to mention her, and it went pretty well, considering. When we got home, Dad didn't disappear into his room. Instead, he sat in the lounge, rolling joint after joint, until it was pretty obvious he was there for a point. I went down and pretended to look for something on the bookshelf.

'You want some of this?' he asked. When I turned round he was proffering the joint. I thought, what the hell, I started this, and took it, sitting down cross-legged on the carpet in front of the couch. I took the shallowest hit worthy of the name and passed it back; he seemed to be getting a pretty good swerve on, so I could get away with only pretending to take the smoke without offending him.

'It was good to see Gavin,' I croaked, as if I was still holding the smoke in.

'Lanky git,' he said, 'he's about a foot too tall to be any cop. Too many angles in him.'

'He used to put me on his shoulders,' I said. 'Go from two foot to eight foot tall.'

'Yeah, he's a good lad,' he conceded, taking a thoughtful puff.

'Be good to see more of him,' I prompted.

He raised the joint to his mouth, then stopped it there, squinting across the room at the two pots by the fire. My mum had made them in an evening class; she thought they were pretty sharp at the time. I used to dust them if the cleaner missed.

'Reckon it's time to adios those?' he said.

They were the last things of hers in the place. 'I'll take them to the loft,' I said.

'Enough crap up there already,' he said. 'Get us a black bag, eh.'

It was time to knock it on the head. Even if I was getting somewhere with my father, it was somewhere I didn't want to go. You see so many people trying to connect on TV that it starts to seem natural to you; you forget that the guests on *Ricki* leave the studio with bruises they didn't have when they went in. You only come out of talking the same as you went in if there was nothing wrong to begin with. There was plenty wrong with me and my dad – more, even, than I'd thought. I had enough issues with my mum without him stirring them up again. If Alita wanted to hear about it, I could lie convincingly.

Besides, I barely saw her that autumn, or any of them. Saturday mornings, instead of hanging with them all in the juice bar after the gym, I was standing in the pissing rain on some manicured prairie out by the motorway. By the time I'd sat around in the clubhouse for two hours on top, stuck for a ride home till Dad was done talking turkey, the others'd had their hang time for the weekend and were cracking into their coursework. Like a spider adjusting for a lost leg without missing a beat, our little unit seemed to have adapted pretty well to my absence, making me wonder how much they needed me to begin with. Whenever I called

Jojo to see if he was up for some PlayStation one-on-one, he was into new games that I didn't know. Even the couple of times we managed meth that semester I felt like some kind of UN observer. It was time to concentrate on what was important in my life, not all this crap my parents laid on me. All I needed was the moment to start.

The Christmas holiday provided. Waking up to free days was like coming out of suspended animation. We got back together in the gym juice bar every morning like in summer, and the rest of the day led on from there. The bank holiday closures were something I was dreading, but Jojo came up with the ace on Christmas Eve. Everything fell into place: suddenly I had the means to seal the deal with Alita.

Jojo was having a party, New Year's. We told him he was crazy, but he went for it anyway. His parents had gone to a hotel at Land's End for the millennium, and had such a blast with the other weekenders that they'd swapped addresses with a view to a reunion a couple of years down the line. Failing to understand that no one's ever serious about this let's-keep-in-touch kind of thing they'd gone ahead and sorted it, and duly decked the Discovery down the M4 two days before New Year's, giving Jojo and his kid sister carte blanche to trash the homestead over the holiday weekend.

They weren't as suicidal as this makes them sound. Admittedly, most parents pulling a similar abdication during the party opportunity of the year ought to book the glazier, the steam-cleaner and an army of Filipinos at the same time that they book their hotel. If they don't come home to find catfood paintings on the walls, the lawn reformatted with handbrake turns, and the snooker table bearing the aftermath of a game played with a dozen free-range instead of reds, then their kids have failed them in a quite fundamental way.

Jojo's parents felt that it was okay to hand over the keys

and jam because they actually did know their kids quite well. Jojo's little sister Amy was hopeless, a fleece girl, a Saffy, resisting the urgings of her totally projecting mother to get pierced, get Kookai'd and get laid: her and her geekling friends' idea of a wild time was a cookie-dough sleepover, with maybe a Leo fest on the VCR if they were really going for it. For love interest, they hung with the studly Jamie and Harper (when they could drag them out of their lab) which tells you pretty much all you need to know. The wall-to-wall nylon twist had nothing to fear, even on the big 3-1, from that quarter.

Neither, as Mr and Mrs Jojo probably knew, would there be much grief coming from us. Whatever frustrations drive normal kids to drink till they puke in swimming pools and punch out windows, we didn't have them. But even so, Jojo was more trusting than Mulder to think that any party, particularly one New Year's, wasn't going to end in tears.

In any town with teenagers, news of a party travels like no-life twentysomethings, spreads like Nutella on a stoner's toast, transmits itself like *E. coli* from the last butcher to hold out against the superstore. There was no way Jojo's party was going to resemble anything other than a Jerry Springer participants' reunion, with undertones of chalet-girl toilet bowl, by the time the chimes kicked in.

'You're crazy,' I informed him, when he announced it in the juice bar on Christmas Eve.

'Testify to *that*,' said Asia, who watched too much Ricki Lake.

'It'll be a blast,' Jojo said. 'C'mon, we'll get a shitload of sangria, make some punch –'

'Why?' said Talya.

'Cos that's what you do,' Jojo said. 'Work with me on this. We never do stuff like that any more.'

'We never did,' Alita pointed out.

'Then all the more reason.' Jojo gestured with his mango-and-guava smoothie. 'C'mon, you want to get to uni and have no stories from back home to tell?'

He had a point. I didn't know about the others, but the thought of uni was tailgating me most of the time. The days when you went for it were supposed to be pretty much over by the time you got to uni (the idea being that you could rechannel that party-power into a 2:1 in Spin Studies and membership of the lacrosse team). I was worried that I hadn't properly exercised those impulses, might consequently fail to rechannel them, and would end up like Shana, dropping out to go crawling to my mother in India. I thought about this now.

'Maybe we ought to make the effort,' I said, but still more devil's advocate than serious.

'I'm there,' said Euan, doing a Jerry-Jerry-Jerry gesture with one arm. 'Party party party.'

'Whoo-*hooh*!' said Asia, who, as I've indicated, had Ricki issues. But it suddenly got infectious; a few suggestions bounced around, and then Alita was returning Euan and Jojo's fives, and starting to discuss party-outfit colourways with Talya.

I sat back, bemused, and let them get on with it. This was something they were going to do whether I was on board or not, and it was just another marker of how far they'd gone in a new direction since I'd stopped being around. Jojo had maybe twigged I was only doing this stuff with my dad to make myself look good with Alita, and if he'd guessed I was going to make the move on her soon, he was most likely setting up the party so he could cop off himself. Why the others were so up for it took me most of Christmas to figure, but of course it was meth. Doing it so little made it feel kind of weird. You either did it all the time, like in summer, and that normalised it, or you laid off for fear it'd go weird on you. That was probably what some of this party was about – a striving for normality, for doing what regular kids did. After such a fucked-up autumn, I could testify to that.

So in the last daylight hour of the year we went to the superstore to stock up on party essentials. It was heaving in there, caught between the post-Christmas restocking rush and citizens like us with New Year mayhem on their minds. We shared out tasks to spread the load, and split up.

I was rolling my trolley down the chips-'n'-dips aisle when Alita shanghaied me from behind.

'Aren't you pizza and salad?' I demanded, hacked off already with negotiating the traffic.

'Done it,' she said, drawing her stacked trolley up alongside mine.

'You work fast,' I said, pleased nonetheless that she'd chosen to come and hang with me rather than any of the others.

'That's because I work good.' She selected a twelve-pack of McCoys and tossed them onto my trolley.

'And I don't?'

'I know Asia doesn't,' she said, inspecting the Kettle Chips. 'I just passed her by the chill cabinets, agonising over whether she wants smooth juice or Florida-style chunky.' I snorted – I could totally see it. 'Wait'll she has to go past the chicken grill by the deli,' she went on. 'I swear, if it weren't for the thought of her reward card dobbing her in as a carnivore, she'd be piling it up.'

I looked back up the aisle and, sure enough, Asia was approaching the grill counter. She paused for a moment, looking hunted, then pulled away briskly; Alita and I cracked up.

'Pretty smart, huh?' I grinned at her.

'I bet I know what Euan'll be doing too,' she said, twinkling her eyes at me.

'Do you now?' I said.

'Fuck you then,' she said, but she still had that impish look in her eyes.

'Euan was munchies, right?' I scanned the overhead signs, sweeping a shelf of Doritos into my trolley to fulfil my obligations. 'C'mon, then.'

We found him in the snack aisle, as appointed, suffering no such crap as Asia. His trolley bore some extra fruits and other perishable items ('New protein-drink components to toss into the blender back home,' Alita remarked from our position at the end of the aisle behind him) and he was propelling it briskly along, his mind less elsewhere than simply idling as his hands reached out automatically for the more heavily advertised products, the kinds that feature cartoon character endorsement on the packaging.

'Betcha he goes for some beer afterwards,' Alita observed; and sure enough, two minutes later, he was balancing a breezeblock of stubbies on top of the piles of Yo-Yos and Penguins.

'How'd you know he was going to do that?' We'd already laid in the lager from the off-licence Asia's brother was working at.

'Because he'll go for the fittest check-out girl, and he won't want to look like a kid with all his junk food,' Alita replied, doing this thing with her hands that meant, It's so obvious I can't believe you had to ask. 'We think this place is like modern, all the up-to-the-minute stuff, but it's primal. You could do a wildlife documentary in here, with people instead of animals.'

I made a tiger noise, then said, in a Discovery channel voiceover, 'The superstore is at the heart of the community here,' reeling off from memory something I'd written for a school project. 'Its wide aisles, richly stocked with produce, replicate the narrow streets of the medieval marketplace, providing a forum for the townspeople to interact.'

'Except there's a lot more to it than that,' she said, sweeping her arm back towards the fresh cabinets. 'Those aren't just pouches of fresh pesto, and shrink-wrapped spatchcock guinea fowl; they're reminders of what might've been, and isn't. I asked my dad once why they left London to live here after they got married: he said, if you live in a city, then you're so worn out by it at the end of the day that you don't have the energy to take advantage of all the stuff there is, and you get sick of having all the cons and none of the pros. It's the same here. If you can afford these products, then all you probably want is comfort food. You'll beat yourself up over it either way.'

My tongue was practically dragging along the floor by this point.

'So how about me?' I said. The first rule of flirting is never forget that all you're really doing is reminding them you exist. 'I mean, say I'm doing my first shop after I've graduated and moved into my new pad?'

'You and Jojo wouldn't be so different from each other,' she said, looking at me in an amused, speculative way. 'You'd both be primed with recipes cut out from magazines. You'd spend a fortune on the ingredients, then you'd take them home and burn them onto the pan.'

'You got me,' I said. 'C'mon, let's go pay.' We went back to our trolleys, and I automatically started pushing mine back towards the main entrance, rather than the logical end, since the queues'd be shorter. I suddenly noticed she wasn't following but standing behind her trolley, grinning.

'What?' I said, breaking into a smile.

'I knew you'd do that, too,' she said, laughing in a way that meant all kinds of things. But mostly it meant yes, I figured. I'd done what she'd asked of me – demonstrated I had what it took to tune in to my father – and now it was time for the payoff. We all knew it; I'd only taken so long to twig because I'd fallen out of step with them. We weren't kids any more, running around tweaking and humping. It was time to take up the positions that were going to get us through the last phase, through A levels and into gap year, and tonight was the night it was going to happen. No wonder everyone had jumped on the idea of a party; having other people around us would mean that our every action wasn't under scrutiny from the others. We could lose ourselves in the crowd, and by the time it dispersed everything would be set, too late to be undone. Tonight was the night.

As if I needed confirmation that something mega-big was going down, we were all totally weird with each other for the next few hours. It would've been so much easier if we all could've just turned up at ten like everybody else, but we had to get the place ready and there was a lot to do. Jojo's house was big, the kind of red-brick mini-mansion that my dad got in on in the eighties, popular in City-boy towns because they were the opposite of the exposed-pipe aluminium towers that the money to buy them came from. There were concrete pineapples on the gate pillars and fun-size columns by the front double doors, and it got worse inside. The concept of stealth wealth never really caught on in our town, so we had to squirrel everything breakable away.

'This is what happens when you don't understand the style section,' Alita remarked while we were packing *objets* off the display shelves into boxes for the loft. Jojo was in the kitchen heaping Doritos into bowls. 'When they say, this is the perfect lamp or spice rack or whatever, they don't really mean that these objects will improve your life – all they really mean is, here's something we haven't had in the mag before. You're not actually meant to go out and buy all the different shit week after week, month after month. Some people are so clueless.'

It could be bookmarked here that Alita and I both lived with single parents, and therefore less stuff. She had a point, though; it made you dizzy just to keep your eyes open inside Jojo's house, and what was worse was that most of it hadn't even come from style mags – it was just a mess. Cherubs on everything: appliquéd, stencilled, moulded, gilded. By the couch, where I sat later, sipping a juice cocktail as the first people arrived, was a lava lamp and a white fake-sixties phone; above it was an awful framed colour portrait of Jojo and his little sister, Sunday-bested on the back lawn at the age of ten or so, aping sophistication but looking like a *Hello!*-magazine shot of a disgraced politician's family. I tried to snap out of it – a particularly loserish way of dealing with party-induced introspection is to keep a coolly distanced commentary of observation going in your head all the time no one's talking to you – but I was as nervous as the rest of us, and was still doing it long after people had arrived.

Maybe ten o'clock, it'd got so bad that I went outside to kill some time. I was definitely going to put the moves on Alita, but there was no point even thinking about it for another couple of hours. No one was going to be up for that kind of stuff until after midnight. I was kicking moodily at some shrubs when a couple of 50-cc Yamahas buzzed up – the kind that compensate for their hairdryer engines with a lot of yellow plastic – and Rob Carter and Dave Long got off.

'Hey, it's gay fuckin' Bay,' said Rob when he clocked me. I'd never heard that one before.

'Yo, Babycham,' Dave said, and cracked up dutifully.

I had some history with these two. Before my dad built our house, we lived down the terraced end of town, in a pretty nice new place, but the other side of the road from a council estate nonetheless. I was too young to know any different and hung about with these kids at infants' school, crossed over the road to go play sometimes. Rat-running through there latterly, I couldn't believe I hadn't noticed how grim it was: rows of semis built out of raw red brick, the colour of dried blood, broken up by patches of tussocky, mud-patched grass and phone boxes owned by telecom companies you'd never heard of. Every house had a satellite dish, presumably so the inmates could tune into the underclass home-shopping channel and pick up style tips: why not accessorise your front garden with a piss-stained mattress and a rusting refrigerator? Why not live on economy oven chips, but never wear the same pair of white Reeboks twice? The Jerry Springer people who lived there considered women who carried condoms to be slags, and men who still sported both ears intact to be foppish popinjays. The word at school was that you could get a twenty-quid Sherman there if you didn't mind the kids watching *The Lion King* in the next room, but I'd never felt the need to verify this.

If Rob and Dave had come to my birthday parties when I was a kid, then that was a dozen years ago. They were total chavs now, into dirt bikes, dope and SAS survival manuals.

They'd left school after GCSEs and I'd heard they were working at the superstore; behind the scenes, obviously, so as not to put the shoppers off. Even if they'd changed, I felt I was basically the same.

'So what's a girl like you doing here?' said Rob.

'How's it goin', man?' I said.

'All your faggot friends here too?' said Dave.

'Just leaves more snatch for the rest of us,' Rob pointed out, clapping him on the shoulder. 'That Asia Cartwright here?'

'Yeah, she's here.' If they got in they'd only give me a pasting for denying it.

'Does she fuck?'

'I couldn't tell you,' I said. I had to handle this carefully. Last party I was at that they crashed, they ended up writing their names on the lawn with their off-road tyres.

'Yeah, course you can't,' Rob sniggered, and his halfwit sidekick joined in. 'So when's it starting?'

'When's what, man?'

'The shagging, dickless.'

'Gonna get high and get horny,' Dave clarified for me.

I almost took a step back. Did they know about meth? They couldn't. I was reading into it.

'So when's it starting?' Rob demanded.

There was no use trying to see them off myself. With a bit of luck they'd get tired of being shot down by women and leave.

'Must've been waiting for you,' I said, indicating the front door.

'You taking the piss?' Dave said. Rob was doing whatever people with one eyebrow do instead of frowning.

'Hey, c'mon, man,' I said, backpedalling. I didn't fancy

trying to snog Alita with a fat lip. 'It's me, Bay. You used to come over my house, remember?'

He considered this a moment, weighing up whether this meant something or whether I deserved a slap for reminding him.

'Yeah, well,' he said after a minute. 'We won't just be playing Power Rangers this time.' They pushed past me, Rob grabbing my arse as they went.

I gave it a minute, let them find their way into the playroom where the music was, then I went back into the lounge. Alita was there but it was still too early; besides, I had to push on swiftly into the kitchen when I clocked this girl Paige from school. Her parents used to be friends with mine, and she'd told me that ten years ago they used to have E-parties at hers, where maybe ten couples would all neck one, get naked and make with the massage oils. This she had watched from the top of the stairs, aged eight or so, she'd claimed to me, stoned, at a party six months before. I'd been avoiding her ever since.

So I was propped against the kitchen counter, satirically eyeing Mr and Mrs Jojo's crockery shelves; specifically a bunch of oversize cups with TEA & MILK stencilled in uppercase around their brims, set off by matching TOAST & MARMALADE-rimmed white china plates. The room was full of people from school getting trashed; suddenly Talya materialised among them, pulled down one of the cups, glugged it full of Diamond White, and toasted me with it. I grinned, grabbed one of the cups for myself, and followed suit from the two-litre she'd brought with her.

'I tell ya, I could do with some of these cups,' I told her. 'Most mornings I swear I *need* instructions on the crockery to remind me what I came in the kitchen for.' This was balls and she knew it; mornings are my best time, but teens are supposed to hate them. Having other people around you makes you less like yourself; this is probably the point of parties.

'Do you think there's much left in the world that Jojo's mum hasn't bought?' Talya said, plucking a remote off the counter. 'Check this out.' She pointed at the window and thumbed the button, and the venetian blinds commenced to roll up.

'Cool,' I said. 'Maybe if we point it at the swimming pool it'll roll back and reveal a rocket launcher.'

'Yeah,' she snickered. 'Or make the trees along the drive fold down to make a runway.' She looked at me over the rim of her cup as she took a swig. 'So. You heard from Shana?' she said.

'Nah. I suspect writing home's a bit low on her priorities at the minute.'

'Lucky cow,' Talya said.

'You think?'

'Shit, yeah. Sun, sea, sand, gorgeous beach bums. Bet it beats business studies.'

'Yeah, I guess,' I said, though I had my own feelings on the subject. When my mum left, a couple of years before, she'd gone on a yoga holiday in Kerala and never come back. I thought this sucked a bit: she was supposed to be leaving my dad, not the rest of us, as she'd pointed out at great length during the many excruciating you've-got-a-right-to-know-type chats she'd made me and Shana sit through during the split. To be fair, my mother'd sent us both open-ended tickets to go visit her, but all I'd done with mine was wonder whether I could swap it for one to somewhere I actually wanted to go.

'Oh, shit, I'm sorry,' Talya said, when I didn't say anything more. 'Is your dad still cut up about it?'

'He hasn't really said much.' This was true, though it was pretty obvious that he was. He'd screamed at Shana down the phone when she rang on Christmas. Me and dad had been sitting in the lounge watching the *Xena* tapes I'd bought him, the remains of two pre-packed Turkey Platters congealing on the coffee table. I'd gone up to my room not to hear the worst of the ding-dong.

'Look,' I said, 'I'm not welling up or anything, but I just don't have much to say about it. I mean, she was at uni anyway, so the fact she's gone isn't like something I'd notice too much anyway.'

'Okay,' Talya said, slipped an arm round my waist and gave me a squeeze. Fortunately Jojo came up with a bowl of McCoys just then, which he proffered to Talya.

'Have one,' he said, 'they're ribbed for *your* pleasure.' Talya laughed, but not hard enough to take her arm back.

'Mr Popular,' I said to him; half the school was there.

'Yeah, they've all just come to see me,' he agreed, giving me an odd look.

'Hey, what's the dip?' interrupted a blonde girl, peering into a bowl on the counter by Jojo.

'Onion burger relish,' he said.

'Ugh. That shit's full of sugar,' she said, and turned back into the throng.

'What is it?' asked another girl, Kettle Chip poised, who'd clearly only half heard.

'Caramelised onion and sweet red pepper extra-chunky salsa,' said Jojo, deadpan.

'Ooh, lovely,' said the girl, and troughed.

Jojo winked at us. 'You like it chunky, huh?' he called after the girl's back, following her away into the party.

'So. Happier topics,' Talya said, turning back to me. 'Who you gonna snog at midnight?'

'Whoever's handy,' I said instead of what I wanted to.

'So I'd better stick around then, huh?' she said, and gave my waist another little squeeze.

'I might be a disappointment,' I said, sure that she knew what I meant.

It was about to happen, and I suddenly understood that all of my old life – being alone, wanting Alita, feeling like it was never going to happen – was about to end. I wanted to talk about Alita, hear things said aloud before they actually happened, get Talya on my side before the event. There was still an hour or so to go before I could realistically make a move. Across the room I could see Rob and Dave, still clutching their crash hats, beginning to percolate in our direction.

'Listen,' I said, 'you want to go somewhere quieter and talk?'

I suppose I was asking for it. I was just making myself comfortable against the headboard, settling in for a long one, and considering whether revealing the facts of the matter to the best friend was in fact the best strategy for furthering this kind of project. I mean, it's so year seven: what did I want her to do once I'd confessed, go up to Alita and say 'My friend fancies you'? But it was a total surprise when she knelt before me on the bed, pulled a wrap of meth out of the back pocket of her jeans and opened it out on the duvet.

Okay. Shock one was that she'd taken that 'let's go somewhere quiet' for the cliché it was. I was quite insulted: I would never have used that line without irony. But shock two, squared, cubed, diced and drizzled with olive oil, was the meth. Our ground rule was that we kept it all in one place to minimise the chance of anyone else finding it. Even if no one else in the country knew about it, we were pretty sure that when they found out, crystal meth would turn out to be class A, and none of us fancied giving Her Majesty much Pleasure.

'Where the fuck did that come from?' I was thinking maybe Talya'd scooped some up when we were using before and kept it back.

'Alita,' she said, like it was nothing.

'Alita *gave* it to you?'

'Yeah,' she said, like I was being retarded. 'We all keep a little for wanking – women need something extra.'

'You *what*?'

'Oh, c'mon,' she said. 'You wouldn't get arsey about a woman using a vibrator, would you? Well then, you shouldn't get arsey about this. A girl needs a helping hand wherever she can find one.'

'But Jesus, Talya, that's so not what we agreed –'

'Oh, bollocks to what we agreed,' she said quickly, then gave me a slow smile. 'Anyway, hark at you. Has Alita slipped your mind?'

I flushed red before I could help it. 'Excuse me?'

'Alita? Dark hair, five-nine, hundred and twenty pounds?'

'Thirty-four, twenty-six, thirty-five –'

'Don't pretend, I know you do,' she interrupted.

'I do what?'

'Tweak with Alita,' she said, taking off her top. 'Euan said.' She was wearing a white Sloggi sports bra.

'Euan said to who?

'Me,' she said, but then seemed to consider a moment before adding, 'and Asia.'

Asia. Right. 'What you mean is, Euan told Asia and Asia told you.'

'Okay, what of it?' she said. 'Jesus, Bay, chill.' She leaned forward off her haunches onto all fours in front of me on the bed; her shoulders were as defined as a panther's. 'It's a party. Don't you want to have some fun?' She lifted one paw onto my thigh.

'It's not that kind of party,' I said.

'There's only one kind,' she said, slipping the bra-top over her head and pouncing. I put my hands up; her breasts were cool and heavy against my palms. 'No,' I croaked, and she pulled back; but only to slip a square of foil from her hip pocket that she began flattening out for the meth. She looked up, licked her eyes over my evident distress, and winked as she busied herself.

'Hold on,' I said, pushing for time, 'when did Euan say that?'

She shrugged, tapping out the crystals. 'What of it?'

'It was horseshit, that's what. I don't tweak with Alita.'

'Then how come every time I call her you're there?'

'Duh-huh!' I said, though I was secretly kind of pleased. If we seemed that tight to people, then they wouldn't have such a hard time dealing with us as an item. Commencing in about two hours. 'Cos we're *friends*, Talya. Jesus! I'm not fucking her.'

'You don't have to shit me,' she said. 'Face it. We're not like other kids any more.'

It was a shock to hear someone say it. While I was being shocked, however, she was flicking the Bic under the foil and taking a hit.

'Stop,' I said. 'Stop it, I mean it.'

She blew it out and proffered me the sawn-off Biro. 'You know you want it.'

'You're wrong. I only do it –'

'To make the drugs work,' she finished for me. 'Yeah, that coy little line lasted a long time.'

'Shit,' I said, finally getting it. 'Yeah, it did. Let me guess. When did Euan tell Asia that Alita and me were tweaking? It wasn't while he was trying to get into her knickers, was it?'

'Maybe,' she said, backing up suddenly

'Oh, Jesus, Talya,' I said, 'don't you see it? And when did Asia tell you? It couldn't have been connected to you catching her with Euan some time, could it?'

Talya's silence spoke a few volumes. She put the foil back down on the bed.

'Fuck it, Talya, I can't believe you fell for it,' I said. 'Euan and Asia were always hot to pair off.'

She folded her arms over her breasts. 'So what's your problem with pairing off?' she said. Then, more quietly, 'Why'd you bring me up here?'

Soliciting her help and advice for making Alita mine till the end of time was plainly as good an idea as expecting to be accepted for a cut-rate credit card without ticking the 'Yes, I want expensive card insurance so you can recoup the loss you make on the interest' box. I was saved by two kids bursting through the bedroom door. Saved like a diver being saved from a barracuda by a shark scaring it. They were a boy and a girl I'd never seen before, a little younger than us, high as the sky and handling each other like sex had a sell-by date.

'Hey, private party, dudes,' I called out, and they broke their snog. The girl gave me a what-the-fuck's-with-you look, but the guy grinned as he checked out first Talya's tits, then the hit of meth on the bed.

'No problem, *dude*,' he said, and produced a see-through Ziploc bag of glassy grey flakes like a conjuror plucking aces from the air. 'We brought our own.'

* * *

I dug out the local paper for the week I was born from the library for a school project once. It wasn't even digitised, just bound up in big dog-eared binders. Scanning among the UPVC ads and Women's Institute reports for evidence of significance to the week of my nativity, I found a news story, more or less the only one in the paper. It was about a firework parade the Saturday before where, instead of a Guy Fawkes, the citizens had burned an effigy of a union leader, this coal-mining chav with bad hair. I found out who he was from *Encarta* and, I have to say, I think that was a pretty fucked-up thing to do. I mean, the guy was alive at the time: that's the kind of thing flip-flopped foreign guys with moustaches do, and aren't we supposed to be better than them?

Now, as I ran down into the party, I was surrounded by the offspring of the burners and they disgusted me. Like my dad was fond of saying, the concept of being different from your parents went out the window with the property boom. I homed in on the first year-ten kid I saw.

'Where the fuck is Jamie?' I didn't slam the kid up against the wall, but I might as well have. 'Huh?'

'Stop it, Bay, leave him alone!' Talya had followed me.

I glared at the little fuck. Now I looked at him, I was sure I'd seen him with Jamie and Harper earlier. But he was wasted beyond belief and probably not much use anyway. Jojo and Alita were nowhere to be seen. Across the room, on the top-whack Technics rig lovingly installed by Jojo's hi-fi purist father, a mangled pizza was spinning briskly on one of the turntables.

I came out of it. It was a pretty greasy one to pull, throwing your weight at a kid two years below you, and I never thought I'd sink to it. So I threw it at Talya instead.

'Are you high? Can't you see what's going on?' I demanded, waving my hands as I rounded on her.

'Hey, time out, come on,' she said. 'Outside. Now!'

I went to open my mouth.

'Now, Bay.' She held out her hand. I took it – realising how much mine was shaking – and followed her out through the garage.

It was cold as a bastard: cold the way the hot tap, when it's too hot, can feel cold when you first stick your hand under it. It was only when Talya wrapped her bare arms around me that I felt it, and the sweat seemed to freeze on my skin.

'I'm okay,' I said, starting to shiver.

'You sure?' Her voice was brisk. She held me out at arm's length to look at me.

'Yeah, sure,' I said, avoiding her eyes.

'Then it's too cold to mess around here,' she said. Pulling her key-zapper from her pocket, she popped the locks on her 205.

I didn't want to drive anywhere, but she said there was no way I was going back inside till I was chilled out, and in the meantime you had to get the engine hot to make the heater work. We skirted the edge of town, the streets as empty as they were on Diana's funeral, when we went out on our boards to bomb the busiest junction in town – the holy grail, the place you could never normally skate – and found it, as we'd guessed, so quiet you could hear the bulbs in the traffic lights blink on and off. Talya got on the old road south, the one the bypass replaced when my dad was a kid, the one that had been used ever since solely by kids decking their mums' cars out to stoner central, the picnic area on the edge of the woods. By the time I finished the breathing exercises Talya insisted I do, we were out on Deadman's Curve, where there were more bunches of flowers by the roadside than there was grass.

I was chilled, but I felt sick; of a number of things, but mostly me.

'Shit. I'm sorry,' I said. 'I would've chinned me if I'd been you.'

'These things happen,' she said, concentrating on the road, perhaps a little pointedly. I felt moved to differ: these things didn't happen, at least not to me. But I kept my trap shut, and presently she pulled into the picnic area.

It was the midnight hour, and there was no one else around. She dropped the locks and killed the engine; and then the only sound was the faint, rhythmic scrape of interlocking branches in the bare trees in front of us, tipped with silver against the black by the lights from the driving range by the bypass.

'I lost it,' I said.

'Yes, you did.'

'It's just, I never really thought about where the meth came from,' I said, shifting round in my seat a little. 'I mean, I knew it was coming from Jamie and Harper, but I thought it was like a hobby with them. I didn't realise they were selling. And Jesus, if Jamie's selling it to shitheads like that – some fucking dolt who takes it to parties and flashes it around – then he's asking to get busted.' I didn't need to add, And if he does, so will we. 'I don't want to see that happen.'

'That's one way to look at it,' Talya said, and pushed the dashboard lighter in. 'But another way is, the more people Jamie's selling to the better. Then, if anyone gets busted, what're they gonna do? Arrest the whole town?' She pulled a battered ten-pack of her mother's Silk Cut out of the door pocket, extracted one and lit it. 'Safety in numbers, Bay,' she said, breathing smoke out. 'Think of some schoolteacher in Guildford looking at chicks-with-dicks on the internet –

there're so many other people doing it that there's no way he's going to be found out. Unless he leaves a big folder marked 'Kiddy Porn' on his desktop and then takes the PC to a repair shop. This tastes like shit.' She cracked the window and pushed the butt out.

'We ought to tell the others,' I said.

'We could,' she said.

'Hey, where were they, anyway?' I frowned at her. 'I didn't see anyone around after we came down.'

'I don't know, Bay,' she said forbearingly, her patience obviously thinning. Usually she'd listen to my crap for hours; everything seemed to be changing too fast. Perhaps this was what growing up felt like; if it was, I didn't like it.

'Alita looked good tonight, didn't she?' I said. If things were starting to change, then they might as well change the way I wanted them.

'Yeah, she did,' said Talya, sounding like her mother a little. 'She's a pretty girl.' She popped her seatbelt and tucked one leg under herself.

'Maybe she's wondering where we are,' I said, 'you think? Maybe we ought to go back.'

'She might not be there,' Talya said, in a way that made it sound like she knew she wouldn't. 'And anyway, it's too late. Look.' She tapped the dashboard LCD: it was 11.57. 'We'll never make it in time.'

I groaned inside. The whole point of the night had been, through some subtle manoeuvring around Talya, to get Alita into a place where, on the stroke of twelve, I could home in for the big one. Now I'd blown it, and Talya was being weirder than I'd ever seen her, and that was my fault too. I'd thought I had everything sussed six hours ago, but now my life was a house built on quicksand and ice cream. And I was stuck in the middle of nowhere while the rest of the country was counting down, making with the breath mints and lip balm. I really didn't want Alita getting snogged by everyone in the room, though that was probably what was about to happen in two minutes. Most of all, I didn't want any of what I'd done to get back to Alita, if she didn't already know about it.

'Listen, babe,' I said, putting my hand on Talya's. 'I so overreacted earlier, and I so appreciate the way you saw it for what it was.'

'That's cool,' she said. 'I was there. I saw what a shock it was for you.'

'You're a sweetheart,' I said, and brushed her cheek with a knuckle. 'But the others might not understand it so well. Me flipping out. I mean, them not being there. Not seeing how it was.'

'You don't have to worry about what the others think,' she said, turning her hands beneath mine so that we were palm to palm. 'They've probably got other things to think about themselves right now.'

Man, did I miss the point of that one. I was suddenly aware of how close our chests were, how far away the nearest human soul was – how heavy her eyes were, how wide her slow smile.

'It's midnight,' she said, and I was about to say something – anything – when she stopped my lips with all of her full mouth, slick-soft and cool. I couldn't help it; my stomach fell away as my groin tugged upwards. What can I say? I hadn't done it enough to turn it down. Her hand went to my lap, my hand went to her chest; and by the time I noticed the clock again, the new year was crawling around in Baby Gap.

So that blew out the rest of the school year.

I think the girls planned it; or, rather, I think Talya did. I think she asked Alita if she could have a clear shot at me, and Alita was so taken aback – I mean, I can see how it'd be hard to stand in the way of your best friend if she called you on it – that she acquiesced. Then, since Euan and Asia had more or less copped off already, Alita made a play for Jojo, to complete the circuit. Joj probably twigged what was going on and, so as not to be left high and dry, he reciprocated, even though he ought to've known how I felt. I swear, we could've used an Athenian wood and a Puck or two, but in their absence we had to muddle along.

My time with Talya turned out to be taken up mostly with comforting her through her parents' domestics anyway. Four of Clubs' husband, having only recently found out about the playing cards, had begun to obsess on her brief tour through the pornographic underbelly, such as it was, trying to outdo whatever sickness he imagined she used to get up to; and she, having forgotten the whole thing long ago, was suddenly required to go, Talya had gathered, to swapping parties and sex clubs, and to accommodate a number of eye-watering sex toys about her person when they stayed in. This made for a low-serotonin household. Those few evenings with Talya that weren't spent with me stroking her hair while she complained against my neck, we spent dazedly watching Michael Douglas videos from her parents' collection: there wasn't much else to do round Talya's.

Eventually I told her that my dad was making me stay in and study for the final push to A levels. This got me away from her, but was its own brand of hell in itself. Ever since he'd lost it one time, when I pushed him too far about Mum, he'd been overcompensating for his moment of weakness, bluffing it out on me. With Talya in the picture, he seemed to be under the impression that I was finally getting some, for the first time in my life. Ironic, since he'd never suspected a thing during my real shagging days. At the same time, he found my having a regular boy-girl-type thing with Talya almost unbearably amusing, and would try and *FHM* me out with manly advice.

'If you're going to smoke, don't use matchbooks,' he counselled me one time, during a late-night sad-lads session. 'Get yourself a solid lighter you can't lose, and use it. If you don't, you'll come home after working late and there's your dinner waiting for you and you're doing fine – but then you finish eating, you go to light up, and there's the matchbook from the place you've really been all evening, staring her in the face.'

This was what pissed me off most about my mother going. I didn't choose to be with him, she did; and yet I was the one who had to deal with him. She chose him; she ought to have been around to put up with his crap, not me. It was such a filthy winter that he was home more than usual too. January through March it rained persistently and copiously enough for him to have to turn all his building crews over from development to repairs, to cope with the damage done to his executive deluxe detacheds with their Kleenex walls and Play-Doh foundations – off the warranty, natch.

In the spring, the rain stopped for the first time since Christmas. Dad started going out more, and so did we. Party season was cranking up; everyone was hot to get out and shake a little flesh, us included. The hot spots were the big ex-hotels out in the middle of nowhere, converted into hollowed-out, four-level monster party zones five years before by – you got it – my father. They were strictly for us whitebread children: the hard kids from the estates went to the church-conversion boozers in the town centre. They came into town, and we went out of it – to Blah Blah's, the ManuFactory, the Sound Republic and the Venue, all a half-hour drive in different directions into the country. We convoyed out every Thursday, Friday and Saturday during the Easter holidays and spent six hours shaking our tits to the hits.

They were pretty stinky parties, but we needed them. We'd all been coupled up for a few months now, and weekend nights had become stilted nightmares of playing grown-up in country pubs, in restaurants. It was a relief to do something mob-handed again on the pressure nights of the week, though it wasn't the same as it used to be. What had been natural and spontaneous at sixteen now seemed to need planning, diarising, negotiating; I'd say to Talya, 'Let's all go out together on Saturday', and she'd say, 'Fine, but what if the others have plans?' Being eighteen is about being so self-conscious that you imagine someone's watching everything you do; you can say this is vanity, but it isn't. It comes with the realisation that everything from now on has to be negotiated, where before you could count on people subsuming their own agendas to the group, for fear of standing out. It's a pain, and you wonder why it can't be the way it used to; you realise, sooner or later, that if you put people in couples, they turn into their parents.

It was on one of these outings that it finally became clear that I had to do something. We were at the Venue, an old brewery surrounded by what used to be hopfields but were now go-kart tracks, paintball arenas and a golf-driving range, twenty minutes south of town. It was a handbag night, with the remmy who passed for a DJ dropping what he billed as 'anthems' – a term he'd probably heard off some frantic TV advert – into the mix with wild inaccuracy, but we danced for hours anyway, the whole bunch of us, fuelled on nothing but energy drinks. It was a relief to be out in a gang, but doing anything beyond dancing – talking, for example – seemed too much like hard work.

I ducked out around eleven to go drink some water. Dancing is some kind of point of honour with women, but for guys it feels very different to how boybands make it look – it's both difficult and boring at the same time. I headed for the chill room instead. Inside, Orbital was playing quietly, as if embarrassed to be there and trying not to draw attention to itself. There were a lot of kids from school sprawled about, flaked out, and richer kids too, the ones who went to the public school two towns away. Both groups were unnerving; the kids from school were younger and harder than us; the rich kids were just from another planet. You felt they were looking at you the whole time. It was a relief to see Jojo wander in at the far side and make his way over.

'Hola.' He dumped himself down beside me.

'Hey,' I said.

'How's it going?' he said.

''kay. How's your mum?'

'Oh, all right,' he said, and that was it. I couldn't think of anything else to say. We'd barely spoken – I mean talked – in weeks. Seeing him these days was like, this is a big deal, I've got to talk to my ex-best friend, who's going out with the only girl I ever really wanted. It sucked.

'So,' he said, after a few pulls at his energy-drink pack. 'You in A-level denial, or is this a reward for revision?'

'Bit of both. You?'

'Total denial.' He grinned, but it faded as quickly as it had come.

'It's different somehow, isn't it?' I said. Meaning us, everything.

'Tell me about it,' he said. 'There used to be something else.'

'Possibility,' I agreed.

'Totally,' he said. Alita and him were as miserable as me and Talya. Excellent; I gloated inwardly as I tried to conjure up ways to make him reveal more. But he tossed away his drink packet and said, 'It's not too late to put things back, is it?'

I didn't know how to play it. 'You have to do what you want to,' I said, hedging. 'Life's too short.'

'Listen to the man,' he said, standing up and dusting off the arse of his cargo pants. 'C'mon. Let's go score some meth.'

I went round to see Jamie first thing next morning. You couldn't get Alita out of bed with a crane on a Sunday, so there was no danger of running into her; her mum worked the early shift at a Shady Pines across town, clocking on at seven to toilet the oldsters who'd woken up (and to bundle the ones who hadn't out the goods entrance, so Alita claimed). Jamie used to get up at six to grab off-peak modem time, and couldn't break the habit for weekends. I rang their bell at seven forty-five, and it was he who opened the door, on my third ring.

'She's not up yet,' he said, eyeing me like the stranger I was.

'No kidding?' I grinned. 'We were gonna blitz some revision today. I thought she was being a bit optimistic about a breakfast kickoff.'

'I'll go and blast her out,' he said, letting me in.

'Whoa, cool your jets,' I said. 'I wouldn't want to be responsible.' We stood awkwardly in the hall for a second, Jamie obviously keen to get back to whatever he'd been doing.

'You want to watch TV?' he offered.

'Actually, while I'm here,' I said, 'my dad switched cable companies last week. I can't get on the net till the new box arrives – and what with school being closed and all. Can I sit in on yours?'

He knew something was up, but I was being just grinny and pushy enough to leave him no option but to let me follow him up to the loft conversion.

'There you go.' He gestured at the PC he and Harper had built from mail-order parts, then went over to the workbench on the other side of the room, put in a jeweller's eyepiece and commenced to tinker with a circuit board. Stacked under the bench I could see a whole bunch of the stuff that I knew was for meth manufacture – kitty litter, stacks of piping. There was a lot more of it than I'd expected to see. I sat down, opened the browser, made a connection and pretended to work.

'We were at the Venue last night,' I said, offhand, after a while.

'Yeah?' He didn't look up. 'Any good?'

'Not really. It was different.'

He snickered. 'How does sucking make it different?'

I dropped the connection. 'Different vibe.' I got up, propped my butt on the edge of the desk, folded my arms. 'No one does coke anymore. Or E much, either.'

He looked over at me sharply. 'Yeah?'

'Yeah,' I said, and held eye contact. 'You know that half the people there are doing meth?'

'Really?' he said, trying to look anxious to get back to his stuff. He wasn't any good at this.

'Yeah, really,' I said, squaring up. 'You know they're selling it out of their cars round the back?'

'Hey, that's nothing to do with me,' he protested, holding up his hands.

'Is that a fact?' I said. 'Because I'd say it's everything to do with you. I'd say it's everything to do with this.' I swept my arm across the sacks of SaniKat, the coiled plastic tubing, the bundles of pH sticks and stacked heating mantles piled up under his workbench like in some bizarre cash-and-carry.

He gave me a sharp, calculating kind of look, then leaned back in his chair, popped the top of a Diet Coke and took a sip. We locked eye contact for a moment, and then suddenly he'd pulled back at the dynamic; I was the hick, he was the homeboy; I was now-wait-a-goldurned-minute, he was get-the-fuck-out-of-my-office. I'd thought I could throw my weight around on him a little but clearly years of being the nerd had taught him other kinds of hardness. There was nothing to do but go for the soft underside.

'Look at all this stuff,' I said, gesturing at the scraps and mementoes of dead projects that he and Harper had decorated the hardboard walls with. 'You and Harper used to have such fucking plans, man. You were the coolest kids I knew. But now you're what, a drug dealer? That's all you want to be now?'

'Seed money, man,' he said with a shrug, using the semi-stoned drawl that sixteen year-olds think sounds worldly-wise.

'You need money to buy *seeds*? You're going to grow *dope*?'

He gave me a despairing you-fucking-greybeards kind of look, like I was the drug fiend, not him. 'Duh. Seed money is what you water ideas with, make them grow.' He gestured around the walls like I just had, taking in the tacked-up diagrams, the elevations, the odd prototype hung from the rafters with fishing line. 'Look at all this crap.' He batted a second-hand Psion with an extra circuit board grafted on, and sent it swinging on its line. 'Ideas'll sprout anywhere, but you want a lawn, you need to spend some money.'

I realised I could be pressing on a raw nerve here unless I played this carefully. Harper came from the crappy estates so there was no input there; Jamie had paid his own phone bill since he was old enough for a paper round; anything the two of them wanted to do, they earned the money for themselves. I couldn't pretend to know what they were doing with their sawn-off Psions and Palm Pilots, but even if all their big talk turned out to be their hormones mouthing off, they did it off their own backs. You had to give them credit for that.

'We're concept-rich, cash-poor,' he went on, giving me a look that was both sulky and proud at the same time. 'We go to uni, earn degrees, get jobs, that's five years down the drain. Either we shortcut or someone else beats us to it; we watch them rake it in while we're still living on grants.'

'So you set up a little drugs lab in the meantime?' I said. 'C'mon, Jamie. Watch a little TV. You get into this stuff, you don't get out again. You're joining a club that they don't let you leave.'

'No, man,' he said, 'you don't get it. We're the only ones making it.'

'*You* don't get it,' I countered. 'C'mon, man, what are you thinking with? Why are you the only ones making it? Don't you think there could be a reason for that?'

'Yeah,' he sniffed, snottily. 'We're a couple of light years ahead of the game. You never see these drugs guys on your TV? Huh? They're the kind of people who run hookers, bouncers. They work in cities, not here. Old-school. You think we didn't check this out? Even E is still a new thing for them. No one knows about meth except us. You stay ahead, you stay safe.'

He was wrong, I knew it, but I couldn't tell him why. I'd always thought this loft was a pretty cool place; for the first time it felt like what it was, the pit of a couple of hormonal teenage boys, the kind of place where you didn't want to touch anything too long. I shifted tack.

'What about your mum? I mean, this is hardly a covert operation you have here.'

'She doesn't know from shit. She sees this stuff, I tell her it's a science project. What does she know?' His voice was breaking all over the place; he must've been the last one in his year. Each sudden shift of pitch made him flush red, the poor bastard. 'She flunked all her CSE science, and she didn't even do A levels. What's it to you, anyway? You've always been happy enough to smoke it.'

'You using it yourself?'

'No.' He shifted his eyes, but I was pretty sure he was telling the truth. 'What're you saying? You're getting side effects? Tolerance?' Suddenly he was the concerned technician, already computing how he might factor in some new isotope to ensure a longer-use market.

'What do you care, if all you're doing is raising seed

money?' I said. 'You don't need it to last forever.' I got up, stretched, made to look absently out the skylight. 'Though maybe you haven't made so much from it yet. I mean, even for a drug dealer, this town's pretty small-time.'

'That's where you're wrong,' he said, taking the bait. 'There's more money here than in some inner-city shithouse, I'll tell you that.'

'So you must be pretty close to getting what you need, huh? Surely you're smart enough not to keep doing it beyond that.'

'What's it to you?' he said, and I knew I'd pushed him about as far as I could go without having him turn his back on me for good. Teenage boys are touchy about the stuff they do, however pointless it seems; the only goals they can reach (since everyone – parents, teachers, girls – gives them a wide berth) are the pointless ones they make up themselves.

'Hey, c'mon, Jamie. I don't want to see you fucked up, is all.'

He studied my face for a long moment. 'One big batch. One shitload, and we're out. That's all we're gonna need.'

'If that's all you need, why don't you quit now?' I said. 'Huh? While you're ahead? If you only need to do one more batch you must have a pile of cash already – and c'mon, man, you're smart enough to know how to make money work for you.'

'You think I hadn't thought of that?' His voice boomed, then shrilled; I pretended not to notice.

'Then why don't you?'

'You don't understand, do you? We've got kids selling for us. People rely on us.'

'Don't give me that,' I said. 'You don't owe anyone.'

He looked at me then like kids look at teachers, and I knew I'd lost.

'I don't need this,' he said. 'I've got stuff to do. Go wake Alita up and get out of my face.'

'I want you to tell me you'll quit it, Jamie,' I said, talking down to him; it was pretty obvious that this was the last time he was going to give me houseroom, so it was now or never. I had to do this. Meth was our mess as much as his; we'd encouraged it by doing it. You play, you pay. You don't leave a kid to clear up your mess. 'It's getting out of hand. Someone's going to notice.'

'Cops? You're kidding me.' His voice was all over the place.

'Someone serious,' I said. 'You just said it yourself. There's a lot of kids round here with a lot of money. You're not going to be the first person to have noticed.'

'You think you're so smart, don't you?' His larynx had settled low, finally, so he was almost growling. 'Well, you're not the first person who's noticed how many people want meth either.'

'What do you mean?' I said, feeling my eyes slit.

'Ask Alita about her college fund, why don't you,' he said, turning back to his desk. 'I bet she's got quite a balance now.'

He was lying. But there was no point getting into a slanging match; I let it slide and made for the stairs.

'She thinks you're a wanker, you know that?' he called after me. 'Why d'you think she's not with you? Why's she fucking your best *friend*, man?'

I obliterated the rest, thundering down the stairs, out the door and into my Clio. I'd done what I could, I told myself as I decked the pedal. The faster I went, the less space there was to think about whether I was right or not.

I found out a month later.

When you're turning eighteen, even if you're convinced you're right, you tell yourself that you're probably wrong. I left Jamie and Harper to it, didn't face down Alita, bumbled disconsolately along with Talya, kept my head down and worked for four weeks. It was one of those weird Mays, full of too early summer, when you know there's still going to be another tranche of crappy weather before proper summer begins. The last Saturday before the bank holiday, I needed a break. I'd been tied to my desk all week, telling myself the weather wouldn't last, but Saturday dawned too good not to think about kicking back; twenty degrees by seven a.m., with the sun in the sky like an egg broken into a blue china bowl. I decided that part of the discipline of revision was knowing when to give yourself a break.

I ate breakfast cross-legged on the sundeck, hit the gym, stopped for petrol on the way back. I was thinking maybe I'd drive to the coast later if I could drum up any support. While I was queuing, scanning the shelves, I noticed a porn star Alita used to like on the cover of an American grot mag, and bought it for her on impulse. There'd been too much grimness lately, not enough kidding. I dropped it through her door on the way back, in a old Jiffy from the floor of my car, with a note saying, 'He hasn't retired, neither have I; sod the revision, come round and play.'

When I got back even my dad was up early, mowing the back lawn before golf. I waved to him but didn't bother stopping to say hi because he'd have to turn the mower off to talk, and he hated to do that; instead I went up to my room to watch the chart show while I coloured in a new revision timetable. Presently I heard the mower cut out, so I went down to take Dad a beer.

He'd beaten me to it, though, and was flopping down on the couch and flipping on the TV as I hit the ground floor. He gave me a wink, then popped the top of his Stella and started paging through the TV channels. I went into the kitchen to make it look like I'd come down for something else. I heard him whistle from the sofa.

'Aye-aye,' he said, sitting forward on the sofa as I came into the room. I followed his line of vision to the TV, which was showing helicopter footage of backed-up traffic on a dual carriageway, fire crews, and a motel spouting flames from its roof in the background.

'That's the Cresthouse on the bypass, isn't it?' Dad said, squinting.

I peered at the screen, but they'd cut back to the local news anchor, who was addressing urgent and concerned questions to a reporter on the spot; then the aerial shot filled the screen again, and I recognised that it was indeed the local franchise of one of the chains of motels that had sprung up on the back of the Channel Tunnel. The news anchor was solemnly advising viewers that sightseeing traffic was making things more difficult for the emergency services.

'Sounds like it's too good to miss, then,' Dad said, putting down his beer and gathering up his keys. 'Fancy it?'

He knew a back way around the woods by the bypass. We parked at the end of a farm road, then walked over a couple of fields, Dad readying the video camera as we went, and got a prime position on a bluff above the motel. He shot a few minutes' worth of footage of the fire-fighters, both of us lying low in the grass, but it was kind of samey. It made me realise how hard news crews have to work to make live reports from disasters interesting. We soon tired of it and stagger-ran down the hard shoulder to join the crowds behind the police tape.

There were the same daft theories floating about as the day the Indian boys fell out of the sky – gas-main rupture, helicopter crash – but we were hours after the event this time, and everything was sealed off. There weren't even any flames any more. Dad was soon strolling around, hands in the pockets of his shorts, networking with other local business types. I spotted a kid I knew from school, though I usually avoided him because we used to post fake messages on support newsgroups in year-seven lunch hours, pretending to be cross-dressing bouncers, dominatrix schoolmistresses and stuff. He was an even bigger dolt these days and it was kind of embarrassing to be seen talking to him, but he told me that he'd seen Alita and Asia cruise by earlier, with Asia's brother Jackson driving; they hadn't stopped, but just peeled rubber back towards town. I didn't have my phone, because Talya was after me the whole time on it, so I found my dad, ponced his mobile and dialled Alita's, then Asia's, to see what they were doing.

There was only voicemail at both, so I called Asia's textphone and left my dad's mobile number and an 0001000 – I'm lonely, give me a call. What I really needed was a ride back: it was turning into a regular networking fest there for my dad, and until he got tired of it and left, I was stuck there. His mobile rang almost non-stop, so even if Alita or Asia had been trying to get me, I wouldn't have known about it. I got talking to one of his cronies, however, and it turned out that he had to take his mother out from the Shady Pines, so he'd give me a ride back if my dad was going to go on for lunch with some of the other guys there, which seemed to be where the money was. I indicated to Dad that I was heading back; he barely looked up from his call, but he flapped his hand at me, so I left.

When I got home, the only messages on the machine were for Dad. Asia had rung my mobile three times, but hadn't left any message; I tried to call her back, but she was busy.

So the options were either to call Euan or Talya and find out what was smoking, or goof aimlessly around on the net for a few hours. No-brainer. By the time I was sick of surfing it was after two, and I could hear Dad coming in downstairs. I jumped up and went down to see if Asia had called me back on his mobile, and found him sitting white-faced on the sofa.

'What's up?' I said. 'Shit, Dad, you look wasted.'

He looked up at me like it was the hardest thing he'd ever had to do – I remember wondering just how he'd managed to fit so much Stella down his neck in under two hours – and said:

'You better call your friends. There's some stuff you need to know.'

Jamie had 70 per cent burns, Harper was worse. It had happened a little before nine. The fire took hold in the wing Jamie and Harper had been dragged out of, and might have been confined there if it hadn't taken the emergency services almost an hour to get there through the Saturday-morning traffic. By the time they arrived, the whole place had gone up.

Jamie and Harper weren't the only ones, but they were the worst. A cleaner and a Belgian couple had also been taken to the hospital with smoke inhalation, along with a couple of the staff who'd piddled at the liquefying motel with extinguishers. They were still in the local BUPA place, but Jamie and Harper had been choppered to a burns unit in London. It had taken an hour for the air ambulance to get down to us and my dad had tried to bribe the news helicopter to take them, but it turned out you needed specialist equipment onboard so they'd had to wait. The hospital they'd waited in was more used to pacemaker fittings and hip replacements than kids who'd been blown through a wall and then flame-grilled. It wasn't looking good for them, was how Asia put it, grizzling down her mobile from a cab stuck in traffic in London.

The next thirty hours or so are smeary in my mind. The fact that we were in a place where time comes in six-hour multiples rather than in days and nights probably has something to do with it; but mostly I've blanked it out of shame. I felt most of the things I ought, but too close behind them was a feeling I couldn't shake, which mounted until it took over. It told me that everything was fucked now, and the world would never be the same again. I felt like a High Street must feel when a superstore opens on the edge of town.

Those hours were the worst of my life so far. I was stuck at home, no one to call, no one calling me, dependent on smarmy news anchors for information, all because I'd been avoiding Talya that morning. Alita, her mum, Jojo, Talya and Asia all went to the hospital in London; I called Euan but he hadn't even known it had happened until Asia's mum called to let him know that Asia would be blowing him out for their rock-climbing tryst that afternoon. The hospital switchboard wouldn't talk to anyone who wasn't family, and it was only after a few hours of not being able to get either Alita or Talya on their mobiles that I found out cellphones had to be switched off in hospitals, like on planes.

I stayed home, climbing the walls, waiting for someone to call. I wanted to drive up to London and go to the hospital myself but I felt I'd be intruding if I went on my own. The others had gone as a group, one that I wasn't part of. I half hoped Dad would want to go up – he could have the stated purpose of comforting Alita's mother – but he'd started smoking as soon as he got back and lit each successive joint with the roach of the last. By Saturday teatime it was taking him anywhere from ten seconds to two minutes to respond to routine questions.

Finally, around nine, Talya called, but she wasn't any more lucid than Dad. I got her to hand the phone to Asia, who gave me the score: Jamie and Harper weren't going to last the night. They were too far gone for the doctors to be able to give them any effective analgesia – drugs that might've been strong enough to alleviate their pain would probably also kill them, and the doctors weren't allowed to do that. We had to hope that they were unconscious; I found out later that this was wishful thinking. Asia wanted me to come up to the hospital and chill Talya out, but I couldn't face it.

I put the phone down and cried for a bit. What stopped me was remembering the grot mag that I'd posted through Alita's door that morning. The thought of it practically trepanned me. Dad was baked out on the sofa, so I ran up there, snivelling all the way, and spent a miserable half-hour trying to get my arm through the letterbox to retrieve it and, when that failed, to break in. Neither worked. My fingers even brushed it. I can't describe how that felt. I trailed back home, flinching, and used what was left of Dad's gear to smoke myself unconscious.

When I woke I found a four-hour-old message on the machine from Asia saying that it was over and they were going home now.

I went up to Alita's after a shower and three Excedrin, to find that Dad had locked the gates at the top of the drive to keep out the news trucks and reporters and photographers who were camped in the street. It was like having a dozen stalkers, fresh out of stalker school and anxious to pay back their student loans, coming at you all at once up there. I went back down the drive and cut through the hedge into Alita's back garden. All the curtains at their house were closed, and I didn't know what I'd find if I went up to the kitchen door and let myself in now that they were back. I went back to ours and tried to call, but all I could get on any of her options was voicemail. I e-mailed her telling her I was home and trying to reach her.

For the rest of that week I sat by the phone in my room and waited. The police had told the TV news, in the first few hours, that Jamie and Harper were cleaning rooms as a Saturday job. Anyone who knew them at all should have found this a little unlikely; they had much better ways of making thirty quid than spending six hours with their tongues down a U-bend. By late on Saturday the police had found the remains of enough stuff – fused glass, melted condenser pipe, reformatted kitty litter – to convince them that Harper and Jamie had been up to something a little more chemically advanced than bleaching the toilets. On Sunday morning the motel company confirmed that they weren't employees but paying guests, and on the lunchtime news the anchor announced that the two boys killed in yesterday's motel explosion were suspected of using the room as a makeshift laboratory.

Game over. I went to my room, wiped my hard drive, waited for the cops. I thought about packing a bag, using the ticket to India my mum had sent me, but I knew I wouldn't get through the airport. I spent the afternoon at the window, watching the drive; after dark, I slipped out to the recycle dumpster by the swimming pool on foot with my hard-copy pornography. I sat up till after one, and then I couldn't sleep. Although I'd long hoarded a bottle of diazepam my mum had left behind, I didn't dare take any; if I was going to be hauled out of bed at four a.m. I didn't want to be too Valiumed to think straight.

They didn't come. Next day it was in the papers. I didn't usually read them but Dad had got them all and left them lying about in the lounge. The general drift seemed to be: Thank God they blew themselves up before they could take the bomb to school, kids who have everything, how could it happen here? That kind of thing. I didn't know if this was good news, disinformation from the cops, or what. I put the newspapers back the way they were and went back up to follow it on the web. One search I made on Jamie's name brought up, on top of the news articles on him, all his posts to chat strands. It was horrible to look at them: flamings, gangsta posing, paranoia. I opened a couple. It was the same whitebread teen stuff CNN broadcasts as the Killer's Secret Net Diary after the latest US high school slayings. Look at me, somebody! Testosterone talking. It wasn't the kind of thing you'd post if you thought it'd be serving as your obituary. It wasn't what you'd want to remember someone by either, but I just kept clicking and clicking, couldn't help myself. I wound up following him into a paranoid strand, people who thought they were being stalked. The tone of Jamie's pronouncements changed. He wanted to know how to be sure someone was following you; he got the usual bag of responses, from Montana militia men to kids talking the talk like he had elsewhere. The posts stopped two weeks before he died. I couldn't look at them; I dropped the connection, wiped the history, waited for the cops to come.

They didn't. They knew I was waiting. They knew what they were doing. Every noise was them; every car that passed up on the road, every crunch of gravel, every breath of breeze in the trees. They knew how to do it. Dad checked on me occasionally, but he didn't know how to handle this. Neither did I; and until I did I lay in my room, breaking my masturbation-abstention record, letting the machine pick up anything that wasn't Alita, which was everything.

On the Wednesday Dad came into my room at eight a.m., told me to do something about the stench and that the funerals were in two hours. My only suit was a linen one, and I was really going to wear my old school uniform, so the channels of communication between me and Dad were tentatively reopened as I negotiated the loan of a black Blazer blazer and grey Paul Smith pants. The lines stayed open on the way to the crematorium, as he filled me in on the events of the last few days – post-mortem, inquest in a couple of months' time, Alita and her mum staying with relatives in London, a photographer he'd got in half a ruck with down our road. We didn't mention Jamie and Harper at all; I thought he was going to ask if I'd known what they were up to, but he didn't.

By the time we were taking our seats – at the back, it was packed, and I couldn't see any of the others – all I could think was, what are we doing here? How could Jamie be dead? He was raised on grilled chicken breast, Petit Filous, iceberg with everything, same as the rest of us. Death is what the poor do, in cities. You have to smoke cut-price fags, gorge on red meat, have violent altercations with the neighbours, and spread your arse in front of soaps for fifty years to end up dead. It had no place here.

And the service was murder. It'd never really registered with me that Harper had a family too, though I knew he wasn't as whitebread as the rest of us. Now here was a whole gang of them, mostly driven in from elsewhere, keen to claim a link with the notoriety in a Jerry kind of way, but it was still pretty shocking how common they were: keening women screaming obscenities when the security tried to restrain them, men with fags between their fingers taking pops at them. It just made things armpit-scorching rather than sad.

The after-party, back at Alita's house, wasn't any easier. The neighbourhood security had put barriers at the junctions of our road and issued passes to residents to keep the press out: they were still gathered round, though, and there was a really suave moment when the photographer Dad had snouted stepped up for a close-up as we went back through. It didn't get much better back at Alita's: cans of warm lager at 11.30 a.m., no music until someone put on that Morcheeba CD that everybody bought and someone else took it off. Alita was tied up with relatives and dropped eye contact immediately every time I caught her. None of the others were there.

I was ready-to-puke drunk by half-one, and I went upstairs to do it in Alita's mum's en-suite, so as not to tie up the bathroom by the top of the stairs. I was in there a while, trying to think about what I could do before the wake broke up. Now was the time to do something, start things moving again, break the freeze-frame I'd been in since the weekend. I couldn't think how, though.

I don't think I ever felt more wretched, like everything was down to me, not even since Mum left. I stayed in there, propped up against the bath with the toilet open beside me, that Morcheeba CD coming from somewhere again, feeling the certainty that we weren't kids any more, and that from here on in there would be consequences for everything we did. Most of all I felt blind burned-moth panic at the thought of us all being grilled by the cops about meth: it was shameful, but that thought was the only one that could dispel the vision of two blistered kids, and I held on to it for that reason.

When it started to get dark I went into Alita's room and got into her bed with all my clothes on. I woke up, soaked in sweat, with her beside me in the pitch black: the digits on her video said 03.38. I needed a drink of water, so I went downstairs as quietly as I could. When I was down there, it seemed like it would be a big deal, somehow, if I went back up. Maybe she'd been irritated to find me in her bed, and had just got in so as not to have to wake me up and talk to me; maybe she'd liked the idea of having someone to hold when she went to sleep, but would find my still being there when she woke a little awkward, with her mother in the house; maybe Jojo would break my face for sleeping with his girlfriend. I let myself out as quietly as I could – the sky was starting to tinge with oxygen-deficiency blue, just enough to see by – and went home instead.

Alita's house stayed dark all the next day, and I didn't dare contact the others. Instead, I worked on how I was going to get out of this without having the cops taint my future.

I started with my father. If I could get him to understand what had been going on, maybe he'd give me money, put me in touch with people, help me to get away until it'd blown over. The day after the funeral I went downstairs to watch some *South Park* reruns with him; I figured, slow build but fast, let it seem to come out naturally, and then we could decide what to do.

The trouble was, he was weirding out worse. The moment I came out of my room, stopped being the invalid, he didn't know what to do with me, and we fell back into the old positions, right there on the couch. By the second time Kenny got killed Dad was stoned, and not long after the third he was wasted beyond belief, started putting his face in his hands, moaning how he didn't know it was Jamie. I tried to bring him out of it, saying that everyone had taken video cameras, all anyone had thought was going down was just a motel fire. It didn't help.

I left him, went up to my room, couldn't sit down. I wanted Alita, I wanted my mum, I wanted someone. I went up to the attic, climbed out the conversion dormer, sat on the roof and looked out across town. It was warm and clear, and the only lights were the main roads and the superstore car park, away in the distance, twinkling through the haze. It was hypnotic. By three I knew what I had to do, but I was still there at dawn. I felt I had to see it, and it was a good one. But then I had to go. I got in my car before Dad could catch me, and drove the twelve miles to the next town.

The cop on the desk looked like a teacher. He took me to a waiting room and brought me a cup of real tea when I started to cry a bit. The cops attached to Jamie and Harper were plain clothes, he said, and didn't usually come in till after nine. He told me to go home, get some sleep, they'd come out to see me later if I wanted; but I'd shown too much weakness already, so I told him I'd wait, do this here and now. He shrugged a whatever, shut the door on me, and I waited.

And waited and waited. It was a little after twelve fifteen when Mackey, the younger of the two, looked at me like I left a bad taste and said:

'So it's not enough for you they're dead?'

'That's not what I'm saying,' I said, for the hundredth time.

'Let me get this straight here,' he said, shaking his head as he got up from the desk, doing a cartoon frown into the air. 'Two lots of mothers just watched their sons get burned to death. Sat in the fucking hospital and watched them die. Were you in the hospital?'

'I told you,' I said.

'No, cunt, you weren't. Your father know you're here?'

I looked down. 'No.'

'You want me to get him on his mobile, see what he thinks of this?'

He was maybe five years older than me. Crop hair, first suit, tendons standing out over his collar; the kind of face that you knew, if you had to sit next to him, he'd have it out under the desk during lessons; threaten to kill you, and you'd believe it, if you ever told anyone. But I could see him as an adult too, and that was the scariest thing; he looked like the actors they have in adverts where they try to intimidate you into being worried about rain damage to your brickwork; he looked like he came from that world, and wanted to protect it. I should've found out who was doing this first.

'I came here of my own free will,' I said.

'You came here because you were shitting your pants, you little wanker,' he said, folding his arms as he leaned back against the wall. 'You know what you look like?'

McCormick came back into the room, carrying a cardboard file. He was my dad's age, but real-looking.

'What?' I asked Mackey.

McCormick dropped the file on the desk and sat down. He massaged his forehead a moment, then looked up, face to face.

'What is it that you'd like us to *do*?' he asked, as if he genuinely wanted to help with whatever mystifying project I had in mind. He didn't seem like a bad guy: he looked like the kind you see making video diaries for holiday programmes (*Mike and Paula went to Costa Rica with Pathtrek Adventures*), the kind you catch singing along to some old Whitney CD in traffic. Section marks on his face.

'I'm just telling you what I know,' I said. 'I didn't want you to have to waste your time coming looking for me.'

'Do you know how to make this drug? Do any of the people you've named?'

'That's what I'm trying to tell you. No one does. We don't have it in this country.'

'You have to appreciate, Bay,' McCormick started, then seemed to change his mind. 'You're asking us to begin an investigation that may result in criminal charges. Against you, against your friends, against everyone that you've implicated so far. You may go to trial or we may decide to caution you, but either way it'll be in the papers and it'll be on your record. It will be an offence not to declare it when you're required to do so: for university, for job applications, mortgages . . . do you understand this?'

'Let's go and see what he's got on his computer,' Mackey put in, grinning viciously at me.

'Have you downloaded anything to your computer you should tell us about, Bay?' McCormick asked gently.

'No,' I said, but said it too hard, thinking how I should've reformatted my hard drive, not just deleted everything.

'I think we oughta go and have a look,' said Mackey, getting into the idea.

'Would you be willing to show us if we came now?' McCormick asked me.

'There's nothing on my PC, okay? I use it for homework. That's not why I'm here.'

'That's not why you're here,' said McCormick. 'You're here because you seem to want to have every employer you apply to, every college you go for a place at –'

'Credit cards, car hire, passport, visas,' Mackey put in.

'For the rest of your life. To know you're a user of hard drugs. Your friends too,' McCormick finished, sat back, spread his hands to me. 'I don't understand why you'd want to do that.'

I started to cry. I was so tired, I couldn't help it. But it was anger too. I was like, Are you cops? Or what? I'd had to use the Yellow Pages to find this place, and it had turned out to be a bunch of Portakabins in the civic centre car park. I hadn't even seen any badges, just heard a load of DS shit. Feeling them watch me cry like they were watching a pisshead wet himself shut it off.

'I'm telling you what I thought it was your business to know.'

Mackey sprang off the wall, planted his fists on the desk, pushed his face into mine over it.

'You're telling me my business?'

He'd had Thai the night before, and took sweetener in his coffee. This was going where he wanted.

'What's your father's mobile?' McCormick said. Mackey stayed where he was, not blinking.

'It'll be busy,' I said.

'You haven't discussed this with him?' McCormick asked like he couldn't believe it. Mackey backed off, grinning at me.

'He's been broken up too,' I said. 'I thought . . . I mean, I didn't mean –'

'And he has a home office? There's a separate phone in there?'

'It's always on machine,' I said.

'Say we sent you home now. Would you check your father's machine to see if we left a message? Would you wipe it?'

'He keeps his study locked,' I said. 'Always has.'

'You don't use his computer?'

'I've got my own. His is in his study.'

'So if we were to accompany you home now and we checked his computer, we wouldn't find any evidence that you used it too? Nothing on the hard drive, nothing in your web browser? No passwords, no downloads?'

'I told you, the study's kept locked. I've been in there like, twice?'

'What d'you think, Phil? You're the computer buff.'

Mackey shrugged maliciously. 'Always turn up something.'

McCormick turned back to me. 'Do you want us to come and look?'

'I don't want you to waste your time. I promise you, his stuff's too important to risk me crashing it. He keeps it all locked up. And he wouldn't let you. Don't you need a search warrant?'

'I'm sure if we called him –'

'You don't need to call him, okay? I'm eighteen. This is nothing to do with him.'

McCormick nodded, like he could appreciate that.

I worked on it. 'This has been bad for him. My mum split with him and he hasn't taken it well. I don't want to put more on his plate.'

'But you want to put more on everyone else's,' Mackey put in from the wall again.

'DS Mackey is right,' McCormick said, like he was finally starting to lose patience. 'It's what we have to come back to. You seem to be asking for us to drag everyone through this, after everything they've already been through. You seem to want to damage people's lives, on top of the damage of this last week, your own included. You want to make sure everyone has to live with the consequences of what you're saying for decades to come. I have to ask myself why you want to do that.'

'I didn't want to cause any more trouble,' I said.

'But you want two grieving families to be branded as bringing up drug dealers,' he said, exasperated. 'You want to turn yourself and your friends over to face criminal charges for possession and supply. Do you like hurting people? Do you *like* hurting yourself?'

'I'm trying to help –'

'The two boys were cautioned eighteen months ago for damaging the school science laboratory,' McCormick said, consulting the file he'd brought in. 'A student teacher had given them access after school, and they precipitated an explosion that required fumigation and repainting of the facility in question. In the intervening time we've been able to trace a file of internet activity that follows United States high-school perpetrator patterns. On my interpretation of the evidence, that's all that happened here; but they were stopped, mercifully, before they could damage anyone other than themselves. Do you understand?'

I couldn't answer that, couldn't look at them. They wanted people to believe it: the misfit thing, the rage thing, the bad-seed thing. Better Jamie and Harper had been twisted losers than garage geniuses. The way the two men were looking at me made me feel like what I was: eighteen, male, unsanitary, trouble. Like you'd only ever want to be where I was not.

'I have no reason to think that the inquest will find any other verdict than death by misadventure. Nor will it recommend that any charges be brought. If what you've alleged is true, then it's over. Do you understand?'

'My colleague asked you a question,' said Mackey.

'Yes,' I said to McCormick.

'Then fuck off,' Mackey said cordially, and held the door open.

'The community pulls closer together' is such a cliché that you suspect stricken people only say it on TV so as to give the news crews the closure quote they want and make them go away again. It did turn out that way a little, however. There's an automatic recoil from young death programmed into our operating systems; a society that didn't recoil from it, a society that didn't find it disgusting, wouldn't be a society for much longer.

But mixed with the disgust was fascination. At the twenty-pump Shell, at the 24-7, wherever I went over the next week, I could feel people looking at me, whispering to each other, giving me space. They must've recognised me from the pictures of us all at the funeral, and as they nudged each other, stepped back out of my way, it was almost like they wanted me to fall to my knees in the checkout queue, spray mucus on the floor tiles, beat my head against the Doritos bins. My father was the same: sticking his head round my door before he went to bed, waiting till he'd seen me eat breakfast in the mornings before he left, ordering vanloads of extra fruit from the superstore delivery to make sure I got my vitamins.

I couldn't take the burden of being the focus; I hated the way the old routine of things seemed so irrevocably interrupted. But it was like when Mum left; the old system may be shot, but only new routine is going to get you over this, the spin of stacked-up days, to-do lists, deadlines. You have to get on with it. The trouble is that when everyone expects you to be feeling a certain way, it makes it harder to do it. You feel like a fake. Every time I thought about the cops I doubled over. And in the time left between I felt like a fake.

There wasn't time to dwell on it. A-level exams started the next week, and though the deputy head had sent a mailmerge-personalised letter around, expressly referring to the 'pressures' of 'this difficult time', it seemed that I was still required to do them. I resurrected, from my broken schedule, a last-minute revision programme, but I couldn't seem to stick to it. I wasn't seeing Talya: I'd spoken to her a couple of times on the phone, but had point-blank refused to meet with her, pleading a need for space and pressure of study. She'd hung up in tears both times, but had the sense not to drive over and force her confusion on me.

The morning of the first paper I slipped into the exam room five minutes late, so as not to have to speak to anyone beforehand. Alita's mum had taken her back to London again after the funeral; it was quite a shock to see her hunched over a desk on the other side of the hall from where I'd been assigned a seat. I spent the first ten minutes studying her profile, then resignedly set about fudging three essays together. At the end she was allowed out while they were still collecting papers, and by the time I got out too, she was gone. Her house was still dead when I went home that day.

I went in to do the second A-level expecting Alita to be there, but it wasn't until we were well into it that I remembered she'd done a different option; the first paper had been the only one we were scheduled to share. I asked around a few likely kids after the exam, but they were weird and evasive with me, in the way that almost everyone had been since it happened. I didn't need consideration. I needed my friends, but I couldn't go and see them.

That was the way it stayed for the next couple of weeks: a stomach-sick blur of feint-ruled pads and buff-coloured booklets, Staedtlers and Pentels, textbooks whose covers were depressingly familiar but whose contents suddenly weren't. In between times I took to parking out by the bypass, by the burned-out motel, watching the cars file on and off the slip roads; if you went there first thing, at drivetime, the bright, low sun hit dirty windscreens straight on, and you could see the line of sleek cars all spouting their washers in turn, like whales in ceremonial procession. Other times I'd drive the strip through the centre of town like it was some way of testing the fates, of shaking the *malocchio*: if I could do it from beginning to end without the sun going behind a cloud, then things were going to be okay again; if the shadows started to lose their definition, to fade at the edges on the road before I reached the last set of traffic lights, then everything was going to go to hell, and there was nothing I could do about it. Tailing the car in front like I was on a cable; taking the car out of gear on the downhill and coasting. That was the best: shifting into neutral, turning down the CD so I could hear the engine running like a bird beneath me. Slipping out of gear in the straights between bottlenecks gave me my quiet place and I needed it, though it only ever lasted till I came back up behind someone and had to engage third again.

I wasn't still kidding myself that the cops were watching us; I was just too much of a mess to do anything but take the path of least resistance. I felt like I was food, like I was an item on a menu that some day someone was going to pull down and activate (Cut-Copy-Paste: Find-Replace-Clear). I worried about my state of mind, for the first time ever. Dad nagged me about Talya calling until I let her come round one night, and then she came round every night, following a set pattern: she cried, I let her, and around midnight we'd bring each other off like we were strangers; then she'd drive home, and I'd frantically try to revise for the next exam.

Finally the A-level board ran out of fresh tortures to throw at me, and a whole bunch of us went to the pub across the road and got blasted. Euan was there, and though he was mostly too busy being a stand-up guy to notice me much, he cornered me by the urinals at one point and did a big I'm-here-for-you-man number on me. I faked up my part in the exchange pretty well, but mostly the incident served only to remind me how calculating Jojo and I had been a couple of years before, getting involved with such a meathead simply because we thought having a quarterback on the team would improve our chances with girls. Now that it had worked, and now that it had come to this, I didn't know what to say to him. I wished him good journey for his forthcoming Indonesia trek with Asia and ducked out.

Alita's house stayed empty and she didn't call, she didn't e-mail, she didn't write. I knew her mum had left an emergency number with my dad, and I tried to get it out of him, but the old bastard had obviously seen a Ricki on the subject: he said I ought to respect her space, that if she wanted to speak to me, she would, and that I had to wait until she was ready to do that. I slammed the lounge door on him and stormed out for a drive, but lying in bed later, I had to admit he was probably right. I hated it, though. I couldn't imagine what she was going through, but I felt like I needed her as much as she could ever need me.

And then one lunchtime at the end of June, I came back in from driving aimlessly around, chasing the shadows, and there was a yellow stickie from her on the fake Victorian lamppost by the gap in the hedge in our drive, saying to come over. I whirled around, expecting to see things like they used to be but it was just the same as before – dead house, shut curtains, closed eyes. Except that Alita's bedroom window was cracked open ever so slightly, so you wouldn't know unless you were looking for it. I had a moment of self-consciousness, thinking she might be watching me, but I couldn't help myself: I had to run in and shave, check my hair and change my clothes, my heart flipping around like Lara in a final level. It was hard not to grin as I trotted across to hers. I knew that if she was watching, whatever state she was in, she'd understand.

'So how've you been?' I asked, as I followed her into the kitchen and sat down.

'Okay,' she said. 'I mean, my aunt's is okay, and Hammersmith is pretty cool. My cousins have been taking me out a lot. There're some good parties.'

I didn't know anything about any cousins. 'Clubs?'

'Yeah, you know. Bit London, lots of attitude. But you learn to adjust for it, you know? It's like my cousin said. You come from a small town, you think London's such a big deal. But then you move there, you soon find out that all London is is just a bunch of small towns.'

I'd assumed that she'd come the same distance, and in the same direction, as me.

'Your cousins . . . they're, what, at uni?'

'One in the first year, one just graduated.'

'Yeah?' I felt sick.

'Yeah,' she said, then got up as the kettle boiled. She made us Maxwell House and handed me mine.

'I'm sorry I didn't call,' she said. 'My mum didn't want me to. And look, Bay, I didn't feel up to it.'

'Hey, no problem, I understand,' I said, trying to sound a little injured, but not enough to be offensive. I took a sip from my mug. 'Did you speak to Jojo?'

'Not really,' she said, leaning her hips back against the counter, holding her mug up under her chin with both hands cupped around it. 'Mum didn't want me calling anyone. The papers and stuff – she thought they were listening to the phone.'

'Did you have it checked?'

'No point,' she said. 'I mean, what would be in it for them? They'd got the story, and it was obvious Mum wasn't going to do any interviews. Is Your Kid Making Pipe Bombs? Tell-Tale Signs for Worried Parents. Whatever.'

'They follow you up there?' I asked.

'No, they kind of lost interest,' she said, sitting down at the table with me again. 'Maybe they'll start again at the inquest.'

'When's that?'

'Not for three months.' She stared down at the coffee in her mug, biting the inside of her lips. I didn't know how to put it but I had to ask.

'Did the cops pull you in?'

'After the funeral,' she said. 'They spoke to Mum before, but all they wanted to ask me was if he ever talked to me about bombing the school. Whether I knew if he had any contact with right-wing groups. I told them that it was their job to find that out and if they'd done it a little better there might not be two sixteen-year-olds in copper fucking urns now.'

‘Christ.’ I couldn’t maintain eye contact.

‘Don’t worry,’ she said, in a hard voice, ‘they’re not going to pull you in. Not you especially, anyway. They’re doing Jamie and Harper’s classmates at the school next week, when the GCSE kids go back for sixth-form induction. I bet there’re a lot of sixteen-year-olds sweating it right now.’ She shrugged her shoulders. ‘If they pull you in it’ll be after that. They know it wasn’t a bomb they were making. I mean, get real, this is Kent, not Kentucky.’

My balls dropped through the floor.

‘They know about meth?’

‘Pretty sure,’ she said. ‘They’re not telling the papers anything different, but they know.’

‘They said so to you?’

‘In so many words. First time I saw them alone.’

Christ. So they knew before I told them. ‘Oh, god.’

‘It’s all right. They’re quite relieved that’s all it was. Nobody else is going to start cooking it. Nobody knows how. It’s over, is where they are.’

‘They ask you if you did it?’

‘I told them I knew nothing, big round eyes. I think they bought it. They’re thinking it was mostly kids their age who were doing meth, not us.’

‘They’re not so wrong,’ I said, not thinking with the relief.

‘What do you mean?’ she said, in a voice I wasn’t keen on. I backspaced.

‘Just, you know, that kid at New Year’s. C’mon, Talya must’ve told you.’ I didn’t want to mention that Jojo had known where to score meth at the Venue.

‘That’s not all, though, is it?’ She squinted at me. ‘C’mon, Bay. Try and shit me and I’ll know.’ She ducked her head under my line of sight, trying to intercept my attempts to avoid eye contact. Then she said, 'You know why they were doing it at the motel, don't you?'

'Don't you?' I asked.

'Only because the police told me, to try and get me to squeal,' she said.

'They were doing one big batch,' I said. She probably knew more than I did by now anyway. 'They went to a motel to do it because it would take too long to do at home and your mum might have found them.'

'Almost,' she said. 'They went to a motel to do it because the bigger the quantity, the more volatile the process. They didn't want to blow the roof off here, so they checked in under fake names.' She pushed her hair back with one hand. 'Fuck knows what the desk clerk was doing, letting two kids register, but she says they spun her a story about a holiday breakdown, parents gone to the garage and joining them later. They booked a double room, cash.' She shrugged. 'It was probably more to stop me or Mum walking in on them. I doubt if they were taking the risk seriously. They were kids, they were boffins, they thought it wouldn't happen to them – if anything started to go wrong, they'd see it and have time to get out. Obviously not.'

I didn't know what to say. She looked up at me sharply.

'So spill it, Bay. You know something else and you're going to tell me.'

I had to be damn careful. I couldn't let her know I'd been to the cops and they'd told me to get lost.

'I had it out with Jamie,' I said.

'When?'

'A couple of weeks before. I was seeing meth fucking everywhere. If I was seeing it without even looking, it wouldn't be long before someone else did too. Someone serious.'

'Go on.' She went to drink some coffee but there was none left in her cup.

'I always used to be able to talk to him,' I said. 'He told me they were quitting, but they were going to do one last batch. He didn't say anything about it being any riskier. Did he tell you that volatility was relative to quantity?'

'The cops did.'

'They know how it's *made*?'

'That's not the point, Bay,' she said measuredly. 'The point is that you knew what they were doing and you didn't do anything to stop them.'

'What could I do, go to the cops?' Fronting it out. 'And anyway, don't give me that. You knew they were still doing it as much as I did. You could've tried to stop them, any one of us could. If I've got to take some of the blame, then I don't see how you're suddenly in the clear.' If it had gone on another second I would have faced her down about how Jamie had said she was selling it too.

'I'm just trying to work out what happened here,' she said, and her voice caught. 'I'm just trying to work out what *happened*.' And then she was crying, and there wasn't much I could do.

'I don't know what's happened to me,' Alita said to the table at the superstore café. She'd summoned Jojo and made me call Talya. 'Not just since Jamie died, because it started a long time before.'

None of us said anything. It was hard enough just having to sit there, having to hold it together for the victim.

'Tell them what you told me,' I said.

'I used to feel about life the way we used to about *Tomb Raider*,' she said simply. 'You remember? When you hadn't finished each sequel yet, and every day there were new levels to explore.' Talya started to cry quietly. 'Now I feel like if I ever play again, there won't be any surprises and it won't be any good.'

Jojo and I looked at the table. Neither of us knew what to say to that.

'My mum's staying in London, probably for good,' Alita said. 'Unless I sort something out for gap year, then I have to as well.'

Talya started the we'll-never-lose-touch stuff, but Alita interrupted her.

'Jojo and I weren't going to think about it until after the exams. Have you two got anything to do in the next year?'

Talya looked at me, sniffing behind a bunched Kleenex. We'd made vague noises about travelling, but I hadn't let it go any further. I'd rather we split up at home than did it in some Thai hostel, where I'd feel responsible for getting her home when she was ready to spit in my eye.

'No,' I said, for both of us.

Six weeks later the four of us were climbing aboard an Air India 727 on the way to visit my mum. When the doors closed and we taxied away from the terminal, it seemed like we were leaving the bad stuff behind; and as we made the brisk, strobing climb through the low cloud it felt as though we were on some kind of resurrection trip, leaving our battered and ill-used corpses on the ground as we ascended, like harp-clutching cartoon characters just before the punchline. It had happened, it was over, and we were getting out of it. It was tough, letting the world think that Jamie and Harper had been losers, and if there was a next world I knew I'd be punished for it there. But in this one, it was what people wanted to believe, and telling them the truth wouldn't do anyone any favours. Us included. Everyone has something terrible happen to them at some point, and you either put it behind you or you let it ruin your life. You do have a choice in this. I believed that.

I'm pretty sure Alita did too. Jojo and Talya, sitting in the row behind us, might have put it slightly differently, but they were along for the ride regardless. Alita was in the window seat beside me with a physical map of Russia open across her knees; suddenly she recognised something outside, squeezed my hand and pointed triumphantly at the map. I grinned, toasted her with my juicebox – we both had 'phones on – and reclined my seat. We'd changed planes at Moscow an hour before, and now it was a straight run to Kerala. Anything that could've gone wrong so far hadn't, and I was pretty sure we were coasting. It had been a grim drag to get there, but we were almost like we used to be again.

When Alita suggested that we all go travelling together, I don't think any of us realised that it would work out like this, but Alita made it happen. Going to my mum's yoga place in Kerala and using it as a base was swiftly decided upon as the most workable option, and within an hour of arriving at the superstore café we had it all worked out. I wasn't mad keen to see my mother, to put it mildly, but I still had the uncashed ticket she'd sent me. Shana would be there too and I figured I could use her as a buffer. The only other problem I could see was our relationships, but Alita had that worked out too. She sent Jojo and Talya off into the superstore to buy munchies for a midnight trip to stoner central to celebrate, then faced me across the table.

'Right, you little shit. I'm not going to get into whose fault it was that you got together in the first place, but this has got to stop. Talya asks to be dumped all over, you're too weak not to do it, and life's too short for her to be miserable like this. Agreed?'

'What can I say?' I was singing inner hallelujahs.

'Then leave it to me,' she said. 'I'll see you there, and you better be ready.'

She got up, and took Jojo's hand at the checkouts. I did the same with Talya, who drove me out to where it began.

And it really was that easy. We parked the cars facing each other: Alita and I sat on the bonnet of Alita's, Talya and Jojo sat on the bonnet of Talya's.

'Talya, you start,' Alita said.

'He won't open up –' she started.

'To him,' Alita interrupted. Talya turned to me.

'You won't open up,' she repeated, simply. 'You won't let me get close to you.'

'Okay,' said Alita. 'Bay, tell us why.'

I felt like protesting how clingy she was; I wanted to expound on her inability to do anything for herself ever, and then substantiate this with the psycho-sexual insights I'd gleaned from ten years of flipping past the Living channel; I wanted to explore the subgroups of her saviour complex, her need for transactional validation, her projection of the fact that if I ceased to be a challenge, I'd cease to be of interest. But the way she was looking at me – the way she'd just spoken, so out of character – made me suspect that she was as briefed on this as I was. So instead I said,

'Sweetheart, it's not like I've chosen not to throw a switch. I don't have a lever inside me with open up/don't open up Dymo'd on it.' I looked to Alita for, I don't know what, approval, but she directed me back to Talya. I took a breath. 'It's different with guys. Girls get encouraged to share, from like dot. It's like . . . I remember this party when we were kids, allowed downstairs for an hour: Shana got asked how many boyfriends she'd had and everyone cooed over her for saying how she felt about each. When they were done with her, they asked me what football team I liked. You know?'

'You're not a kid any more, Bay,' Talya said, sounding tired, looking older than she was.

'Okay, another way,' I said. 'Can you think of many women who wouldn't be comfortable discussing their feelings with their mothers? But can you think of any guys who would?'

Talya shrugged, though not as disgustedly as she could have done, and looked at the floor.

'All I'm saying is – Jesus, I don't know – okay, the getting-close part, the being able to open up: it doesn't just happen because you decide that's the way it is. If it's going to happen, then first you've got to find a level by just doing stuff together, establishing a baseline intimacy.' I hoped this was getting through to Alita; I couldn't have been putting it more pointedly. 'And face it, Talya, we're not good at doing stuff together, so the next level isn't going to happen.'

Give a speech like that and never come out of your bedroom again. But after a while, with Talya riding the crest of her sobs like a kid riding a sneeze, Alita put her hand on my shoulder and squeezed it. I gathered she'd already done her part with Jojo on the drive.

'Let's go back, okay?' she said. 'We've forgotten who we are. And forget what happened, it started before that. First there was meth, and all we were was bodies; then we take the meth away, and suddenly we're like suburban bloody marrieds. Is this what we wanted? Talya, sweetheart, stop it now. You guys used to mean the world to me. I would've died for any of you. But the last year we've barely talked – just humped at each other, or played at being grown-up. Let's go back.'

If someone offers you the chance to be sixteen again, you're not going to say no. Not when you're eighteen and everything's gone to hell; and certainly not when the person offering it is walking the kind of line Alita had been since her brother died. So, murderous as it was, we did a group-huggy kind of scene, Jojo apparently accepting that Alita's speech meant that she and he were toast, too; then Alita drove me home, and Talya drove Jojo.

The next time we got together it was planning, and the

next and the next, trying to pretend we weren't waiting for something to happen with the cops all the while; but it didn't, not even when we got our visas. And then we were on the plane; and then we could see, clustered at our two windows, that the polygraph line of cloud below was shadowing the coast; and then we were landing in Trivandrum.

One bad thing about getting taken on foreign holidays every year since forever is that flying quit being exciting a long time ago. It gets like Christmas, as you negotiate your early teens; however much you try to feel what you used to, it won't work.

One good thing about being carted off to the Balearics, the Costas, the Canaries and the Caribbean every year is that the oven-door rush of heat that hits you as you step off the plane becomes less of a shock; we'd all worn layers to travel, to insulate against the snowmelt cabin air; but now, as we returned the stewardesses' smiles before stepping down the quaint CinemaScope-era gangway that had been wheeled across the apron as we taxied, we took off our sweats and fleeces and bundled them into the spare ruckies folded into our hand-luggage especially for this purpose.

Our fellow travellers hadn't been so prudent, I noticed, as we loped across to the rickety baggage reclaim; saronged and sandalled for the plane, the gang of desperate-looking thirtysomethings who'd embarked with us had shivered through the flight, bothering the cabin crew for blankets that they didn't have, and were now blowing their Lonely Planet cool as the opposite hit them. They weren't very good with the locals either: first off the plane in order to jockey for position at baggage reclaim and money-change, they were the first to be caught by the beggars too; and were forced to fumble through their money-belts for low denominations, exposing huge bundles of notes in the process, which the urchins clustered around relieved them of as we breezed past. Several of them, consequently, found themselves having to ask us – whom they'd eyed with disdain back at Heathrow – if we had change for the coast bus; we pissed them off further, as we sat waiting for the driver to arrive, by spritzing each other's faces with Evian mist and sipping Diet Sprites, bought icy-cold in the departure lounge and cool-bagged, while they sweated, drinking steaming *chai* from the vendors outside and chewing duff-looking Bombay mix.

Eventually the driver arrived, apparently surprised to see us, and took a mystified roll-call. Several of the sports-sandal brigade turned out to be going to my mum's place too, and though they were excitedly buddying up with each other, there wasn't any point in our making friends with them. Shana had told me in an e-mail that Mum's place was almost exclusively a regular turnover of two-weekers, and since we were going to be there for four months, we'd soon be watching them come and go like natives.

So all there was to do was sit back and enjoy the ride. It was certainly pretty, but if you've ever spent more than a few hundred a head on a holiday you've already seen pretty, and without the swarms of beggars and other in-your-facers making you regret being outside of a secure Western compound. On top of this, everyone in India smokes, you swiftly find out, our driver included. It was fucking disgusting. I was damned glad when we got to the line of hotels that signified the coast, and our bus pulled up at the top of some building works. A path to the beach was just about discernible through the middle. We collected our bags and followed it down to some whitewashed shacks arranged in a semicircle between the trees and the beach, where there were people sitting around. Alita asked one of them for directions and he pointed us at the largest building.

'In there, man,' he said, fucked-up blue eyes narrowing at us over his beard. 'Charlie'll sort you out.'

The large building was made of wood, like all the others, but it had a flat roof with a bamboo canopy over it, accessed by stairs going up one wall. Alita assigned Jojo and Talya to sit with the bags, and dragged me through the screen door. Inside, a woman was tapping at a computer behind a counter, a curry-house ceiling fan turning lazily and ineffectually above her.

'Help you?' she said, smiling up at us. She was wearing a linen suit and full make-up, her blonde hair combed back into a French plait. She looked like an air hostess, except that she was smoking a joint the size of my johnson and making no attempt to conceal it.

'Hi,' I stammered.

'Hello,' Alita said, 'is Cassandra around?'

The blonde looked quizzically at me. 'Are you . . .'

'I'm Alita and this is Cassandra's son Bay,' said Alita.

'Hiiiiii,' said the blonde professionally, offering her hand as she flashed on a smile and stood up. 'I'm Charlie. I run the office here. Bay?'

'Right here,' I said.

'Cassandra is in Trivandrum today on business. She said to make yourselves comfortable and chill out, and she'll see you at supper. You're in 12 and 16 – here are the keys. Lunch was a couple of hours ago, but the cook can usually make something up for you.'

'No, I fucking can't.'

Shana came out of a door behind Charlie, carrying a towel, with sunglasses pushed up over her hair. She was wearing a sarong and a bra top the same colour as her nail varnish.

'You're the cook?' I said.

'The old one did a bunk two days ago,' she said, regarding us sulkily. It was typical of Mum to make Shana work once she got bored with having her around. I would've laughed out loud but for the thought that she'd probably do the same to me. 'Hi, Alita.'

'Hey,' said Alita.

'You got here okay?' Shana said. She looked terrible, like an aromatherapist; like someone who, having downshifted from being normal owing to a failure to reach unrealistic life goals, has now convinced herself that what the economy really needs is another scented-candle shop. Alita's mother did it once – in fact, she did more or less all of them once, reflexology, naturopathy, angels-on-your-body, you name it – and wound up practically sticking her business cards in phone boxes to hawk for punters.

'No trouble at the airport?' Shana went on.

'How d'you mean, trouble?' I asked, suddenly reminded of Interpol, passport controls, global police computers. I'd assumed we were home free when we got our visas, but maybe that was what they wanted me to think.

'We get grief from local kids stoning tourists off the plane,' she said.

'Hindu extremists,' Alita nodded.

I didn't know what they were talking about.

'They don't like Westerners coming here,' Shana said. 'But you obviously got lucky. Here –' she handed me a roll of mega-C vitamins – 'neck these.'

'Why?' I said, examining them.

'People get colds after long hauls,' Alita said. 'Now there's no smoking on planes they don't have to bother conditioning the air like they used to, so it gets recycled round and round. You end up with less oxygen, your lungs have to work harder, and if anyone's carrying an airborne infection, the whole plane'll get it.'

'So I'm not getting special treatment,' I said to Shana.

'Just share them out with your little playmates, okay?' she said. 'I don't want your fucking germs.' She pushed her sunglasses back down onto her nose and made to hit the beach. I turned and raised my eyebrows at Alita.

'Let's go unpack,' she said.

I'd had enough mystification for one day and agreed enthusiastically. Slipping a smile to Charlie (she really was quite tasty, in a scary kind of way), I followed Alita back out to Talya and Jojo, and we hauled our packs down the line of cabins under the palms.

Jojo and I were in the fourth one we came to, the girls two along. We pushed open the door of our whitewashed shack to find a bare plank floor, an Ikea-type canvas wardrobe thing, and two wooden beds with mosquito nets. I turned to Jojo.

'Christ,' he said.

'Where am I going to plug in my ultrasound?' I'd bought, at Heathrow, a state-of-the-art mosquito pisser-offer, with built-in light-sensor and timer, which slotted directly into the electricity outlet for convenience and efficiency.

Jojo shrugged. 'You reckon we can get some smoke off Shana?'

'I wouldn't count on it,' I said, dumping my pack out on the bed to unpack. 'You see her? She's got a crimp in her butt about something.'

'We remind her of home,' Jojo said. 'She's come out here pretending she doesn't come from anywhere, then we show up. She'll get over it, in a day or two.'

‘Yeah, I guess,’ I said, and started to unpack.

‘Whoa,’ said Jojo, coming over to inspect my holiday outfits. ‘You shoulda tipped me off, I could’ve bought shares in the Gap.’

He had a point. My dad had taken me to Bluewater and bought me three of everything I picked out, without even attempting to impose his Floral Street neuroses on me. This had certainly been refreshing, but I wasn’t quite sure how to take it. Ostensibly his bounty was rooted in relief at seeing the back of me for four months, so he could get on with the business of bringing home Australian and Japanese girls from his weekend forays into London. He’d held off a few weeks after Jamie and Harper died, probably because of the police presence in our neighbourhood; but in the last month he’d started going up to the Ministry again, bringing back bulimic backpacker-trash girls younger than Shana. I didn’t mind so much – they almost always pissed off back to London by Monday lunchtime – except they’d inevitably try to make friends with me before they left. Like, yeah, I’ve just listened to you noisily fucking my father all night, and now I really want to discuss the full-moon parties in Phuket with you. Now I was gone he’d have them there almost full-time; but the real reason for his largesse, I suspected, was that he didn’t want my mother thinking he couldn’t make sure I was dressed good.

‘Yeah, yeah,’ I said, putting some folded shorts onto shelves, ‘you can talk. If you haven’t brought half of Ted Baker, I’ll wipe your arse for you.’

‘Where are the bogs, anyway?’ he said suspiciously. ‘They make you go in the bushes, or what?’

‘There must be some kind of shower block,’ I said. ‘My mum definitely wouldn’t shit in the woods, I can tell you.’

‘Yeah, but is she a Catholic,’ Jojo muttered, turning out

piles of connoisseur sportswear onto his bed. 'Where is she, anyway?'

'Fucked if I know,' I said, which pretty much summed up my relationship with her for the last few years.

This was her fault, not mine. She started this crap. If she wasn't happy with us, then fine, but things that you start, you see through until you've borne out your responsibilities. You don't go off and enjoy yourself and leave your kid to clear up your mess. This is what they taught us in civics at school, and they taught us for a reason. I'd had to take all the strain with my father, and it had messed up my own judgement.

'C'mon,' I said to Jojo, 'sod this. Let's round up the girls and hit the beach while there's still some rays left.'

'UV sounds good to me,' he said, stuffing a handful of underwear back into his pack. 'And if I pull first, you're sleeping with your mum tonight, man.'

She wasn't around anyway. We had the beach to ourselves all afternoon because, as Alita had found out from somewhere, most people slept through the hottest part of the day.

We'd found the girls already chilling. They'd unpacked in half the time it'd taken us, and apparently met half the locals too.

'The deal is this,' Alita said, sitting up on a sarong she'd spread out on the sand about two metres from the Evian-clear water. 'Two hours yoga from 6.30, then breakfast on the roof of that reception building.'

'Can you eat it?'

'Oh, aye. It's all organic, fruit and yoghurt and stuff, eat as much as you like. Then you do what you want all day – they run classes in salsa, ceramics, creative writing and stuff.

Lunch in the same place if you want it, another two hours yoga at four. Then supper at seven, and as much of the local shit as you can smoke while you "watch the sun sink into the sea".' She said this last in an exaggerated loverman accent, and Talya giggled.

'What's the joke?' I asked.

'That was Ranj,' Alita explained, and did his voice again. 'He was just here. "*You want smoke, you want show round? Anything ladies need, they come see big Ranj.*"'

'He runs the beach bar along the bay,' Talya said. 'I think we're in there.'

'Hey, if you want to wake up sold into slavery, you go for it, babe,' I said, in a tone I couldn't quite figure out. Was I feeling a twinge at Talya copping off with someone else? I didn't know. I mean, it was pretty obvious this was the place for flings; some of the old witches on the bus from the airport had been almost drooling as they gave me and Jojo the once-over. Take a posh white bird who won't swallow at home, put her under a palm tree by the ocean, and you practically have to beat her off with a cattle prod, my dad had informed me, slipping an economy-size pack of Extra Safe into my luggage. I didn't doubt him. I checked out the back of my eyelids instead of dwelling on it, and when I woke the sun was going down and it was time to go in.

Supper was pretty good. I'd thought that the food would be a nightmare, and beverages even more so – no Sunny Delight or Sprites for a thousand miles – but it was just like the juice bar at the gym: roasted veg and rice, raw salad, mango juice, piles of weird fruit; I figured I could make this trip into a monster detox session. The witches and the bulletheads from the airport bus all sat in a circle and talked loudly about their jobs in offender rehab and law and spin and so on. Shana still seemed arsey enough about something to pretend to be interested by them rather than us, so we sat in our own little circle to eat, on the far side of the flat roof.

When the after-dinner stashes came out, however, Alita collared one of the witches while she was getting some more juice; she obviously made friends pretty quick, because the harpy led her back over to where the bulletheads had begun making with the Rizlas. Talya went over to sit beside her; Jojo had the decency to raise his eyebrows at me as he rose to his feet, as if to ask if I wanted to come too, but I looked away and let him join the others. I should've thought about this before, but I hadn't. I didn't know how long I'd hold out, but I was damned if I was going to start smoking on the first night. In the absence of anything else to do, I sloped off downstairs in the vague hope of running into that Charlie lady.

I sat down on a wall with a bottle of Vittel; it was pitch dark already, but there was a moon like a motherfuck and you could still see pretty good. The office was all closed up, but there were lights on in the biggest cabin and a radio jabbering mad Indian shit from inside; there was obviously someone in there, but I knew it wasn't my mother. She hated the radio. Maybe it was her cleaner or something.

I lay back along the wall and stared at the moon awhile, trying to feel good about myself. When that didn't work I fell to thinking what I was doing, bringing Alita here, when what drew us together was at home. I didn't like how far away the horizon was here. I didn't like the London types upstairs with their little lacquered hash boxes. I didn't like the fact that they'd paid for their own flights, that they'd already negotiated all the tough stuff, and that they had lives to go back to. I hadn't let myself think about what came after, and it made me remember why we were really here. I groaned Jamie's name out loud – I'd got to feeling like he was watching me sometimes – and only then did I look around, the way you do when you realise you're talking to yourself in public. There was an Indian guy chilling his buns on the other end of the wall.

I had to look twice to check he was a native because he was dressed like the money. He clocked my scrutiny and I sat up, wondering how long he'd been there.

'You a married man?' he called along the wall to me, out of nowhere, crinkling the corners of his eyes. I held up my left hand, palm in, fingers stiff, to show him.

He shrugged with his eyebrows and glanced out to sea, twisting the silver band on his own wedding finger reflectively. 'Too tight. You plan to get married?'

Was he some kind of weirdo? I gave him the polite smile you use on strangers.

'If you do, go somewhere cool for your honeymoon,' he said. 'Cool, I mean cold. Prague. Reykjavik. Temperate.' He looked down at his ring as he turned it around, trying to make it more comfortable, the way a first-day-of-term schoolkid will run their finger irritably around a new collar.

'Why?' I said.

'You see guys on honeymoon, they never wore a ring before and they've gone somewhere much hotter than they used to. Their fingers swell up in the heat; the ring that fit nicely at home is too tight now. Spend their whole time twisting it on their finger like a gangster. You're English?'

'British.'

He nodded slowly, then took a carrot-size joint from inside his jacket and fired it up. 'I spent a summer working the beach in Sri Lanka when I was your age. Lot of weddings. Lot of English couples. Lot of guys playing with their rings.'

It was hard to tell if he meant the joke. His accent was almost London; if he occasionally sounded Indian, I got the impression it was because he wanted to.

'You get English couples here?' I said, making conversation. 'I mean, for weddings by the ocean and stuff?'

He snorted. 'Just English women,' he said, taking a reflective pull. 'You should see how they sell this place to the rest of India. "Come see the white women having sex on the beach. Free live porn show."' He seemed to find this pretty funny, so I laughed ha-ha to be polite.

'I'm Tjinder,' he said, and offered me the joint.

'No thanks. And it's Bay,' I said, not proffering my hand as I got up. I was thinking he was probably some kind of cop, or some kind of crook; my travel book had said you should steer clear of people offering drugs in India, even if all the locals seem to be doing them and nobody minds, because the moment you take a puff you're vulnerable to extortion. Or maybe he was a 'mo, I thought, what with that last remark, the kind who's not that keen on women. Maybe the wedding ring was a pretence the faggots had to make here, with all the religion and shit. His clothes, too; the man could clearly shop, though where I didn't know. Did he work here? I started back towards the main building.

'Later,' he called after me.

'Sure,' I called back, thinking, yeah. In your dreams, freakshow.

The stoners' circle had thinned out a little when I went back up, and the sounds of at least three different configurations of sex were floating around from the cabins below, forming a part of the soundtrack with the hum of the ocean, the chatter of insects. Jojo and Talya were still in the central loop but Alita had joined a satellite group, dangling her legs over the edge of the roof and back-chatting over her shoulder to two bulletheads and some saronged PR witch with a chest out of *National Geographic*. I sat down next to her and started humming circus music, der-der-diddler-der-*der*-der-durder, under my breath. Though it was a pretty bratty thing to do, she giggled; it was always easy to get her when she had a swerve on.

'Behave,' she worked into the tail end of her snickers; and I made a face at her, but it seemed to have worked. The freaks had shifted onto their other hips, effectively turning away from us, and I had her all to myself.

'So where'd you vanish to?' she said.

'I hit the beach to catch the sunset, but its answerphone was on already.'

'Leave your message after the solar flare.'

'And there was some Indian git trying to puff your feelthy reefer down my throat,' I said, but I was thinking: good clothes, knew Europe. Maybe he was from London and here on holiday too? Or somewhere better than London. 'What's with this Rizlarama anyway?' I said irritably.

'When in Goa you go for it.'

'This is Kerala.'

'Same difference,' she said.

'So that's your plan?' I asked her.

'As good as any,' she said, looking at me as she sucked on the roach. 'What's yours?'

I shrugged, looked at the floor. I didn't want to be on the spot like this. 'I thought, y'know. Maybe we could start again here. Go back to where we were, before it got screwed.' I couldn't look at her.

'You want some of this?' She held the jay roach-first towards me. Had she been listening? I shook my head. 'I don't know why you won't. You could use loosening up. Helps you get on with people.'

I didn't want to get on with people, I wanted to get on with her.

'But if you don't want a part of stuff around here, y'know, that's good too,' she said. 'It's what we all need. Find our own space. Meet some new people. Start moving on.'

'I don't want new people,' I said.

'Snap out of it,' she said. 'I mean it. I've got enough on my plate, okay? I need to forget home. Something broke for me there. It's not a good place for me now, and I want to move on. I love you, Bay, but I'm not going to be able to do that if I'm hanging with you twenty-four-seven, okay?'

I didn't know what to say. Or, I did know what to say, but I wasn't going to do myself any favours saying it. Could she have told me this before we came? I'd thought we were okay. I'd thought we were getting better together. I'd thought that was the plan.

I looked away, trying to see where Talya and Jojo were at, a last ditch to deflect this thing with Alita right now; but they were on the far side, not close enough to attract their attention; then, beyond them, I saw my mother's head bobbing up the stairs around the side of the building. She didn't see us for a moment, but Alita saw her; and, with a grimace to me, she got up and walked over to the bulletheads. I didn't know if she was angry at me, or meant to let me have the reunion alone.

I hadn't seen Mum in eighteen months, and she had different hair; a Rachel cut, like they used to wear in the nineties. This was so true to form that I almost laughed, despite everything. She always missed it somehow, however much she tried. My father told me once that when he first came on to her she explained that she worked in a Thomas

Cook currency exchange because she loved the buzz of the City. This was in the eighties, when everyone loved the buzz of the City. The closest she ever got was doing Dad's books for him, and I was surprised he'd managed so well without her. I'd never heard him complain, at least. Her Rachel cut, years after everyone else, was totally in character, and actually quite suited her. She was still a pretty good-looking woman. Jojo used to fancy her, he'd told me once, in possibly the most awkward conversation I'd ever had with him. I looked around for him now but I couldn't see him.

I watched her doing a swift meet 'n' greet with the croaks via Shana and then she saw me. There wasn't any kind of TV-movie moment, which surprised me; instead, she continued with the kiss-hugs and chit-chat, as though she knew these people. Only when the gnarlies were done slobbering all over her did she come over to me.

'How's my special guy?' she said, giving me the same hug as she gave all the others. I kissed her cheek and let her hold me at arm's length while she checked how I'd grown.

'You're benching, what, one-ten?'

'One-twenty,' I lied.

'Whoa,' she said, massaging my deltoids approvingly. But then what Dad used to call her gimme-line appeared between her eyebrows. 'Gonna do some yoga? Feels like you need it.'

'I'll stick with my training,' I said. I'd planned to keep up my programme with swimming and sand-runs, pull-ups and push-ups. Yoga is a girl thing. The bulletheads were only doing it to get access to vulnerable women, the same way guys join pro-life groups.

'You really need to stretch some of this crap out of your muscles,' she said. 'This group here' – she dug the tips of her fingers in painfully – 'feels like it's packed with gravel.'

'Well, I just got off the plane,' I said. Honestly, this was my mum all over. Pick up on the effect, not the cause, and you get to float through life, pretending you care but never having to deal with the rough stuff. 'And it hasn't been the easiest couple of months.' I could have said years instead of months but it wasn't the time to get into one.

'I know, baby,' she said, changing her face, 'but you can't let it make you ill. You've got to let it out.'

As if she'd like it if I did. This was where I decided to give it up and go home. I hadn't come out here to have it out with her; I'd come out as part of the break-up deal with Talya, so I could get things back on track with Alita. But now Ali had cut me off. She needed time with me not around. I didn't want to leave her out here to cop off with backpackers, but there wasn't much option. If she was going to do it, she was going to do it whether I was there or not. I'd give it a week for the sake of decency, then get on a plane back.

'That's what I'm here for, Mum,' I said, playing up to her, but she was already looking round for someone to change the subject.

What was she like? Honestly. It was like when Diana died; she'd turned into a total Diana freak for a month, practically camping out at Kensington Palace, and then forgotten about it a month later. Diana had been a bit wasted on me, but Jamie told me that a lot of younger kids'd had a real problem with it: your parents tell you that when people die on television you shouldn't get upset because it isn't real; so when Diana died on television . . . They made us keep a scrapbook for school about the mourning, and Alita hung on to hers. A week before we'd flown to India, she'd been back from London to sort her stuff out; I'd gone round to help, we'd ended up talking about Jamie, and she'd dug it out of a box in her wardrobe.

'Remember this?' she'd demanded, brandishing the Diana scrapbook at me. 'Remember how we all had to go into special assembly the first morning back at school, and anyone who didn't cry got kept behind until they did?'

I'd been one of them. We weren't let out until we let it out.

'That was all such a bunch of crap.' She began flipping the pages. 'Look at this: "A Nation Grieves". Oh, I cried – who didn't, we were encouraged to – but grief? My arse. I remember exactly what it felt like. You cried for teacher, you cried for Mummy, and they patted you on the head, and you felt warm and squishy and included. They told us that was grief, but if it was, then god help me for what I'm feeling now.'

I hadn't known what to say, at the time.

'Was there an inquest?' my mother asked, still massaging my shoulders.

'In a week or two,' I said. 'I mean, that's partly the reason Alita's here, if you remember.'

'Oh, sure,' Mum said, but her eyes were starting to wander. 'Where is she, anyway?'

'I think she went to bed,' I said, though I had no idea. 'Shana's being totally prickly around her, I don't know why. It was giving her a headache.'

'She shouldn't take any notice,' Mum said. 'Shana's just used to being the youngest girl around here. She's probably worried Alita's going to steal her thunder with the boys along the beach. Speaking of which,' she went on, and suddenly, behind her, there was the spooky Indian guy from before. 'This is Tjinder,' she said. 'My husband.'

When I was a kid I had a bit of a lisp; I wasn't so hot at pronouncing stuff, and foreign words were the worst – croissant, guacamole. It was the same with the name of the Indian kid whom my parents sponsored through school, the kid whose biannual letters, A-starred report cards and future-gazing graduation photos had adorned our fridge door for as long as I could remember: Tjinder I couldn't manage, but Tinder I could. So to me he was always Tinder; and just because my mum had married him now, I didn't see why I should change.

He didn't seem to mind. He even seemed to like it; maybe he saw it as evidence of how far we went back together, in an odd kind of way. Family was very important to him, he told me a month later. If it hadn't been for him I would've skipped the country weeks before. He was amazing, an incredible guy to me. He'd worked in India's silicon valley, built his own business and sold it at twenty-six, and now he wanted Munich, Milan, Stavanger, Stockholm. The marriage to my mother was just to get green cards, Mum told me, so that she could expand the yoga place and he could work in the EU. He'd run into my mother almost by accident, she said. They hatched the visa plan, got married a month before I arrived;

he was at my mum's place because of the wedding. They'd meant to take a honeymoon, to make it look to immigration like they really were married, so he'd cleared his diary to do it; but then the staff walk-out that had led to Shana becoming cook meant that my mum had to stay at camp. Tinder was left at a loose end, and happy, eager even, to show me around.

I was happy to let him. Each morning he'd come pick me up in his Range Rover, and we'd drive away under a sky that was too blue to look at. Maybe I should've thought it was slightly odd that someone who was twenty-eight should be so keen to buddy up with a kid of eighteen. Something you learn as you grow up is that the kind of adults who want to involve themselves with children – camp leaders, drug dealers, teachers – aren't necessarily the best adverts for adulthood. But I figured that thinking in terms of age differences was something that belonged back in the playground; and if there was any unhealthiness it was probably on my side, wanting to spend so much time with him.

Even if he hadn't been the Third World kid whose photograph on our fridge had been an incentive to eat my greens all through my childhood, now he was a blueprint for who you want to be. He had a gait that made it look like he was walking on softer ground than the rest of us, turf instead of tarmac, red carpet instead of a bare dirt road. That was the way he'd chosen for his life; he made me feel that I could choose it too. Every day we drove: into the hinterland, into the spice towns, around the bays. Tinder was from Bombay: he was a street kid, before the charity found him, and so uneducated that he'd once strayed onto a Bollywood set without knowing it, assuming that this was just another part of town; he'd never had Disney videos or storybooks, so having never seen palaces, he didn't know there was anything special about them. He'd found an appetite for scenery somewhere, though; he seemed to get as much out of our jaunts as I did, chilling on the backwaters, the bays, and he knew everyone up and down the coast too. One evening we stopped at a beach café on our way back; next to us at the bar sat Tinder's buddy Vanu, snowing some backpacker girl.

'It must've been cool growing up so close to nature,' she said, lighting a roll-up.

'I remember childhood as a magical time,' Vanu said, while Tinder and I tried to keep straight faces. 'I remember my mother, on a night just as this one, leaning over my crib and saying, "Hush, my darling – be still, my darling – the lion sleeps tonight."'

'Whoa,' said the girl, round-eyed.

'He grew up in Birmingham, the cunt,' said Tinder under his breath to me, and I had to fake a choking fit so as not to blow the guy's pull.

'I hardly remember my parents,' Tinder told me later, over dinner. 'Dad kicked my mum out when I was a baby – I think he caught her turning tricks for the housekeeping, and his pride wouldn't stand it. We lived in the same room, but we could have been on different planets. His life was a mystery to me.'

He turned his fork in his dhal, and I thought about my own parents, who, for all their dumping us at the grandparents', had had all the videos on child development.

'I hated that time,' Tinder went on, still poking at his food. 'The boredom, the frustration of being a kid; not being able to accomplish anything, you know? I had to stay at home, look after the other kids, while he worked fifteen hours a day in a tannery. I wanted to get out into the world. Hungry for it, y'know? I needn't have worried. He died when I was six – the chemicals killed everyone soon enough – and then I had to grow up pretty fast.' Tinder raised a forkful to his mouth, chewed and swallowed. 'Of course, two years later I'd had enough and wanted to be a kid again. I got to the mission school, though it nearly killed me, and your family paid for me to stay there.'

'*Your* family,' I said, trying to bring him out of it, though it took him a moment to get it. 'So do I call you Tinder or Pop?'

'Do you call Cassandra Mother or Cassandra?'

'Cassandra. Unless she's doing something embarrassing; then it's, like, *Moth*errrrr!'

He didn't smile. 'And your father?'

'Daddy dearest.'

'You must have become very close over the last couple of years,' he said, with a certain something in his voice. A reproach, maybe; I certainly felt, suddenly, like he was a man and I was a clown. You get so used to doing the teenage thing for adults that it can take a while to accept it when they want to treat you like an equal.

'Yeah, I guess so,' I said, trying to come back up to his level. 'I mean, we do stuff together. Probably more than we would if, you know, I wasn't the only one there.'

'And you'll follow him into his business.' It wasn't a question, and I suddenly got where this was going. When my dad was wasted, he'd air the odd vague sentiment about me working with him some day; I just took it as the dope talking. I'd never doubted that my future was going to be a long way from home, even if it was in the same town. I gave Tinder a hard look. If my mother was putting him up to try and pressurise me into doing what my dad did . . .

'No fear,' I said. 'I don't know exactly what I'm going to

do but, you know. Lots of options. And Dad's very different from me. His stuff isn't my stuff –'

'Your father doesn't share his business with you?' he asked, almost incredulously. 'He doesn't want you to follow him?'

'No,' I said, a bit freaked. It was difficult to keep it in mind that things were so different here. 'I mean, most fathers don't. Back home. Hardly anyone ends up doing the same thing as their dad.'

'I see,' he said. Even though the father-son thing hadn't worked out for him, he probably took it as read that, in other people's situations, where the father was well-off, the son would automatically follow the stairway to bucks that had been constructed for him.

'My dad's been, I don't know, a bit hard to get through to, the last couple of years,' I said, trying to make myself look a little less dysfunctional. 'I mean, he's still kind of broken up about everything – Mum going, and then Shana. It's got in the way of how we ought to be together.'

Tinder was looking really closely at me, nodding in the right places, but not making a move to say anything. It was like the way teachers keep shtum in assessments when they want you to keep talking.

'And then a couple of our friends died,' I went on, trying to close it off. 'Alita's brother. The dark girl? That's kind of why we came out here.'

'No, you came to see your mother,' he said. 'You won't be a son to your father until you see things with your own eyes, not his.'

'I don't want to follow him in his business,' I started again, but he cut me off.

'I'm talking about your family, man,' he said. 'You can still have one. She's concerned for you, you know that?

She needs you to understand her. You have a chance to do this.'

Was this the only reason he was taking an interest in me? Because she put him up to it?

'You should talk to her,' he said, pushing his plate away. 'It's meant a lot to her, your coming here. She's waiting for you, you understand?'

'There isn't much to talk about,' I said, feeling sick at having to face him down.

'You're wrong,' he said. 'You want to be like me? I have no one. This isn't good for a man, to come from nowhere.'

Actually that sounded pretty good to me. The relief, if the only crap you had to put up with was your own. It'd be nice if either of my parents ever behaved like parents, but until then . . .

'I need to move on,' I began.

'You can't until you know what you're leaving,' he said. 'You're going to sit down with her, eat dinner, talk. You'll do this for me.'

Everyone was trying to make me get on a plane. First Alita, now him. If I didn't do what he said, that was going to be the only option.

'Okay,' I said.

'Good boy,' he said, and ruffled my hair.

He fixed it up the next night, drove us round the bay to a palmetto-roofed restaurant on the beach, and left us there.

'Do this for your mother, then it's done,' he said, as I got out of the car. My mum was already kissing cheeks with the guy behind the bar, and continued gabbing it up with him while I watched Tinder drive away. They seemed to know each other pretty well. Even when we sat down he was still fluttering around, trading clever remarks in Indian with her.

I had no idea she spoke it so well. He finally got round to asking who I was, and then made a big deal out of it, your son come all the way from London to see his mother, a dutiful son, a fine son, and so on. I felt like smacking him one. Finally he pissed off to get our food and I was left alone with her.

'Friendly guy,' I said.

'I give him a lot of business,' she said, pouring out some bottled water. 'If it weren't for my trade he'd go under. But if it weren't for him, my guests'd have nowhere to go to. These new places they're putting up –' she nodded to a building site along the beach – 'hotels with air-conditioned restaurants, waiters in dicky bows, my trade doesn't want that. They'll pay to avoid it.'

'Quite the businesswoman,' I said.

'Somebody has to be,' she said. 'Tell me, your dad still living like a student?'

I looked away. She took a deep breath, as if to launch into one. Instead, she said:

'I'm sorry. That isn't the way I wanted this to go. I'm as nervous about this as you are, okay?'

I looked hard at her, but it seemed like she meant it.

'Okay,' I said.

'I don't want to get into a slagging match with your father,' she said. 'There're some things you ought to know –'

'Mum,' I said.

'But this isn't the place. Can we start again?' She smiled, trying.

'No problem,' I said.

The guy brought us some mango.

'You're getting on with Tjinder,' she said, ignoring hers, lighting a joint. She'd taken that up too.

'Sure,' I said.

'I'm glad. He's really taken to you.'

'It's good to spend some time with him.'

'Your age, you need some male company.'

I put my fork down. 'I have Dad, remember?'

She put the joint in the ashtray.

'I know you're angry with me,' she said, 'that's natural; and I'm sure your dad's made me out to be the whore of Babylon, that's natural too. But I want you to know that I'm grateful to you for staying with him.' She picked the cigarette up, watched me through the smoke as she took a puff.

'What else could I do?' I said sourly.

'You could have come away too,' she said.

'You didn't tell me that at the time,' I said. 'You didn't tell me much of anything, as I remember.'

'Bay, can you try and work with me? You don't want to hear bad things about your dad? Fine. But he was there too when this happened, okay? Try and see the corner I'm stuck in here. Please?'

It was hard to say what I wanted to with her across the table from me.

'It's easy to see his side,' she said. 'He's got you there, you're both in that little town, I bet it all looks pretty black and white, doesn't it? Let me finish. You can't know until you've moved on yourself, but the way things seem to you right now is not necessarily the way things are. Things are different there. But everywhere else is where you have to live your life, and it's not so simple. Can you try to see that?'

There wasn't much point arguing. I wanted it to be tomorrow, off somewhere with Tinder, him pleased with me for doing the right thing.

'Okay,' I said. We both went through the motions with the mango for a while, then the guy brought our curry. We both sat and looked at it.

'I had a chat with Alita,' she said when he'd gone.

'Oh, christ, Mum –'

'It's all right,' she interrupted. 'She told me what you've been through.'

'Mum . . .' I groaned.

'It's my fault too,' she persisted, 'that's what I want to say to you. If you hadn't been left to sort out your father, then things might've been different there. You had too much on your plate to see what was going on.'

'I don't know what you're talking about,' I said, meaning *Please. Drop it now.*

'She told me, Bay, it's okay. You knew what Jamie was doing, but you didn't have anyone to go to.'

I'd sat on it so successfully that now it came out without warning.

'There's something I haven't . . . haven't told her,' I said, and it was because she was a woman, not just my mother.

'Alita's coming round to it,' she said. 'She knows there was no one you could tell. She just needs a little time, that's all.'

'I can't have her finding out. I can't.'

'It's growing up, baby. Everyone has to do it. Once you leave home you have more people to deal with. They all want you to be a special person for them. You can't just be yourself for everyone like you could when you were younger. You have to be different people to different people. You were going through it already. You had to be one person to Alita, another to her brother.'

'I shouldn't have done it.'

'Better that you're telling me. Just don't ever get involved with the police. You don't know because we've kept you away from them. For that, it was worth paying to stay in that town, I can tell you.'

Finally. 'I don't understand.'

'I mean that everyone does things that they'd find it hard to stand up in front of strangers and explain,' she said. 'If they got unlucky and found that they had to. You know what I'm saying?'

I wasn't sure I did, but I dipped my head.

'The police are in the business of taking a snapshot of people's lives and developing it in black and white. They don't look at the colour, they don't look at the light and the shadow. They don't need to see how you got to be in the frame. They'll just hold up the picture and say, Look. And everyone can see what it looks like.'

'I spoke to them.'

She put her joint down. 'You never.'

I told her. The lot. It took a while. When I was done, she exhaled *wooh*; then fired the joint up again, took a long suck on it, looking out to sea.

'But you think they knew anyway?' she said, when she was ready.

'They really weren't interested,' I said. 'You have to understand. I couldn't stand people thinking that way of Jamie and Harper. I knew the cops really knew. I thought they were just waiting to see what we did next, if we made it any worse for ourselves.'

'But they'd rather people believed the easy option,' she said. 'File closed instead of fifty kids to pick up. I can see that.'

'And if no one else knew how to make it.'

'Right,' she said, 'sure. What were their names?'

'Mackey,' I said, shaking my head, 'he was a bastard.' I looked up. 'And some guy called McCormick.'

'What did he do to you? My God, is there something you didn't tell me?'

'It's all right,' I backpedalled, 'really. He just kept saying he was going to come and look on Dad's computer, see if I used it, you know. For over-eighteen stuff, when I was underage.'

'Mackey,' she said, like she hadn't been listening.

'Why?'

She snapped out of whatever she'd been in. 'Nothing. You just usually know people's names round there. Brothers, sisters you might have gone to school with. It's nothing.'

'He was only just older than me,' I said.

'Well, there you are,' she said, back to herself, 'it's going to be okay.' She put her hand over mine. 'Just don't ever do anything like that again, okay? I mean it, Bay. Talk to your mother first. Not strangers. And definitely not the police. You hear me?'

'You're not going to tell Alita?'

'I'm on your side –' she squeezed my hand – 'like I said. Someone sees a picture out of nowhere, it's hard for them to see how you got in it. Don't worry about her. She just needs some space, sort her head out. In the meantime, you've got nothing to beat yourself up about. It's my fault. If you'd had anywhere else to go to, you wouldn't have gone to the police. I know what your father's like.'

'It's so *hard*, Mum,' I said, my voice breaking a little with the relief of it. 'He's been like . . .'

'I know,' she said.

'And I was trying to bring him out of it, really I was,' I said, needing her to see it all now, 'but I was so busy with that I didn't know what to do about Jamie. And he was like, he was making out like I was *his* father laying down the law, and I'm like, come again? What do I know about fathers? I don't even know how to be with my own.'

'Bay, you're out of it now,' she said.

'Am I? Because it really doesn't feel like it.'

'You can come to me now. You should've known that, but it's my fault you didn't. You do now, okay?'

'Okay,' I said, wondering how far she meant.

'Then okay,' she said. 'Forget it. Forget about everything, start living your own life,' she said. 'Believe me, this is the place to do it.'

Five minutes earlier I would've jumped down her throat for that. 'I just want to be a normal kid,' I said. 'I want to be making decisions like, should I take my date to a horror film or a comedy.'

'Yeah, yeah,' she said. 'And the horror film she gets to shrink against you, and the comedy you get to do lines from to each other afterwards. Girls know this.'

'But they like it, right?' I tried a weak smile.

'You didn't ask for any of this,' she said, rubbing my hand. 'You know something Alita told me? She said you talk about your father like he's the kid there, not you.'

I put my face down so she wouldn't see me welling up.

'He's going to unload on you forever if you let him.' She gripped my hand in hers, her rings digging into me. 'Shana left him to get on with it, and you need to do the same. Your father's a big boy, though he doesn't want to admit it. Do like your sister. I can't say she's everything she can be yet, but she's worked out for herself that no one gives out prizes for being selfless in this life. She's doing what she feels like until she knows what she wants, and so should you. Start living for yourself.'

'I want to.' I really did.

'Then I want you to think about staying out here,' she said. 'Hear me out. It's not fair you taking your father on your own. I thought he was big enough not to unload on you, but obviously not.'

I did this once not long after she left. I really let go to this teacher after school and suddenly they were like, I'm going to refer you to this guy and make you an appointment with this woman; but I was like, It's okay, it doesn't seem that bad now I've wailed about it. Can't we just forget it?

'And what with everything else,' she went on, like it was already settled. 'It isn't healthy, having all that pressure. You're better out of it. Do your gap year here. You can help out around the place, go travelling if you want. You need to be with people your own age.'

'I like Tinder,' I said.

'I didn't mean that. Anyway, he'll have to get back to his life soon, free you up to mix more. You'll like it. I wish I'd done it when I was your age. Then, it was just money money money.'

'I'll think about it,' I said, thinking about commuting to an office job through the sleet. Working somewhere everyone already knew each other because their parents got them the job. Staying here would be my parents getting me the job. I'd be made up. 'I'll really give it some thought.'

'I'll feel a lot better with you here,' she said, 'you know that. But of course you don't have to make a decision till you're ready.'

I already had, but of course I shouldn't've yet. Maybe she was thinking I'd cramp her style; and if I was here, she'd watch me like Dad never did. I stared down at the green sludge on my plate. She pushed away hers.

'Tell you what. How about we go back and I cook you something? Don't tell Shana, but I've got some lambchops in the back of the freezer. What do you say? I'm sick of bloody curry even if you aren't.'

'Okay,' I said. I hadn't had chops since before she left.

'Good boy,' she said, and signalled the guy for the check.

'So how'd it go last night?' Tinder asked next day.

I'd woken that morning thinking, screw it. Time to live for me, not for anyone else. I could do anything I wanted, so I started by taking my breakfast with the others, something I hadn't done since we arrived. They hadn't taken much notice – Jojo'd been out all night, Talya and Alita were talking to Shana – but I stuck it out until I felt I'd made the effort. Then I took some juice to the beach, sat down with a Lonely Planet I'd borrowed from my mother, and that was where Tinder had found me.

'Pretty good,' I said. 'I'm glad we did it. Thanks, man.'

'Welcome,' he said. 'I'm glad you did too. What you reading?'

I showed him the cover.

'I thought I'd mug up a bit,' I said, 'so you wouldn't have to explain everything.'

'Man, I like to explain,' he said, taking it out of my hand, flipping through it with a sour expression on his face. 'And don't you want to get it from me, not some public schoolboy who was here for two weeks once? Look at those guys.' He gestured at a group of yoga tourists sprawled on the beach, all reading paperbacks with beaches on the front. 'Reading travel books *while* they're travelling? It's like watching porno at an orgy, man. I tell you what,' he said, squatting down. 'I gotta go to Delhi, business. I'd take a plane but there're guys I could see on the way. Old investors of mine, you understand? Money men, country estates. I'm thinking, why don't you and me drive there, stop off on the way? What do you say? You see the country. You see what everyone else only flies over.'

Wow. 'How long?' I said.

'I'm thinking, a month, round trip,' he said. 'I don't want to take you from your friends . . .'

I could've hugged him. There was always, with him, a slight air of you-must-have-better-things-to-do, though he knew I hadn't. Jojo's parents did it a lot too; adults can be so kind. We packed up the Range Rover and left the next day.

Looking back, I swear, it was just like the way my parents used to persuade us to go to our grandparents' so they could go to a weekender. You want to go round to Nana's and play with all the new toys, or stay here and play with these old ones? But at the time I was like, what am I leaving? Alita was still weird with me, but given time to herself she'd get over it; Talya I still wasn't easy with since we broke up, and probably never would be again; Shana, having apparently decided that Alita and Talya improved her chances of pulling (since the blokes on the beach worked in groups too), hung with them 24-7; and Jojo, when there were no computers, PlayStations or TV to mediate between us, wasn't much fun. If they all wanted to do their own stuff, fine; here was my chance to do mine, be a real traveller and not just some waster on a beach.

And this was the way to do it. Backpacking off from my mum's place was hardly enticing, though she got a lot of kids our age using her place as a base. I'd assumed that we'd be all-gap-year-together with other kids out there, and it wouldn't be a big deal, but it was. They were slicker than us, somehow, more out there, more self-assured. They came from very different places, or seemed to. It gave me a look at what it might be like if I did go back for gap year, or afterwards, at uni. After the first few times they'd made me feel like I was some kind of hick yokel loser even though my mum owned the place, I kept clear of them, and soon learned to steer Tinder away from them too. Their mere presence – lounging around, drawling anecdotes, trying to cop off – was enough to set him off for an hour at a time.

I found out why the second night of our trip, when we stayed at his apartment near Goa. He'd got a beach-view place and pumped it up with money into a Bond villain's gaff of CCTV, satellite streams and banked monitors, only to find the beach below his terrace overrun, within a couple of years, by vomiting Belgians and spaced-out Swedes, full-moon parties every night of the week. I asked him why he didn't sell up; he said it was the principle of the thing.

'Sink lickers,' he snarled, surveying a beachful of them from his balcony, practically spitting. Back at Mum's place I'd seen him blank the yoga tourists when they tried to chum up to him, get advice from the horse's mouth about the cheapest way up the coast and so on. Now, on his balcony, I called him on it.

'C'mon, man, aren't you like, flattered? These people are prepared to live in the same clothes for months on end just to get to know your country better.'

'Are you proud that Bangladeshis live in hostels to experience your country?' he countered. He had a point. 'These are rich children. I don't care if they're poor students at home, any Westerner is rich here. So they should behave like rich visitors; not pretend that they are poor as Indians and entitled to haggle for native prices. They make a show of avoiding the beggars, yeah?' Tinder went on, grimacing like he had something bad in his mouth. 'I've heard them say it, "Be like the Indians, they never give money to them." Do you see that the beggars wouldn't be here if they weren't? Your mother's guests – they pay luxury tourist rates for their authentic yoga experience, and Cassandra employs local people with the money, buys local food. But these freeloaders I can't respect.' He gestured disgustedly at a ring of backpackers sitting cross-legged on the beach, getting a swerve on while some dreadlocked German patted his bongos. 'But enough,' he said, breaking it. 'Get much older than twenty and attitude starts to look like bad digestion. Let's drive.'

I had to keep reminding myself that he was a successful young guy who'd made a pile in his chosen profession; at home, my meeting someone like him as an equal would be too unreal to imagine. And though he was so like a regular, stand-up guy with me, I had to remember that here he was a sophisticate, one of the elite. Everywhere we went, as we pushed on northwards, he seemed to know people; the ones who owned the bars and hotels, and they all wanted to throw their facilities at our disposal. It was kind of embarrassing at first, but it wasn't hard to get used to it.

By the time we got near Bombay it had even started to get a bit samey. All the way up the coast there had been the same crappy roads, the same palmetto-roofed beach shacks, the same bamboo-panelled bars, the same grinning guys in flip-flops telling me that any friend of Tjinder's was a friend of theirs, before they disappeared into back rooms with him to pray in front of their shrines (I was never allowed). I think Tinder began to notice; out of nowhere, he'd suddenly say that the real India was inland, that the fascination with the coast was a Western thing.

He pumped me up so much that I didn't even want to go into Bombay, I was so hot for the interior; but then, almost as soon as we headed into it, I was desperate to go back. Where there were no tourists, India was a toilet, worse than America; nothing to see all day except fields, nowhere to stay at night except khazis – nothing in the whole country between a Ritz and a roadhouse, a Hilton and a hole, and there was no Ritz or Hilton between Goa and the Ganges. It's supposed to be a developing country but I tell you, I didn't see much developing going on. You should see where these people go to the bathroom. And as if that wasn't enough, everyone smoked, everywhere, all the time. You couldn't get away from it. I damn near puked about a thousand times a day.

There wasn't even that much to see. There was the odd MTV moment as we rounded a bend and hit a sky filled with wind-farm turbines, but mostly it was a load of nothing. I tried to be polite and everything but it was almost a relief when we stopped for his business calls – overnighters at big, deluxe Southfork-type ranch compounds – and I could just go chill by the pool while he had meetings with the hosts. I ate with them in the evenings, of course, but they all talked in Indian after they'd asked me a few token how-do-you-like-India's and what-are-you-studying's; and after dinner, while they talked and smoked, I'd go work out or swim until I was tired enough to sleep.

It was all totally disorienting. India is like nowhere else, once you get inland: no motorways, no services, no logos on the trucks, no billboards. Just country. There's so little to look at that you feel your brain kind of floating free. I could see, after a week of it, how people go to India and end up joining a cult. I said this to Tinder, when he asked me how I was liking it for about the hundredth time and I was sick of saying 'fine'.

He laughed. 'I get you, man. I like that. You've got a special way of seeing things.'

'I'm just so not used to this. It's so alien,' I went on, feeling duty-bound to expand, in my celebrated special way. We were drinking *chai* on the veranda of the place where we'd slept the night before.

'That's what I wanted to show you, man,' he said, putting down his cup. 'I want to do for you what your father did for me. You know, when I was a kid this was all I knew –' he waved an arm to encompass the dust, the *maidan*, a cur wandering in front of some shacks over the way – 'except this would've looked like heaven, a garden, to me. All I knew was alleys and streets. Your father took me out of that, put me in school, had me taught that those streets led to motorways if you walked far enough.'

I wanted to say that it was no big deal. I mean, what did they charge to sponsor an Indian kid in the eighties – a fiver a week? But thinking it made me see how spoiled it would've sounded. A fiver, loose change, a handful of shrapnel – it had been the difference between death and life to him.

'I know you've been through a rough time at home,' he went on. 'Those poor boys, man, those friends of yours. It's a terrible thing, for youth to be wasted like that. Before it's even had chances to prove itself, you know? I would have been wasted too, if it wasn't for your father. That's why I'm glad you wanted to come with me, man,' he said, putting his hand on my arm, letting the self-consciousness of what he was saying push him towards a grin. 'On this little jaunt, this little tour of ours. I wanted to show you another world, and let the broadening of horizons open up the world to you, just as it did for me. And, when that's happened to you, when you're flipped out of the alley you were born into –' he pantomimed blinkers, tunnel vision, with his hands – 'then you're free. Then you can make your mark on the world, man. Then you can make some money. C'mon.'

He got up, peeled some notes from a roll big as my fist, dropped them on the table and led me back to the 4x4. When we were inside he took out the map and tossed it into my lap, then reversed onto the track and spun the power-steering back towards the road. 'Look at it,' he said. 'Look at the map, look out the window. Look at the people we're meeting. This is where I can put you ahead of the game, man. This is how I can repay your father.' He chuckled at that – the tone of it was a little disconcerting to me – but then he said, 'This is where the future is.'

This was the kind of crap we used to do for GCSE geography, where the textbooks were saying, yada yada yada the twenty-first century belongs to the Pacific Rim, while on TV every night there were Asiatic executives weeping their way through press conferences about the failure of their banks.

'I thought India was, like, poor,' I said.

'No, it's been kept poor, man,' Tinder replied heatedly, grimacing at the road as he swung us back onto smooth asphalt. 'All these famines, these floods and droughts; where do you think they came from?'

'Global warming,' I said without hesitating. 'Over-population.' I'd got a B for geography.

'No, man. That's bullshit. That's what they tell you in the West because they can't tell you the truth. All these temples, these palaces we've been seeing – does it look to you like the people who built them were paupers? Huh? So stinking poor that every time there was a storm or a dry season, half of them died out in the open fields from having nothing to eat?'

He had a point. We had gone past some pretty Disney stuff.

'But that was before the population explosion,' I said lamely.

'Look out there,' Tinder said, gesturing out the window at an empty landscape. 'Think back over the last couple of weeks. This place look overpopulated to you?'

I had to admit it. Everywhere we'd been had looked like a bunch of nothing, because there were no people or franchises around; what there had been, now that I thought about it, was a whole lot of lush.

'Everything you think about when someone says "developing nation" – the floods, the disasters, the droughts you've seen on the news – they were engineered, man. They were made to happen. The Third World became the Third World because the West wanted it that way.' He switched the transmission from manual to automatic, and shifted his shoulders back into his seat. 'Listen to me,' he said.

Three days later we were in the living room of a flat that could've been in London; sitting in dog-eared armchairs while the owner, a small, spectacled man maybe twenty years older than my father, made us tea in the kitchen. Outside, whatever went on in the streets of Delhi went on, unsuspecting heads passing a few feet below the room's one window; inside, Tinder was sitting calmly opposite me, urbane and reposeful in one of his cream linen suits. He'd made me wear mine too, though it was considerably more lived in at this stage than his fresh one.

I didn't like this one bit. I did not want to be there, but Tinder had left me no option. He wouldn't tell me what it was for, just that there was someone he wanted me to meet. Everyone else he'd introduced me to had lived in, like, palaces, or at the very least the thriving bar business they owned; this was some crappy flat up a side street in a stinking city. The air outside had been like smoking a whole pack of cigarettes, every breath I took. It was something very different, and I didn't like it.

Our host came back into the room we were in, and set a tea tray on a side table piled with books; he had to move some out of the way, butting them with the tray, to set it down. The room was infested with them: on shelves, covering every inch of wall space, on the floor, even stacked on top of the TV.

'Your wife's books?' Tinder enquired of him.

'For the most part,' he said, his back to us as he poured tea into china cups.

'The books of a suicide,' Tinder said with a sudden grin, like it was a big joke. 'Perhaps if you were to read them in the correct order, you might catch the virus yourself?'

The man snorted. For a moment I thought he was crying, but when he turned round and handed Tinder a cup, with what seemed to be a kind of mockery of servility, he was flashing his grin back at him.

'Be my guest,' he said lightly, and turned to me. 'Milk? Sugar?'

As the guy was handing me my cup, Tinder said, 'Tell us about your wife.'

He stiffened. 'What could be of interest that you don't know already?' he said.

'Start from the beginning and we'll tell you,' said Tinder.

'She was an economist,' the guy said. He didn't pour himself a cup.

'Did she work for a bank?' Tinder said sneerily, like he

was tormenting the guy. 'Was she a part of the world she studied?'

'No,' the guy said, in a tone I couldn't get at all. They were playing a game that was way over my head, though the accents didn't help; Tinder's had suddenly gone much thicker, more Indian. 'She was an academic.'

'Tell us what kind of economist she was,' Tinder said, more politely now, but still in a voice I was glad he never used with me.

'She was a free-marketeer,' the guy said, and to me, 'Do you know what that means?'

I nodded earnestly, but inside I was like, oh, I *get* it. This was why we were there. It had to be connected with the freaky stuff Tinder told me as we drove there. It'd totally blown me away, and if I'd heard it from a stranger, I wouldn't have believed it. But I'd seen the kind of respect he got, everywhere he went, and I knew the way he carried himself. I had no option but to see the plausibility of what he said.

The way he told it was that the Third World had been invented after colonisation got unfashionable and the natives were allowed to run themselves. My dad had told me that nothing ever happens unless it's to someone's advantage; I could see the reasoning here. Of course the Raj or whoever wouldn't have just cleared out when they were on to such a good thing unless they had a plan B in reserve, to keep things much the way they were; and this was what Tinder had told me.

When Western governments left the colonies, he said, Western business took over. The economy was still based around farming, but where the governments had provided an administrative base, the corporate conglomerates provided money; piles of it, heaps of it, and there for anyone who wanted to modernise, as they put it. 'Modernising' meant jacking in rice or wheat, and taking up coffee, rapeseed, anything that we wanted in the West – and not just ordinary coffee or whatever, but new, high-yield strains that were super-resistant to disease or adverse conditions, provided the plants were fed with the fertilisers and pesticides that the same companies were willing to provide, and at special rates. To begin with, at least. Basically you got your first fix free.

The crops were grown in India but exported raw, and only turned into the finished product once back in the West; so enough coffee to fill a two-quid jar was bought from the natives for tuppence, and the other £1.98 was put on through processing and distribution. Naturally the farmers got wise to this after a while, and complained; and the corporations said, Fine, you don't like it, go back. And of course it was too late: they'd totally changed their fields over to the new production, using the machinery, fertilisers and pesticides that the very same conglomerates had lent them money to 'modernise' with; and they had to keep buying, using and maintaining these if they didn't want their crops to fail.

A country that'd had one of the most successful, self-sufficient economies in the world suddenly no longer grew enough food to feed its own people, because it grew beverages and mega-yield cotton and industrial lubricants instead. And the next time the weather got a bit iffy, the irrigation and support systems that had existed forever were no longer in place, having been dug over to accommodate combines and tractors and maximum-yield agriculture. The land slid in rain, dried out in sun. Even before the crops started to fail, all the farmers had were pesticides, strangle-hold contracts and debts.

I could buy it, even if I didn't see the point. I'd heard all about Third World debt and how we ought to let them off it and stuff, but I'd never thought about where that debt came from. And it was certainly easier to believe than what the famine reports on TV seemed to imply – that all this disaster happened by itself, out of nowhere. I was coming to see that nothing comes from nothing; I had, after all, just done twelve years of school about the greenhouse effect, about soil erosion and deforestation, about landslides and flash floods and butterflies flapping their wings. So I figured that we'd come to this economy professor's flat in Delhi so I could get it straight from the horse's mouth, about the corporations who'd made India what it is. Trouble was, the horse seemed to have gone to the glue factory, and there was just this husband left. Tinder gave me a kind of nudging look, like I ought to say something.

'Your wife – she was successful?' I asked the guy. I mean, she'd obviously read a lot of books.

'Yes,' he said quietly. 'Yes, she was. If success is to be measured by the enmity it arouses.'

I looked at Tinder; he nodded, as if I ought to go on.

'She wasn't so popular?' I asked.

'Not in certain quarters.'

'What did she do?'

'She studied the effects of state intervention in free markets.'

Tinder said something to him in Indian.

'Specifically the one-time free markets in narcotics,' the guy said.

I'd thought everything had already fallen into place about why we were there; but that tossed the pieces back up out of their slots and into new ones. The weird thing was, they fit even better this time.

I was confused at first; he said 'one-time', but I was under the impression that there was a free market in drugs right now; unregulated, letting dealers pass off aspirin as E. But this guy, or rather his wife, said that because drugs were prohibited by the state in the West, then it was an unfree market, one that the state had intervened in.

'Most Western medicines of the nineteenth century contained heroin, morphine, cocaine or all three. Users bought their drugs in pharmacies, at prices that were determined by the market for medicines rather than by the greed of black-market dealers. Their use was therefore much less visible, since they had no need to resort to crime to feed their habits. The spectre of the "addict" – malnourished, unhealthy, criminal – is a post-prohibition phenomenon.'

His wife's work had focused, he said, on the paradox that those countries most protective of freedom of the individual and freedom of the markets were also those that were most virulently opposed to those freedoms where drugs were concerned. It was quite interesting, though you could tell that the guy was only used to talking to academics. There was loads of stuff about self-medication – cancer patients smoking dope and so on – and the way the doctors and drug companies got together with governments so that people couldn't be allowed to treat themselves. I remember that part because we'd done it at kid school, one Halloween, when Miss Garrett-Palmer told us how witches were only really women who knew midwifery, and the doctors in olden times put it about that they were witches because they didn't like the competition. I'd loved all that kind of stuff, and what this guy was saying was more of the same, if you could understand it.

It tied into all the stuff that Tinder'd been telling me earlier, about the way Indian farmers got screwed by the corporations. By the time they got wise to the catch-22 they were in, the only options were to stay a slave to it, go under or turn their fields over to the biggest cash crop of them all.

'So farming drugs helps the farmers compensate for what was done to them?' I asked the guy.

'Cannabis, poppies – these supply a profit margin. Farmers don't need to spend all they earn on fertilisers and pesticides to bring them to harvest. Turning over to narcotics freed them from the cycle of growing in order to buy the chemicals they needed to grow, yes. But then came the West's "war on drugs". Covert spraying of herbicides by your militaries. Collusion with terrorists to attack hill farmers.'

And off he went again. He cited practically every human-rights bogeyman I'd ever seen news about – the regimes, the fundamentalists, the guerrillas and militias – and named the tune to which Western agencies were funding them. I glanced across at Tinder from time to time, but his eyes were hooded, his hands folded in his lap. When the guy was finally done, Tinder looked up.

'Tell us how your wife died,' he prompted, in that same tone he'd used earlier, when he spoke to the guy in Indian.

The guy lit a clove cigarette and sat back in his chair. 'She committed suicide herself,' he said, looking at me through the rising smoke. Suddenly he looked less the academic, more like someone's granddad, in a council flat near a bypass somewhere.

'How?' Tinder pressed, though I could tell he already knew.

'She shot herself in the back of the head. Twice,' he said.

* * *

Before we left I went to the loo to splash water on my face, try and dull the spikes in my temples; when I turned the grinding taps off, I could hear the guy talking furiously in Indian, calmer undertones from Tinder; the guy rising into English with the heat of his argument, saying, 'I don't need it, take it away'; Tinder saying, 'I know you do.' They stopped when I came out, and the guy walked to the door, held it open. Tinder shook his head, and went out and down the stairs outside. I was too embarrassed to just run after him.

'Thank you,' I said to the guy, who was still holding the door open.

He regarded me for a moment, and then said, 'That isn't necessary.'

He didn't seem to be being rude; he said it in the same tone, polite but guardedly disinterested, as he'd used with me at the beginning. I really didn't know how to take it. He seemed to soften on my confusion, because he went on, with the air of someone clarifying a point, 'Your friend has *tor* – do you understand? – respect. When you are visited by someone with *tor*, you open the door.' And with that, he shut it; and I followed Tinder back out into the toxic air.

He was waiting for me in the car.

'Do you understand now?' he said.

'I don't know what you want from me.' My voice cracked.

'I had no choice,' he said. 'This was what my education paid for.'

'I don't know what you're talking about.'

'It was work this business or go back to the gutter,' he said. 'I was sixteen. You have to understand that.'

'I need to get out,' I said, shaking my head. 'I need some air.'

'Man, you need to listen,' he said.

This wasn't the first time India had been the preferred destination of white wasters from the West, the way he told it. Thirty years ago it'd been the same: the hippies had started taking stuff back with them, and pretty soon routes were up and running through Turkey and Iran. When the Ayatollah kicked out the Shah in '79, exporting opiates and hash to the West was such an accepted way of making money that the ruling class changed their money into heroin as they fled, to make sure their savings were still worth something where they settled, flooding Europe with pure, cheap smack at the start of the eighties. But then the religious crackdown in Iran and the war in Afghanistan meant no one could get the stuff through in the quantities they used to. The wasters of the West turned to South America for coke, and to home-grown labs for E and whizz. Then the Soviet Union broke down, closed borders were suddenly open, and Tinder and a thousand others started putting hard currency into hands that, after a century of being clapped against the cold while they queued in line for potatoes, were more than happy to take it. And at the other end, the coke kids had grown up; now what they wanted was come-down shit. Weed through the week, smack to take the edge off on a Sunday night.

'Your mother knows nothing,' he said. 'She thinks my money comes from computers. When we found out she was here, I flew down, introduced myself as if by chance, watched her, checked her out. She runs a yoga business and nothing more. I grew to respect her. She's built something of her own here, but she needed a work permit. I saw a chance to pay her back, to pay your father back.' He smiled, but there was that edge to it, that grimace, that I was seeing all the time with Indians now. 'She knows nothing, and we're going to keep it that way.'

I asked him to let me go. I asked him to stop. I asked him why he was doing this to me.

'I need you,' he said. 'The people I've introduced you to, they're powerful guys. They buy from the farmers, I co-ordinate its journey west. They have sons, nephews, cousins in London, Birmingham, Manchester, watching where their money goes. The return on their investment is not what it was. Part of our market is here now, with rucksacks on their backs. They ask themselves, why spend millions trucking the product across continents when we can sell it on the beaches of our own country? But the tourists won't buy from brown hands. Too much extortion, too many police lining their pockets.' He mimicked Ranj's accent, the one he used when he was copping off with eurotrash. 'Hey, take a toke on this, man. Good shit, huh? Now give me five thousand rupees or I take you to my brother-in-law the cop.' He grinned. 'We need white faces to sell for us, and I need you to recruit them. I've shown you to the men with the money and they approve. If you want to become rich, I am offering you this.'

He drove me straight to the airport and put me on a plane to Trivandrum. He had a few more people to see, he said, but would be back at my mother's in a week, and would expect my answer then. Fine. We weren't due to leave for another two weeks, but a week was plenty of time to sort another flight and get away from the mad bastard and his fucked-up country for ever.

You're supposed not to be able to think straight when you're scared stupid, but I found there was nothing like it for concentrating the mind. I'd never heard such a load of bollocks in my life. Christ knew what game he was playing with me or what kind of a kick he got out of it but that really wasn't my problem. All I needed to concern myself with was putting as much distance between me and him as possible, and suggesting to my mother that she do the same. The bastard was psychotic. He needed help, but as far as I was concerned he could get it somewhere else.

I'd been up for about forty hours when the cab from Trivandrum dropped me back at Mum's, but I marched straight over to her cabin and hammered on the door. There was no answer, so I dug Charlie out of the office.

'Hey, man, what's up?' she said. 'You miss breakfast?' It was a little after nine.

'Where's my mother?' I said.

'Bombay. Some legal stuff she needed the embassy for. Said she'll be back Friday but I wouldn't count on it.' She bent to her clipboard. Bombay? Well, whatever. I couldn't stay now anyway.

'Thought so,' she said, looking up. 'There's a parcel for you, came by FedEx last night. Hold on.'

She disappeared into the back, came out with a bulging A3 Jiffy bag swaddled in parcel tape.

'It might be her,' she said. 'You want me to open it?'

I took it to the cabin. The return address on the outside was Tinder's apartment in Goa. Inside were a dozen taped wads of five-hundred rupee notes and a Nokia. When I opened the phone up, one menu button had a gold sticker on it. I pressed it, and it speed-dialled. I held the phone to my ear, listened to it ring once.

'So you see, I'm serious,' Tinder said. 'That's two million rupees. Take it out of the country and, as you know, it's worthless. Stay here, work for me, and double that money in a month. The entry code for my apartment I've reprogrammed as your birthdate. Spend the week there, spend some money. I'll meet you there seven days from today at noon. Have an answer ready for me.' The line went dead.

Mum's place was between seasons. The last of the drongs, the office types who had to take their two weeks after everyone more important had cherry-picked the prime times, had been and gone; the next big influx wasn't for a month or so, when the Christmas escapees would start to arrive. It gave the place a seaside-in-winter air – stripped back to basic functions, no one there who had a choice in the matter. Shana had quit after a guest had to be hospitalised with a couple of monster tapeworms and had threatened to cause a stink. ('Shana's cooking turned him from an eco-warrior into an eco system', Alita said.) Shana had packed up in disgust, gone to Melbourne–Sydney–New Zealand for the winter. A shifty-looking couple from Brighton had taken over the kitchen work from her. The word was that they were stuck in India after making a false accusation of rape to try and claim off their holiday insurance; he'd caught her with a local, was my guess, made her do the fraud to get back at her.

There were only two guests: a Swedish girl called Anna, who, when I first ran into her and asked her out of politeness if she spoke English, replied that if I was going to tell her something stupid or boring, then no, she didn't; and a rich old American woman in her seventies, who came to live there six months of the year; she spent the other six in Vegas and her morning cough had come to sound like dice rattling in a cup. It seemed like she only spent so much time out of the States so she could smoke as many cigarettes as she wanted. I don't know why she picked a yoga camp, because she never did any. Alita, on the other hand, had done so much that she was starting to resemble Lara Croft, with flat planes of muscle that looked computer-generated. There hadn't been much else for her to do: Jojo's father had called ten days before to say he'd fixed him up with a gap-year job in the City if he could get on the next plane, which he did; Talya had buddied up with a group of backpackers and headed off to Goa.

'Why didn't you go with her?' I asked Alita when she was finished filling me in.

'They're heading up to Agra, Jaipur, be gone a month or two,' she said. 'I need to get back.' She shrugged, and looked ruefully out to where the ocean played softly, ten metres away from us, so calmly that the tiny waves didn't even break, but just rolled out onto the wet sand as though they were a fluffed duvet settling over it. What she meant was that she was out of money. 'So you gonna tell Mama where you took yo' bad self?'

'Ah, y'know,' I said. This felt like a last chance. She always did. 'There wasn't so much to it. Travel's always a bit like work – planning, playing off options. You feel like you ought to be paid for it.'

'Like you feel in the gym after a shitty day at school,' she said, a kind of smile that I hadn't seen before playing round her mouth at the memory. 'Like, stinking tests all day, and I've got my period, and I overslept in the morning, and my hair feels dirty; and I get to the gym and it's dark outside and

I think, Couldn't this bastard Stairmaster at least be hooked up to a turbine? You know? And maybe the National Grid could bung me a fiver for all the kettles I've boiled.'

'I get days like that,' I said.

'And we're going back to it,' she went on, smiling still.

'We must be out of our minds,' I said.

'How'd you get on with Tjinder?' she asked.

'Okay,' I said.

'He's a bit intense,' she said.

'Yeah, you could say that,' I said. Before she could ask me anything else I jumped in with, 'So, what'd I miss here?'

She shrugged. 'Shagging.'

'You what?'

She giggled. 'You remember that lot we arrived with? The women all hairy-legged and wholemeal? You should've seen them by the time they went back. Three weeks of sex on the beach with Indians, and they were buying ill-advised bikinis in Kovalam and painting their nails to match. One of them told me I ought to go into the ocean more – this was a woman who'd told me two weeks before that if you stayed in the water long enough you felt the mystical ebb and flow echo in your womb. Now she was telling me I ought to go in the sea "because it makes your hair go ringletty". Spunk-drunk, Jojo called her.'

'Pottymouth,' I snorted. It was an old expression of his. 'He still smoking so much?'

'All the English guys were,' she said. 'None of them were getting any. They could hardly cop off with Indian girls – not unless they want a dozen brothers and uncles showing up, machetes in one hand and visa forms in the other.' She snickered at the thought.

'How about you? Make any new friends?' I tried to make

it sound like banter, but even with everything else it hurt like hell to ask.

'Oh, yeah,' she said, 'lot of people passing through.'

'Passing through, huh?'

'They come down from Goa, this is the last stop before they fly to Thailand. I swear, it feels like everyone under twenty-five is out here.'

'Scary,' I muttered, remembering what Tinder had said about the party market being here now, not in England.

'Depends how you look at it,' she said. 'Another way is, there's more gap year work for those of us who go back.'

There was silence for a moment, just the sound of the ocean.

'I'm going to go back in a week,' I said, to fill it. I hadn't told Mum this yet. 'Charlie's sorting me a new ticket.'

'Okay,' she said. 'Get her to make it two.'

'Don't just because I am.'

'No, I've had enough,' she said. 'I'm chilled. I've had time to put what's happened away somewhere. Now it's time to go back and get on with it.'

'What're you going to do?' I asked. It wasn't as though her father was going to sort her a job in the City.

'I'll think of something,' she said. 'Maybe Harrods for the sales. My cousin did it last year. How about you?'

'I think I'd better talk to my dad,' I said. 'You need any money? I've got loads left. Didn't get much chance to spend it.'

'Well, you better,' she said. 'You can't take rupees to Thomas Cook. Why?'

'I've still got a couple of hundred quid's worth left.'

'You can start by buying me a beer up at Ranj's,' she said.

'You got it,' I said, and got to my feet.

* * *

I left my mum's place the next day. I told Alita I was going to hang in Trivandrum a few days, meet up with some people I'd met with Tinder, knowing she didn't have enough money to come. Sitting with her in the bar, not being able to tell her a word of it, had been murder. She took my silence as confirmation of how much we'd changed. She told me this was a good thing.

I had a number for my mum in Bombay, and I left a message on the desk saying I'd try later. In the meantime, I took the bag of money and a change of clothes up to Tinder's apartment in Goa. I needed some time to freak out, and I couldn't do it in front of Alita. I don't know what I expected to find there; as it was, when I let myself in, I was too scared to touch anything, not knowing if there was CCTV or bugs or what. I stashed the money under his bed, locked up, and checked into a hotel in north Goa with what was left of my own bog roll of rupees. There was no phone, but it didn't matter. I wasn't about to ring my mother again because I didn't know what I was going to tell her.

I spent the week on the beach, trying to get my head round it. I couldn't. At the end of it I went back to his apartment, a little before noon as appointed, got the money out from under the bed, took it to the couch in the living room, sat down. There was no sign that anyone'd been there since I last was. I sat there for maybe forty minutes before he came in.

'I'm glad you're here,' he said when he clocked me. 'You just arrive?'

'Let's talk,' I said.

'Okay,' he said, dumping a garment-carrier and his keys on the table. 'A drink?'

'No thanks.'

He shrugged, walked through to the kitchen, got a Coke from the stainless-steel fridge. Cokes were the only thing in it. 'So,' he said. 'You saw your mother?'

'Briefly.'

'You speak to her?'

'You kidding?'

'How about your friends?' He flopped down onto the white couch opposite.

'They're gone. Except Alita.'

'Alita. Such a pretty girl. So alive. What's the word?'

'She strikes a lot of people that way.'

'Vivacious,' he said, and took a long swallow. 'She hasn't let this thing, this disaster with her brother, spoil her.'

'The money's in the bag,' I said. 'It's all there.'

'Bright girl,' he said, as though he hadn't heard me. 'It could've ruined her. She's at the critical age.'

'What're you talking about?' Was that supposed to be some kind of threat? I looked at him, trying to make my face keep still.

'The critical age for anyone who needs to make their way in the world.' He swiped the cold can slowly across his forehead. 'Where you are now. I remember it myself. Seventeen, eighteen: I was lucky to come out of school with all the certificates and connections to walk into the civil service, as they'd trained us to. But any one of my classmates could do that, like their fathers before them. I'd seen real life before I'd even gone to school. I knew what was below them. Now I wanted to know what was above.'

'And that was running drugs?' I spat.

He tilted his head, lifted his shoulders, let them drop. 'I was where your friend is now. Where you are now. There's a time in every successful man's life when you get your head down, Bay. When you find out where the rope is that can guide you through the future. It feels like you need one, yeah? If you're going to come off the path.'

'I don't understand what you're saying.'

'The path that leads nowhere. The path that joins its end to its start. The path that keeps you walking circles, never leaving the nowhere you were born in.' He drained the Coke, tossing the can into a brushed-steel bin next to the couch. 'Why don't you ask your father?' he said, and began to laugh.

I left a message for Jojo as soon as I got back, but he was away for the weekend with his parents. While I was waiting on him I cleaned up the house, slept off the jet lag, told my dad it'd been cool but I was damned glad to be back, and slowly climbed the walls. When Jojo finally called me back on the Sunday night I asked him if he could get me a gap-year job where he was. I said I'd overspent in India and my dad had cut off my allowance out of spite at my going to see my mother to begin with. This was a scaly one but it wasn't so far from the truth; I guessed Joj was still a bit pissed off with me for hanging with Tinder so much before he left, and I needed to lay it on thick with him. He said, no problem, they hired kids all the time, he'd speak to his supervisor the next day. I told him I owed him one and I'd wait for his call.

All I was thinking was, get out. Job, flatshare, and gone. Don't get involved, don't get talking, don't listen to the story. Like the way people were with the white beggars in India – ratty-looking wrecks meandering along the beach, trying to sell squashed packs of cigarettes for breakfast money. You couldn't treat them like the Indian beggars, couldn't wave your finger in their face and growl *No*. The white ones you just cut; it was hard at first, but after a while it was easy. You looked away, you quickened your pace, you held your book up in front of your face. You know what I felt most when Jamie died? *I didn't ask for this and I don't want it.* On Moviemax once this babe found a sports bag full of fifties on the street, walked off with it, and then she was surprised when it dropped her in it up to her implants. You know what most people would do if they found a bag of money on the street? Walk away. Run. Forget about it. I was most people. I didn't ask for this, and I didn't want it.

That didn't make it go away. From the moment I got back, it was like Tinder said. When I paid off the cab from the airport, Dad's car was in the drive and the lights were on, but ringing the bell produced about as much response as e-mailing an online contact ad; I had to dig down through my pack to find my keys. As I walked in, I thought we'd been robbed, the place was such a khazi. I found him passed out on his bed, TV going with the sound off, a burned-down joint between his fingers. I knew the signs well enough; every couple of years some project would screw up even more spectacularly than usual and he'd go into this state, spend a few weeks in front of Sky Sports till he started going out again and doing what he did. If the shit was about to hit with him, like Tinder said it was, then he seemed to know it. I'd expected him to turn the house into a shag palace while I was gone, with no one around to cramp his style; but I found out, when he woke up, that even the cleaner (who'd had to deal with what was effectively two teenage blokes ever since mum and Shana left) had resigned in disgust at the way he'd let things go; and though he claimed to have advertised, he hadn't found it in himself to clear up sufficiently for even the most desperate skivvy to want to take the job once they saw the place.

It was, even by the standards I'd let my room slip to in the weeks around A levels, beyond gross. But I was like, cleaning I can do. I spent the first twelve hours after I got back with the windows wide open and the thermostat jacked up, black-bagging a landfill of ashtrays, takeout cartons, glazed-on plates and wadded socks. It was like Tinder had said: the man was a mess, couldn't deal with what he'd done. It seemed that was true for the most basic level. When you're feeding the need, you want to think that the fallout is erased with a toss or a flush, but it's there for anyone with a pair of Marigolds, I thought as I bagged it and went to the kitchen for the Vileda. This was the *fajita* he ate, this the crumpled Red Stripe can he snuffed his post-dinner roach into. It isn't thieves or Scuds or nailbombs we ought to fear, with their sudden, incisive erasures; but auditors, listeners, painstaking reconstructors who collect and collate, creating in order to destroy, hunched over our card statements, our web trails, our garbage, in the dead of night. The question was, was anyone except some Indian psycho interested in the guy?

I didn't want to be around to find out. Though I almost felt like calling Tinder up, saying, Here, you telling me this is a drug lord's trash? See how the man lives: the nearly done crossword, hangman notes scrawled in the margin; the racing page, double underlinings and asterisks; last Saturday's TV, the circled exposé. Tinder would've said, Just goes to prove. The guy never knew what he was getting into, couldn't handle it when he did. It started with him buying for himself; then he was helping out a few friends, people he wanted to impress, ravers without kids and a mortgage; then it was a short step to putting money up front to guarantee delivery; ten years later he had a syndicate fronting hundreds of grand a year, selling it through his brickies, sparks, chips and drivers, washing the returns back through yet more construction, losing most of it, but with no way out once he was in. Tinder would've looked at my dad's trash and said, That's what I told you. Small-time, but since you can't get out, you wind up big-time whether you can handle it or not. I wasn't in so far yet that I couldn't get out. I dumped the bags in the bins, called Jojo, and started digging my escape tunnel.

Joj called me back the next night. He'd fixed me an interview for a different department to him, saying it was the best he could do. He was on salary, in the exhibitions department; the job I was interviewing for was commission only, selling ad space in trade magazines. I told him no worries, I'd take anything. The interview was a breeze, some Jigsaw babe who, the moment I said where I was from, started hurling names at me: you must know Julian Cartwright, you must know Sophie Dearborn, you must know Giles Marston. I was like, oh yeah. Old Sophes, old Jools. Used to play tennis together; I name-checked the country clubs around town. It seemed the interview was mostly to check I didn't say 'innit' at the end of every sentence. My crappy school caused a bit of a pause when she saw it on my CV; I told her my parents were Old Labour, terribly embarrassing but what can you do. 'And who's your father?' she asked. 'BBC,' I said. 'Wants me to work in the real world before I go up to Cambridge. Do I get the job?'

Yes, I did. It was called media sales. I sold my Clio, bought a month's season ticket, caught the 7.08, hit my desk at eight every morning to show willing. I got a list of magazines I never heard of – *Derivatives Direction*, *PEP Performer, ISA Age* – then cold-called people who worked in derivatives, PEPs and ISAs and listened to them asking me not to call again. After work we went to the All Bar One round the corner and shouted and laughed like everyone else. I tried to keep up.

Most of the other guys – there were four women but they had lives to go back to after work – wanted to give me advice. It was all about confidence, they said. Call up, ask for the MD by his first name. I tried it a few times, my armpits on fire, but I just got the MD telling me never to call again instead of the receptionist. I could have cried. All I wanted was to be good, to be productive, to be useful to somebody: this didn't seem to be the point of my job. The guys all said that if you could stick it for a month, they gave you better leads. This was what sorted the boys from the men. Forget uni, make some money, get a flat, get a car, surf the voicemails for all the women you want. Be traffic; be the city. You could do it if you wanted it.

I wanted it. More than anything. The only thing in my way was money. Even after two forty-hour weeks had dragged past, my OTE was sweet FA. This was supposed to be something you just put up with: you told your parents you had a top job in the media and they forked out for your rent until you either got lucky or your year ran out and you were off to uni. I had enough left from my car for a deposit and the first month's rent in a flatshare, but after that I could be on the streets. I couldn't take the risk; I could really see my dad letting me come back a month after I'd walked out. I kept calling Mum, but Charlie's voice on the machine was all there ever was.

In the meantime I was still at home, where Tinder knew the address. I had two weeks left till I was supposed to get back to him. I looked up from my desk the second Friday and thought, Stop messing around with this. I'd dialled Alita's number almost before I knew what I was doing.

My problem was I was trying to start over, which was

stupid. The only thing I had going for me was what we used to have. Even if my job reeked, it was where I came from that had got me the foot in the door here, and lots of people didn't have that. I saw kids come in for interview every day – they were the ones carrying briefcases – and I never saw most of them again. They didn't come from where I came from. I was crazy, trying to walk out on it completely. It wasn't even like I wanted to: there was still Alita, and I couldn't let that go. I needed to find some middle ground between getting out and keeping what I wanted.

Dad wasn't around that weekend and I had plenty of space to think. By Monday I'd got it. I called Alita up, asked her if she fancied a day out to the coast the next weekend, get out of the city.

'Why would I want to get out of the city?'

'Sea air. Whelks. The pleasure of my company.'

It took some doing, but I got the date. I'd thought a lot about that night with my mum back in India, when I told her how bad things were at home and she offered to help me. This was a new her; before she left home I'd had to do a lot more than that. When I was a kid I could tell her that I was broken up about something until I was blue in the face, but she'd really listen only if I cried. She'd only intervene with whatever it was if I showed her how wretched it'd made me. Mum had changed, but Alita hadn't. I needed to show her what a mess I was in. When we'd talked about the return to reality – on the beach, back by the ocean – she'd been waiting for me to say something more, but I'd been too messed up with Tinder to know it. Now was the time to tell her the way it was going to be. I just had to make her feel it was her decision.

I wasn't going to tell her anything about my father, or anything about Tinder; just me and money, and where the lack of it was pushing me. I'd got the idea from when I started to duck out of going to All Bar One after work: when the others got arsey about it, like I was letting them down, I just told them I was more of a smoke man than a Boddies man, which shut them up nicely. If in doubt, play the cooler-than-you card. But after that I was Howard bloody Marks round the office, people giving me the soul shake and humming Bob Marley when I walked past their desks. I remembered what Tinder had said about everyone my age being on the other side of the world. Anyone who wasn't an arsehole, clearly.

So suddenly I've got this rep of being like ganja man, and a few people try and score off me. Blah blah blah new flats in London, haven't got round to sorting a reliable supply yet, maybe I can help them get their hands on some. I tell them I'm dry for now, but pretty soon this guy Andy – on salary, nice shirts and cufflinks, been there a couple of years – offers me a score. He tells me he sometimes drives down to the coast to buy, since it's cheaper when it's straight off the boat; same stuff you get from your friendly neighbourhood dealer, but without the mark-up for shifting it up the M3. Since we all start off earning jack shit, he said, we need to economise.

I could see the guy meant well – the brotherhood of smokers – so I'd taken the mobile number from him, but just tucked it into my broken-down desk drawer. Now I dug it out; and after work I caught up with Jojo in All Bar One, asked him if Andy was for real.

'Sure,' he said, when I finally got him away from the circle of Caffreys-swilling salesboys. 'Used to be a premier-league stoner. Sold round the office when he was on commission. Doesn't need the hassle any more. Since when did you start smoking?'

'While I was on the road out there,' I said. 'Wasn't much else to do. Got a taste for it.'

'Wonders will never cease,' he said. 'You want some? I can get you some.'

'Where from?'

'Home, man. It's all got sorted while were away. You dial this cab firm, they send it over in a Jiffy bag. Like Federal fucking Express. You have to do it when your parents're out, natch. You want the number?'

I told him I already had one.

I called it the next night, was told to ring back Sunday. I did, and four hours later I was meeting Alita off her train at the station down there.

She looked a lot better than I did, but then she hadn't been grovelling to uninterested executives for three weeks. We'd swapped a few e-mails, and I knew she had some kind of work-experience thing going with her cousin's uncle, who handled the advertising revenue of a group of local newspapers in London. I'd been pretty dismissive about it, since I'd assumed she was into the same dead-end kind of crap I was, but in the cab from the station she was all fired up.

'Double page, I got,' she said, 'my byline at the top and everything. Went into six of the group's titles.'

She explained the terms 'byline' and 'title' to me.

'Angela – she's the group editor – said if I'd got any ideas for stories, she'd listen to them. She doesn't have anyone under thirty working for her, and she wanted one.'

'So you do, like, club reviews and stuff?'

She snorted. 'Hardly. These are for the burbs, where the eighties people went to bring up kids. They want to forget they used to do that kind of stuff. Angela wants stories that are, like, this is what your kids get up to when you're not looking. So I did one about how much dope and sex backpackers do, used some of my holiday snaps. What's this?'

The driver was pulling up, as I'd directed him, outside a pub called the Crooked Billabong. I paid him off and led Alita to a rough wooden bench in a scrappy bit of park opposite.

'I've got to do some business,' I said, 'a score. Won't take a minute.'

'You're *what*?'

There wasn't a good way to put it. 'I'm skint,' I said. 'I mean, it was sweet of Jojo to fix me up but I'm earning nothing. Really. It's commission only and even if there is a way to make some money at it, I'm not holding my breath. My dad's gone into one and I don't think he's coming out this time. I need to get some money together, get out. This is the only way I can see.'

'You're buying drugs,' she said flatly.

'Hash,' I said, 'half London prices. I've got people queuing up at work to buy off me.' I told her about my dodge to get out of after-work drinks, and the rep it'd got me. I'd seriously thought she might blow up on me for involving her in this kind of stuff but she didn't say anything, seemed strangely cool about it. I wondered if she'd started going to score with her cousins.

'They're in that bar over there, apparently,' I said. 'We sit here; if they like the look of us, they call my mobile, tell us where to go to pick it up. Okay? Or do you want to go and wait somewhere while I do it?'

'No, that's okay,' she said, in this weird measured tone I'd only heard from her once or twice ever before. We sat down, zipping up our jackets. It was a little after two in the afternoon, getting dark already, and freezing.

'So what're you going to do with the stuff?' she asked, hands thrust deep into her Puffa.

'Flog it at work, like I said.'

'You going to keep some for yourself? Make the days go quicker.'

She had a point. 'Why, do you want some?' I asked her.

She shook her head. 'Hash is hash. I can get it in London.'

'Is that what you do? Of an evening?'

'Only to get to sleep,' she said. 'London is like, god. Not the way it was when our parents chose not to live there. It's like, it's been invented for people like us. You walk down the King's Road and think, oh, okay. I get it now. So many bars, cafés, clubs . . .'

We had a Café Rouge at home. And a Wetherspoon's and an All Bar One. She'd never wanted to go in them before.

'. . . and everywhere like, full of people you want to be. You see so many choices you can make, every time you go out. There's a lot of grotty men, y'know, the ones twice our age who think all this is for them too, that it's all too good to pass up before they give up . . . how's your dad, by the by?'

'Just a reason to go,' I said, trying to pull it back to me. 'You know how he used to get when something went down the pan on him? Like that but worse. I've seen him maybe twice since I got back. He's had some investments junk on him or something. It's . . . not good there. I need to get out.'

'Same old same old,' she said. 'So go. Get out of there. It's a hothouse. I never saw it until I went up to London, but all of this, I swear –' she pushed her hair back with her hands – 'everything that happened, it's because things get too intense there, from there being nothing to balance them. There's too much to do in London to let any one thing get out of hand. It's what you need. Why don't you move up, get a flatshare?'

'I don't know anyone. Unless we . . . you and me . . .'

'You're probably right,' she said. 'In fact, I know you are. Glomming on to what I've got isn't the answer. It's like my dad's other women. He told me. He said it was just getting a glimpse of someone else's life when you weren't happy with your own and thinking, Well, that's different, I won't see the downside of that for a while yet if I don't get too involved –'

'But you're my life,' I said. 'I – *ow*.' I'd meant to try and take her hand in mine, but as I pulled my hands out from under my thighs something caught in my left and dug in. I turned it towards me and saw a shard of grey wood in the drumstick under my thumb, blood welling around it.

'Splinter? Here,' she said, slipping her shoulders out of her backpack and opening it. She pulled out a Clarins zipbag and from there a pair of tweezers. Holding my wrist hard in one hand, she made one deft movement with the other, and then she was holding the bloody sliver up for me to see.

'There,' she said. 'Drill a hole in that and you could drive a truck through.'

'Ow,' I repeated, sucking on the wound.

'C'mon, it hurts less already,' she said, blowing the splinter off the tweezers and wiping them on the cuff of her fleece. 'The function of memory is to contextualise pain. Even the worst kind. It hits and you're like, agony. But five seconds later the pain is different – worse or less, but different. The fact that you can identify a change means it can change again. And if it can keep changing, then it can end too. Hello?'

I took my wound out of my mouth and looked up.

A solemn-faced fat kid in a grubby sweatsuit looked down

at us. It was difficult to tell whether it was a boy or a girl. It was ten or so, brown hair and brown eyes, freckles across its nose. Its knuckles were blue on the handlegrips of its cheap mountain bike.

'Help you?' it said, snuffly.

'Where do we go now?' asked Alita.

'Ten minutes, Castle Lane car park. In the gents. Go in a shitter 'n' wait.' It wiped its nose on its wrist, then returned the hand to the grip.

'Thank you, sweetheart,' Alita said and pulled a five out of her jacket. 'This is for you.'

The kid took it, looking around a little warily, but didn't have anywhere to put it – no pockets in the sweatsuit. Finally it folded it into a palm, applied the palm to the grip to make a seal, and rode off, standing on the pedals and throwing the bike from side to side like little kids do.

We called for a cab on Alita's mobile but the guy couldn't promise it'd be with us fast enough, so we got directions from him and walked. It only took five minutes anyway. Alita parked herself in a kebab shop; I crossed the car park and went in. There were only two cubicles and they were both empty; both crappers, however, were vandal-proof, all-in-one steel jobs, the kind that don't have lids or seats but a sort of raised, fag-burned plastic rim bolted onto the edge of the metal pan. The floor tiles around both were puddled. I went into the right-hand cubicle and shut the door behind me. It stank. I tried to take really shallow breaths through my nose, but within a couple of minutes I was panting, panicky and underventilating, so I made myself breathe slower and more deeply, trying not to retch. To take my mind off it I read the graffiti on the back of the door: specifications, dates and times, crude drawings of the kind that there had been a vogue for scrawling on each other's exercise books in year six or so. Was this sort of thing in public toilets at home? I wasn't sure if there were any. Did this *cock fun* ever actually happen, or was it the advertising that they got off on? When the door to the outside opened and someone came in, I didn't notice until it had happened. Only when the cubicle door next to mine snicked closed and bolted did I understand that this was it.

A bundle of carrier bag – an unbranded one, no logo but just Thank You Thank You printed in a freeware font down the middle of it – appeared under the partition. I pulled the roll of notes out of my pocket and held it by the gap, but not so far that someone would see it if they weren't looking for it. An oddly white, knuckly hand with a tinny-looking wedding ring on it appeared, and cupped under the gap. I put the roll of notes into it, two hundred quid, half of what was left from selling my car. Too late I remembered that I was supposed to get my hand on the bag first. I made a grab for it. There was no one holding it back. As the bolt on the other door slid back, I scrabbled the bag open, and there, wrapped in clingfilm, was a brick of hash, more than I'd ever seen in my life.

The door to outside banged shut. After a brief panic about whether the other guy had faked leaving or not, I realised that if he hadn't, then I was screwed if I went out, screwed if I stayed put. When I finally fumbled the cubicle door open, the relief that he was gone would've had me sinking to my knees, had I not been leery of getting them wet on the floor.

Outside, I walked briskly over to where I could see Alita behind the steamy plate window of the kebab shop. The guys behind the counter were ignoring her as she played the fruit machine, an untouched tray of fries on the shelf next to her. I rapped on the window and jerked my head when she looked up; she left the machine in mid-play, flashing for nudges.

'You got it?' she muttered, walking away fast without looking at me.

'Down the sleeve of my fleece,' I said, following hard.

'This is psycho,' she said to herself. 'They could be waiting to jump us, get the hash back.'

'Chill,' I said, 'honestly. If they were going to rip us off, they could've jumped me in the bogs.'

'Let's just get out of here, okay?' she said, and her tone was so new on me that I didn't argue.

She didn't chill till we were at the station, when she gave me her Karrimor – I hadn't thought to bring one – and I took it into the men's to stow the hash inside. Then we got hot chocolates from the platform concession but went to a bench right at the end of the platform to drink them, where there was no one else around. Her paranoia was starting to get to me, and I kept scanning the length of the curving platform for uniforms. But Alita seemed a lot calmer now that we were somewhere public.

'So how much have you got?' she said, keeping her face turned down into her thermoplastic cup.

'A fucking loaf,' I said

'How big exactly?'

I felt the edges of it through the toughened nylon. 'Half of a videotape?'

'Hmm,' she said. 'And how much are you going to sell it for?'

'Enough for a ticket to Sydney,' I said, watching her.

'You're kidding.' She sipped her hot chocolate, looking at me over the rim.

'I don't think I am. But it's what this year is supposed to be about, isn't it? Pushing yourself, finding out what you want, what you're going to shoot for.' Thinking the converse, thinking that maybe it's called gap year because you can fall down it. I needed to say it fast if I was going to. 'And here isn't the place to do it. London isn't used to supporting gap-year kids. They're all in Chiang Mai, Phuket, Sydney. Working bars, selling tat. Not working in London. It's the wrong place. The only thing to do is get away again, you know? Find some space, live some life.'

Even as I said it, I felt the plates shift between us: the tarmac crumble and slip, the mains rupture and spray high and wide. We were in different lanes: if she just touched the accelerator she'd be away from the gap, could slip back into neutral, let her momentum carry her where it should. In my lane, there was nowhere to go but gridlock.

'But that's excellent, Bay,' she said, 'you're surprising me now. Frankly, sweetheart, that's the last thing I expected of you. Sounds like you got bitten, when you were off with that Tjinder guy.'

'Yeah,' I said, 'I think I probably did.'

'Then go for it.'

'I want you to come with me,' I said, and didn't let her answer. 'I need to do it, but I don't want to do it on my own. If I've come this far – and God knows, I was the last person who'd want to do this a year ago . . .' I'd practised this but it wasn't coming out right. I took a breath. 'I've come this far, and I need you to help me make the leap. Into who I want to be,' I finished, and watched her without looking at her. 'We could go to Oz, New Zealand. I sold my car. When I sell this I'll have enough to get us there –'

'What makes you think this is about you?' she cut in. 'Bay, I thought you were meant to be helping me. Even if I barely saw you while we were away, even if you've practically hid from me since we came back. I know seeing your mum again's probably mixed it up worse now you're back, and we can talk about that when you're ready – but until you can top what I've got, you have to let me have room to recover.'

'I want to help you,' I said, but it came out whiny instead of sincere.

'You have,' she said, putting her hand over mine. 'I'm going to write this up. *When your kids convoy down to the coast to go wetboarding, are they really going to buy cheap hash?* Scandal of the seaside drug supermarkets. That kind of thing.'

'You're kidding.'

'This is my best option now. Mum and Dad are spitting blood at each other over the maintenance. I'm thinking, Why not just get out, not have to rely on either of them? If Angela bites on this one, and the next and maybe the next, she'll put me on staff. If I can stick it for three years – y'know, writing up council meetings and weddings, doing my shorthand and the professional diploma course at night school, then, best-case scenario, I can move up to a bigger paper. Worst, I go to uni and start again, and I get the full grant independent of my parents. Three years on your own and you count as an adult.'

'What about me?'

'You weigh that stuff exactly when you get home, okay? And e-mail me the figure. I need to see just how cheap this is to start looking at the mark-up.'

'The mark-up?'

'Yes, the mark-up. How much is put on every time it changes hands inland. It's *cheaper* here, remember? It comes off the boat, people buy it here and sell it to their friends, who sell it to the people they know, who sell it to the people they know, and so on till everyone's got some, even in the middle of the country. And each step further inland, it puts on a quid or two. You see? You've just saved, I don't know, two, three hundred? Buying in that kind of bulk. It's not enough, though.'

'It isn't?' I thought she was still talking about the money.

'I need to come down again with a camera,' she said, looking up as a train appeared beyond the end of the platform.

'You what?'

'You won't have to come with, don't worry. I just need photos of the bench, the toilets.' She stood up. 'It's all bollocks, though. This is small-time. The real movement's done in truckloads, not jumperfuls.' She turned to the train and started to get on.

'Hold on, this isn't us,' I said. 'We need the stopping one. This is fast all the way.'

'Then this is my train,' she said.

I grabbed the door as she opened it. 'Can't I come back with you?'

'With that? Are you kidding?' she said, and put one foot on the step up.

'So that's it?'

She turned and put her hand on my arm. 'I appreciate this, Bay. Really I do. This is just what I need, and the editor'll love it. I might even be able to push it on one of the tabloids.'

'Can't I do it with you?' I was begging now and she knew it.

'Oh christ, Bay,' she said. 'Listen. I need to find my way out of this now, okay? India, I could feel like it wasn't real; back here, that's not an option. It's like, Jamie's funeral, okay? One of my uncles said to me . . . he was pissed, right? And he was saying, blah blah blah, puts your own troubles in perspective, and shit. And I was like, yeah yeah, fuck off and leave me alone, but he kept at it. And he said, "What this shows you is that you have to live every day like it's your last one." And you know what?'

I didn't know what. I searched her face.

'It's shit,' she said, her eyes shining. 'You can't live every day like you're going to die tomorrow. The only thing that gets you over something like this is routine. Is work, is wearing yourself out. I need to get my own routine, can you see that? I need to lose myself in work now. And I can't have things reminding me of what's happened every day. And I'm sorry, babe, but you're a part of all that. I can't help it. You're home, and I have to leave it.'

She got on the train, pulled the door shut behind her, pulled the window down and leaned out.

'I love you more than anyone,' she said. 'We go back forever. But going back is no good any more, Bay. Too much has happened. It's broken. Here.'

She fished out her notebook, scribbled something on it, handed it to me. It said homegirl247@hotmail.com.

'Talya's address while she's travelling,' she said. 'She writes me once a week, always asks after you but she's scared to write to you.'

I looked at it, aghast.

'You made a mistake there,' she said. 'She's a good girl. She's in Goa, doing henna tattoos on the beach, but she'll get sick of it. She'll be back soon. Think about it.'

As if that was all that was wrong with me. She vanished into the train, but I didn't move. I was still there long after it pulled out, holding the paper in my hand.

I hit the pit that night. When I got back in my room, it was hard to believe it was the same one I'd left that morning. It was like when I'd come home after the New Year's party: it was hard to believe everything could have changed so much since the last time I was there. I sat down and stared at the photo of Alita and me clip-framed above my desk. All her shiny new life was down to me. If she was the girl everyone wanted to be around, it was only because I'd given her a taste for being appreciated. I couldn't look at it.

I'd tried calling my mum all week, but had just got weird engaged-type tones I didn't understand. It was the same now. I put the receiver back, cleared my desk, slapped down an old *Sky* magazine and started trying to hack lumps off the slab of hash with a pair of scissors. I had no idea how dealers did it; maybe they had special tools. If they did, I didn't; it splintered and crumbled a lot, but I soon found out it was easier to do if you heated the blade over an oil burner. Three hours later I had a sore neck and a lunchbox full of clingfilm wraps, a sugar-cube amount in each. At work next morning, I went down to the smoking room, put out the word that I was holding: Amsterdam shit at superstore prices. At the end of the day I sold direct from my desk, in the hour after the supervisors had gone to relieve their nannies. I charged twice what I'd paid; if these people had it, I was willing to take it. They all had better leads than me anyway.

I got my money back and the same again in a couple of days. People were buying for themselves, for their flatmates, for their friends. The way it went in London seemed to be, if you see dope being sold by someone who doesn't scare you, you buy it. My wallet was so fat with tens that it bulged out my khakis, but what would it buy me? More of the same. Another couple of months of commuting, tops. And then what? I couldn't see myself getting off commission onto basic. I was hopeless at the job. I'd taken to spending longer and longer every day calling the government, so I could sit on hold for hours with the LED on my phone showing a live line. Even Jojo was embarrassed of me; the day after I started selling at work he cut me dead at the coffee machine, and I couldn't do anything but stare at his back as he walked away. And now that Alita had closed off the one bypass I'd seen signposted, I had to get through to next September somehow. Even setting everything else aside, I had to earn enough for the commute to do it. I toyed for a moment with the thought of e-mailing Talya, finding out when she'd get back, seeing if I couldn't do the same with her as I had with Jojo – I was pretty sure her father'd fix her up in London just like his had – but like, yeah. That'd be about as smart a move as calling Tinder.

I was sick, sick of it all. The only pictures of the future I'd ever seen had been of me and Alita at uni, maybe getting into rock-climbing or kick-boxing or something, and then passing seamlessly into some shiny big chrome and glass office complex, fountains and glass lifts and stuff, and the suits I was going to wear, and lunchtime workouts at the company's state-of-the-art facility. This was all I could think about. There was this movie on Sky where the guy's life is going down the pan: his wife's walking out, his mistress is screwing her fitness trainer, his kids are screwing each other, and his boss is about to find out he's had his fingers in the till. He's got an escape bag under his desk and his plane leaves in an hour, but all he can think about is this wasp stuck inside his window; he trashes his whole perfect office trying to swat it. Uni was my wasp on the window; it was the only thing I could see. I could get there without Alita, but I still needed the tuition and maintenance from Dad; to get that, I had to stop things getting any weirder with him and keep working; to keep working, I needed to get money for the commute. The only option I could see was to make some more scores.

I didn't get the option. The day I was due to get back to Tinder, I was pushing my bike home from the station because it was too cold to ride, maybe eight o'clock on a black December night. I'd stayed late at the office trying to put together a promotion idea: a themed page in a metals-trading mag for aluminium-processing-catalyst manufacturers to advertise on. It wasn't too likely, but I'd done some digging around: the price of their raw materials was the highest it'd been in a decade, thanks to a guerrilla war kicking off somewhere; and there was a trade fair in Korea in two months' time that I could hang the whole thing off. The production department on our title said they'd give me the page if I could sell it, and I felt it was worth a punt; it was the first thing I'd had to work on that had even the slightest chance of paying off. I'd been hammering away at it all day, and on the train home too; I'd done all the figures, how much I needed to charge per column inch, and as I walked through the dark I was just on hold till I could get home, snap the floppy in my jacket pocket into my A-drive, and have another go at the draft of my pitch letter.

I almost felt useful. I knew the project was probably a piece of crap, but it was my piece of crap; even if it only paid off a tenth of what I was hoping it would, someone might notice my initiative. If they did and I got on salary, I was going to put away half my pay a month for uni, along with the wad in my wallet; open a new account, I thought, feeling the weight of it in my breast pocket as I put one foot in front of the other. Wasp on the window. I didn't even notice the white Corsa creeping along behind me until it pulled up ten yards ahead. A uniformed cop got out, put his hat on.

'Bay Beecham?' he said, and opened the nearside door.

'We sent you a letter asking you to come in, detailing the consequences if you failed to contact us,' said Mackey, enjoying it. 'You want to give us cash or a cheque? Or would you rather have the fourteen days?'

'I didn't get any letter.' It was all I could do to sit in the chair.

'He didn't get any letter,' Mackey informed McCormick.

'It's been with you two weeks,' McCormick said, and I came down off the ceiling. Whatever this was about, it predated my little trip to the coast. 'The reminder went out seven days ago.'

They couldn't know anything. The money was still in my wallet, but the dope was all sold; if they searched me and asked me where I got the thick end of a grand in cash from, I'd tell them my dad gave me it to buy a suit. I'd scored a hundred miles away, I'd sold fifty miles in the other direction. I'd done nothing here. It was off their patch.

'I don't get post,' I said. I didn't. There was always a pile in the hall but I never looked at it, except on birthdays. 'Anyway, what's with you suddenly? Last time I came here you told me to get lost.'

'That was before you went to see your mother,' said Mackey.

'My mother? What's she got to do with anything?'

'How is she these days? What's she up to?' McCormick asked, like he was catching up on an old friend.

'She's fine,' I said slowly, looking from one to another. 'Her business is going pretty good.'

'Better than your father's,' said Mackey. He meant it to throw me and it did. I sat still, breathing.

'Bay, do you know what your father does?' McCormick asked gently. I turned my face to him.

'You know what he does,' I said, trying to keep my voice level.

'But do you?' he asked, softly again, holding eye contact with me. I didn't say anything. So then he started to tell me.

I didn't have to fake horror: I was feeling it. The room had swum away and I was back on the train from the coast, feeling the brick of hash through the backpack on my lap. It had felt so everyday, so inert; but every mile inland, every time we lurched into a station, thrummed a while, then lurched out again, it put on pounds and pence; but mostly pounds. I'd taken it into the bogs, got it out and looked at it, expecting it to morph somehow – expand or pulsate, glow like an alien's brain during telepathic transmission – as it put on value with every set of points my lightweight hopper-train skimpered over. Now, sitting in McCormick's Portakabin, Mackey outlining the details of my father's investment group, I heard Tinder echoing him: *hundreds of grand a month to bring it in.*

That was where it went: on diesel for trucks, petrol for speedboats, kickbacks for dockers, backhanders for border guards, money for muscle every inch of the way. All that money went on shifting the stuff. So if someone was making shit in your own backyard . . . I heard Tinder saying, *He's out of control.* McCormick had finished talking and was sitting back looking at me.

'I need some water,' I said.

'Take a look at this first.' He slid a photocopy across the desk at me. I picked it up, tried to focus on it. It was some kind of legal thing, a land deed, dated three years before, signed by my mum.

'She's a clever woman, your mother,' said McCormick. 'We don't see many women know how to wash money.'

'We're calling her the Washerwoman,' said Mackey. 'Make a good headline, don't you think? When we get the bitch.'

I couldn't have said anything even if I'd wanted to.

'Never wondered why your dad's been such a wreck since she left, have you?' Mackey said, tipping his chair back. 'He don't know where to start with this shit. Spends most of his money paying off accountants to clear up after him. Your mother had a real feel for it. A gift. Didn't pass it on to you, though, did she, dipshit?'

'He's like his father,' McCormick said.

'You don't even know what she's playing you for, do you?' Mackey grinned.

'She wanted me to stay with her,' I said, 'she wanted to get me out of all this.'

'So you knew what your father was up to?'

'I need some water.'

'You'll get it. What was your mother offering to get you out of?'

'Just my dad. It's been . . . he hasn't been the easiest person to live with.'

'And why didn't you stay with her?'

I looked at the floor, trying to hold it together. I couldn't tell them what Tinder had told me.

'I want to live my own life.'

'You do, eh?' said Mackey, and slid another photocopy across the desk to me. 'How badly?'

I looked down from his stupid, smug face to the sheet of A4 in front of me. It was a statement, undated, with my name on it and a space for me to sign. The first paragraph said that I'd been paying Jamie and Harper commission to make crystal meth for me to sell. I didn't read any further.

'Fuck *you*,' I exhaled.

'Aren't you the one that's fucked?' McCormick said it like he genuinely wanted me to believe it.

'What do you want from me?'

'Do you know, that's the first time he's said it,' McCormick said to Mackey. 'Sit here listening to him for hours at a time, and this is the first time he thinks we might have a job to do.'

'Just tell me.'

'We'll cut you a deal,' he said. 'Get your mother back here, we'll forget the meth.'

'You already forgot the meth. You told me the first time.'

'That was before we interviewed most of the GCSE year at your school. We got, what, twenty statements?'

'Nearer two dozen,' said Mackey.

'All didn't mind telling us how close you were to Jamie. How you threw your weight around, looking out for him.'

The party. That night at the Venue. The bastards.

'It's your choice. Sign the statement or bring us your mother.'

'What do you want her for?'

'What do you think? We know about her setup over there. She's one end of the line, your father's the other. We want to collect the set.'

They didn't know about Tinder. They thought it was her. Then they couldn't know much. 'Why don't *you* go?' I said.

'Why should we?' Mackey shrugged. 'When we can have you do the monkey work for us.'

'I don't know where she is,' I said, and it was like waking up from a meth head. I hadn't got back to Tinder. What did I think he was going to do? Let me get on with my life, knowing what he'd told me? 'You have to help me,' I said, looking at McCormick. 'She married some guy out there.'

They sat, arms folded, looking at me like I was spinning them a line while I told them everything I knew.

'Where is this Tjinder character now?' asked McCormick when I was finished.

'At his apartment in Goa. I can give you the address. I can give you the entry-pad code to his building. I'm supposed to be there.'

'And where's your mother? At the yoga camp?'

'I keep trying but I just get the machine.'

'She's not with your sister?' McCormick consulted his clipboard. 'Shana?'

'I don't know where she is.'

'What do you mean, you don't know?' Mackey frowned.

'She's got a round-the-world ticket. She's working her way round. I don't know where she is.'

'Well, where was she starting?'

'I don't know. Australia, maybe?'

Mackey tipped his chair back, exhaled. '*Christ* what a fucked-up family.'

'You're not exactly inspiring confidence, Bay,' said McCormick, 'you can see that, can't you? You're trying to tell us that your mother's missing, but by your own admission you don't know where in the world your closest family members are from one year to the next.'

I was wearing down. 'I give you a global drug ring and all you do is try to frame me?' I said. 'I want to see your supervisor.'

'I want to see your signature on this,' Mackey said, and slid the statement forward again.

'Look,' I said, pushing it straight back. 'All I'm telling you is that Tinder wants me to go back and deal for him, and if you don't do something to help me, then that's what I'm gonna have to do. Unless I sit here and wait for him to send someone to get me.'

'Your mother wasn't with him when you left?'

'He's been off doing business. She doesn't know anything about what he really does. She wouldn't have anything to do with him if she did.'

'But she married him.'

'Only for a green card.'

'Only for a green card. Indian immigration would be pleased to hear that.'

'Oh, c'mon, what's it to you?'

'If she gets deported, comes back here, then she's our jurisdiction.'

'So?'

'So we can talk to her about this,' McCormick said, tapping the title deed on the desk.

'She's not the one you *want*, man,' I said. 'She doesn't know anything about it. If she signed whatever this is –' I pushed the land deed back to him – 'it's because my dad told her it was something else. Tinder's the other end of the chain, not her. And if he finds out I've been talking to you, he'll get me.'

'How's he going to "get" you?' McCormick said disgustedly. He sounded like a teacher.

'He's got people here. He knows everything my dad does, he told me. He's got people watching him, and they'll be watching me too now. I need protection.'

Mackey pushed the meth statement back at me. 'That'll protect you. Read on.'

I did. The second paragraph dropped Alita in it too, said we were both egging them on to make more and more.

'You've got to be kidding,' I said, beyond it now. 'Don't bring her into this.'

'She seems pretty good at bringing herself,' Mackey said. 'We've been watching her. Gets about, that girl.'

'You what?'

He looked down at his clipboard. 'Friday the fourth, twelve days ago. Leaves nightclub in Islington with Julian Wright, a character well-known to our friends in the Met. Driven in Wright's BMW to his flat in Tottenham; leaves flat at seven-ten, takes Victoria Line, then changes for Hammersmith.'

'You're watching her?'

'Just the guy she's fucking.'

I sat back, breathing.

'Seems there's a lot you don't know about the women in your life.'

'All right.'

'Your mother, your sister, your girlfriend –'

'I said okay.' I felt like breaking something. I made myself stay in the chair. 'So why's Tinder telling me she knows nothing, that it's all my father? That he wants to protect me from him?'

'Because he needs white faces to sell for him out there,' said McCormick.

'You said so yourself,' Mackey put in. 'Think you'd be good at it? You getting some practice in round the office?'

I blanched then. 'You're watching me.'

'Wouldn't you?' said Mackey.

'If you were us,' McCormick pointed out.

There wasn't anything they didn't know. 'What do you want from me?' I said miserably.

'Get a message to her, get her to call you,' Mackey said. 'Tell her what Tjinder told you. Tell her you're being followed. Get her to come and get you.' He picked up the statement. 'Then we tear this up.'

'If she ran like you said she did, she's not going to come back.'

'That's where you come in.'

'We're not talking about the same woman.'

'Then you're on your own, mate,' said McCormick crisply.

'Except you're never on your own,' said Mackey, and laughed.

It was a day or two before I understood that last remark. In the meantime I was chasing what had kicked off in my brain while Mackey was telling me about my dad.

The cops drove me back to where I'd left my bike. When I got home he was making a sandwich in the kitchen, as though he was waiting for me. It was the first time I'd seen him for most of a week.

'Working late?' he said.

'Yeah,' I said automatically, couldn't think of anything else. I remembered the disk in my pocket, took it out for him to see. 'Brought some home. Some new business I'm working on.'

'That's my boy,' he said, putting one hand flat on the sandwich while he cut across it diagonally. 'You want one of these?'

'I, uh, I got a crêpe at the station,' I said.

'Suit yourself,' he said, picking up one half and taking a bite. 'I got a new cleaner,' he said through it. 'Angela. Nice lady. She sorted through some stuff today. Found a letter for you.' He nodded towards the table. There was a brown envelope lying in the middle. I stared at it. ON HER MAJESTY'S SERVICE was printed in capitals across the front.

'Aren't you going to open it?' he said, swallowing, taking another bite.

I walked towards it like I was under water, picked it up and tore the flap, trying to look casual. It was the letter from McCormick, requesting I come in to assist an inquiry. 'Just some tax stuff,' I said. 'Now I'm working.'

'You want to watch them,' he said. 'Maybe you ought to go and see Terry.'

'Terry?'

'Beckton. My accountant. See if he can't swing your salary as consultancy. Then you can claim your travel back. Got to think about these things now, kidder. You sure you don't want some of this? Pastrami. Just opened it.'

'No, I'm all right,' I said, putting everything I had into staying on my feet.

'Suit yourself,' he said and, picking up the other half, started towards his room. 'Don't work too late, you hear? Save some for the morning.'

'I will,' I said.

'I mean it,' he said and disappeared into his room, flipping the door shut with his foot as he went.

I sat down at the table, put my face in my hands. His TV went on in his room, making me look up. How could he not know? How could I know, and still be there? Because there he was. The guy who'd done for Jamie and Harper. I didn't have a doubt about it now. The money was all in importing shit. Someone makes some other shit locally, and they're threatening your investment. Jamie had people selling it all around town: Dad heard about it, can't have registered who they were, and sent some bozos off one of his crews to frighten them. They just chose the wrong moment to do it. They push their way into the motel room while Jamie and Harper are cooking, the pipes overheat, the whole thing goes sky-high. The gorillas get away, the boys don't. And then he finds out exactly what it is that he's done.

I remembered how he was after it happened. I hadn't been dealing with it, couldn't feel anything except that I didn't want to know. He was so unfakeably cut up that I was taking pointers from him; but he'd been like that because he realised what he'd done. He'd realised that the kids he'd told some hod-carrier to go and scare were the kids next door. The kids he used to try and play football with, till he finally clicked they weren't interested. Christ.

There was only one way to deal with it and that was not to. My dad had faffed his way into heading up a drugs syndicate: put it away in a box. He'd killed Alita's brother by mistake: put it away in a box. Some Indian drug lord wanted me to come and work for him: put that away too. Alita was screwing petty criminals in London: room for some more in there. My mother was christ-knows-where and if I couldn't find her I was going to prison: shut the lid tight and sit down on top of it. I went to bed, got up, went to work; came home, dodged my dad, went to bed. My promotion idea even started to pay off; by the end of the week I stood to make twelve hundred in commission. My supervisor called me into his office and asked me to look at doing the same on three other titles. 'I'm on top of it,' I said, and meant it.

What I wasn't on top of was the car that was following me everywhere. At the station in the morning, at the station on the way back, buzzing me as I rode my bike in between. I could go home at six, or I could stay in the office till the cleaners came, then trudge the downloaded City till the last train back; it didn't matter. The same white Corsa was always parked opposite the station entrance, where no parking was intended. You're supposed to go over, thump the bonnet, demand to know what's going on; but in real life you just can't believe it's happening, something so out of order, two strangers following you with their eyes like they have a right to do it. I just walked over to the racks trying not to look at them, unlocked my bike, felt their eyes boring into me as I clipped on the lights, stood up on the pedals to get to the road; heard them start the engine, buzz me from behind as I pumped up the hill homeward, come round and do it again as I pedalled, sweating inside my coat even as my skull shrank and my teeth ached from the cold.

It was the wasp on the window. I had a hundred other things to process, but it was the Corsa that hogged all my RAM. They knew what they were doing. As long as that was on the desktop, there wasn't room for anything else. It went on through Wednesday, Thursday, Friday; I stayed home all weekend, locked in my room, with Dad off on one of his pulling weekends. Didn't call anyone, only used my modem to see, hope against hope, if there was something from my mum. There wasn't, and there was nothing I could do. Mackey and McCormick wanted her here; if I went out to try and make sure she was okay, they'd assume I'd gone to warn her, and get me good when I came back. Monday, when I rode my bike down to the station, the Corsa passed me twice. When I came back from work, there it was. Tuesday morning it was there. I kept my phone clamped to my ear through work, didn't get up from my desk, didn't go for a coffee in case I had to talk to anyone. Tuesday night the Corsa was there, Wednesday morning. And then Wednesday night . . .

No Corsa. Not in the station, not as I rode home. It was as though a basic law of the universe had been broken. Every time a car came up behind me I got off my bike, ready to fall to my knees, wrists extended, pulse-point to pulse-point – but the white Corsa was nowhere, and I had disappeared. Fallen out of the world. I saw how well things could manage with no me: turn one variable and my mum ovulated early, nineteen years before; skew the worldview one click of a degree, and I could see it, world without me, as I pushed my bike through the dark, too sick to ride it.

And then I really did see it. Before we had cars I always used to cut round the back of Alita's house to ours, and that night I did it without thinking, wilful almost, glad I was going to get my feet wet to the ankle. I was halfway across the overgrown back lawn to the hole in our hedge before I saw our security lights were on, flooding the front of our house above the privets. Even a fox could trip the infrareds, but I knew this was something bigger. I stopped on the sodden long grass, dumped my bike, crept over to the hedge, soaking the cuffs of my trousers as I went.

I could see the cars in front of the house before I was even close: two Corsas, one blue, one white. There were two shadows in the blue one. As I watched, a uniformed cop came round the side of the house and leaned down to the passenger window of the blue car.

I didn't fanny about. I put my mountain bike on my back so there wouldn't be even the hiss of Shimanos as I wheeled it, and scurried with bent knees round to the side of Alita's, leaving the bike in an alcove where it couldn't be seen and ducking into the garage. The spare key was still in the old Maxwell House jar that her dad had filled with nails in more optimistic times; I let myself into the utility room, then ran for the burglar-alarm panel, barely able to believe that the warning buzz wasn't audible outside. I hit the buttons with seconds to spare – 1397, the four corners of the keypad, the only combination Alita's mum could be guaranteed to remember – and it cut out suddenly, leaving a silence that was even louder. I didn't want to do the next part, but I had to. Jamie's room was the only window high enough to look over both our place and the road; I needed to see where the cops were.

They'd left it mostly as it was. His clothes and books and computer were gone, but the furniture was still there, and all his stuff still crazy-taped to the walls. I crept to the window and looked out. The cops were still parked down at ours, but the road, as best as I could see in the pooled light of the streetlamps, was clear. My dad had always said that the bend in our drive was the best security device there was: we never got turned over because burglars like to know that their escape route is clear, and the fifty-degree kink halfway up our drive meant they could never be sure that someone wouldn't be coming down it when they were trying to get back up. This was what the cops were using. If anyone came down the drive, they wouldn't know the cops were there till they were right on top of them, and then it'd be too late. The road was clear because a cop car there would've spoiled the trap. It was good to realise this, but such evidence that they knew what they were doing was not what I needed.

I sat down on the bare mattress and dug through my pack for my wallet, hoping to Christ I'd got it. There it was, and inside was my cash card, the dope money and my passport, which I carried against getting carded in London. I flipped through and checked the visa: valid six months, stamped multiple visits as standard – to let backpackers come and go, I guessed. I sat for a moment trying to think of another option, but there wasn't one. It was time to go.

Outside, the road was still clear and I went, lights off, in eighteenth gear, for the mouth of the nearest footpath like I was riding a Scud. There were four more stretches of road after that but I had my cashmere scarf wrapped up to the bridge of my nose, and within twenty minutes I was pumping along the nature path, the old branch railway line that led out of town. An hour later I locked my bike in the superstore car park, called a cab from the freephone by the trolley pick-up, and extracted the forty quid to Heathrow out of the money I had. I put the rest of the notes inside my passport, and hung around the side till the cab turned up.

I got to Heathrow around eleven. After some agonising whether McCormick and Mackey would've frozen my account, my suspicion that they'd need a court order to do that was confirmed as I withdrew the two hundred that was left from selling my Clio, leaving a balance of seven pounds and change that I couldn't get at. I checked the board on the concourse to see which airlines went to Bombay and headed to the desk of the one that had the crappiest logo. The ticket, one-way, still took the thick end of what I had; a rucky (and twenty two-pounds-a-pop paperback classics to put some weight in it) left me with only sixty quid, but I figured that was probably sufficient to get me a train all the way round India, not just to Kovalam. I checked my bag and got my boarding pass; so far so good.

There was a choice of a bank of passport controllers. I chose a thirtyish blonde because they try to get you talking to see if you're nervous about anything, and I figured that instinctively she'd be reluctant to get into conversation with some surly-looking teenage guy. The fear of what I was doing caught up with me as I queued, noticing, too late, that the other queues were thinning quicker. I pretended to be lost in the paperback book I'd saved for the plane like I was too busy reading to notice I was in the slowest queue. When I finally got to the front she looked at the passport, looked at me – I tried to look like I'd come on to her given half the chance – then gave it back. I was through. I walked away as casually as I could, tucking the book into my back pocket, but my armpits were microwaving and my guts felt like I'd had my balls kicked up to my collarbones.

There were still five hours till the flight and I passed the time sitting next to a noisy family, pretending to sleep, with my collar up and my scarf wrapped round my face. I figured that if anyone came looking for me, I might get away with looking like I was just the oldest of their kids, in a huff that I'd had to come with them instead of being left to party at home. If someone did, then it worked. My flight was called and I left them there, still waiting for their delayed charter to Lanzarote.

It caught up with me on the plane. As it lurched off the ground I felt like ordering a drink, ordering champagne, but it was a no-frills deal and I couldn't have anyway. Besides, by the time it arrived I wouldn't have wanted it; fast on the back of the relief, as if towed on a short cable, was the anger. I felt ready to puke with it, even got the sickbag out from behind the laminated safety card. How could they have ruined it for me? Your parents are supposed to give you what they didn't have: in my case this was apparently wretchedness, mortal terror, the loneliness of the universe and a future that could only get worse. I should've had it out with my dad already but he was tough to talk to about the weather. So much for getting to know him while I still could.

I drifted, after the seatbelt light went off, wondering if the cockpit crew privately rehearsed what they'd say over the PA in the event of a tailspin. Which facts they'd reveal, which loves they'd declare. I wondered how long till McCormick and Mackey found out I'd skipped the country, what they'd do when they did. Screw 'em; they'd have to find me first. What would my dad say when they got hold of him, if they hadn't already? Maybe they'd given up on me being able to get to my mum. Maybe they'd just been pulling me in so they could put the screws on my dad, see if he couldn't do it. The thought didn't make me feel any better.

How long did the cops keep you in their in-box for? How long till Mackey and McCormick were working different jobs, had forgotten all about this? It might mean five years before uni, it might mean more, but it didn't make me sad to think about it, just tired. It wasn't fair. I'd waited so long already. I'd have to come clean to my mother, but she knew what it was like being around my dad. She'd understand what made me do it. She'd look after me. And fuck it, it was her fault. I was running from what she'd done, from what she'd had to run from too. I supposed she'd started the affair with the yoga teacher because she'd known it was all going to hell, and needed to give herself a few more reasons to make the final push. It'd be something we could talk about.

I saw in some cop video, Gary Busey or someone, that they always know who's guilty if they keep you in the cells overnight: the ones who're innocent stay up all night, weeping, banging the bars; the ones who know they're nicked figure, what the hell, might as well get some kip. When I woke up, properly woke up, it was four hours later, and a fat Indian guy on my right was asleep on my shoulder. I felt better, despite him. I ate a fibre bar and thought, well. I'm getting out. There was a relief to that. No uni, but no more London either. What was I missing? It seemed like everyone who ought to have been at uni was on that stretch of coast anyway.

I wished I could've looked out the window, seen what I was leaving behind, but we were over Russia now. When I thought of not being in that town any more, in England any more, it was like when you see the fields alongside the M25 and can't believe that they're always there, unchanging, in fog and frost and dawn light, even when you're asleep or in school. Silly things: Chupa Chups in convenience stores, clip-art flyers tacked up on the community pinboard at the superstore. I supposed I wouldn't know till I really missed it. That could come later; first I had to find my mother. Maybe she'd backed off because I was so weird the last week I was there. She'd understand when she knew, and I'd tell her; tell her all that crazy shit Tinder'd told me, how he'd tried to mess me up, get me away from her. We could go off together, leave all this behind. I held on to that, feeling the plane seem to warm already as we crawled over the curve, following the red line over the surface of the globe eastwards.

The last time I landed in India it had been hot but overcast, hung over from the rainy season, but now it was blue sunshine, just like when we left. The concrete on the apron shone brilliant white back at us as we taxied, and when the door finally opened, the surge of warm air into the icy cabin felt like a new start. I trooped across to the terminal with the others, taking off layers and tying them round my waist; I picked up my bag so as not to look suspicious to the mustachioed guys with guns, but distributed the paperbacks among the kids outside, thinking maybe they could sell them. They grabbed at them like they were wedges of banknotes, the ones who got them darting away from the mob of others. The attention of the ones left behind forced me to get a cab to the station, which I hadn't wanted to do since they knew you weren't in a position to haggle at the airport.

The train was not like our trains; or rather, it was, but only that one carriage that you hurry through, looking for a seat among the laptops and glossy magazines, away from the single parents on weekend access, the guys with thick fingers and faded tattoos, the foil-wrapped doorstops spread out on the tables. All of this train was pitched somewhere between the stench of an intercity smoking car and the insane overcrowding of the commuter line. It was almost the last straw, but I toughed it out, trying not to think that everything was going to be like this now. It was beyond a relief to get off it, but then the bus to Kovalam was more of the same. The best cab available at the other end was a moped, owned by a too friendly guy who wanted me to sit closer to him than was necessary. He kept telling me to put my arms round his waist, going no-hands to demonstrate; I only gave in to stop him shooting us into a pothole. He hadn't known where I meant on the beach ('The yoga camp? Yoga. Jesus, white women! Topless, yeah?') and I suspect he thought I just wanted to go see some naked chicks, but I pointed out the turns over his shoulder and we were there inside half an hour. It was such a joy to see the place that I gave him double what he'd asked for and packed him off. I wanted to kiss the ground. I'd been through it, and I'd got away with it, and the time when I had to bear it alone was ending. I could share the weight of the problem now, let Mum take the strain a little; it was about time she did. We'd be laughing about this in a few hours. I ran a hand through my hair, felt the good summer sweat in it, so different to the sweat you get in the gym. I walked down the trail through the new hotels towards the people on the beach.

But bad times are never over until you've gone to the bridge with them. It hadn't been hard enough yet. All of Mum's shacks now had Hotel Janahki signs on top of them, and a decking walkway had been built back towards a big new hotel, a hundred metres down the beach. The main building, the one that'd had the open roof, wasn't there at all. Instead there was a guy in a Janahki T-shirt sitting in a new bamboo booth, fluffy white towels piled around him. Almost immediately he came out and trotted over the sand towards me.

'You staying at the hotel, sir?'

'What hotel?'

'This is private beach, sir.'

'Hold on. Where's my mum? Cassandra. Where's Cassandra?'

'Staying at the hotel?'

I realised what a state I was in, same clothes for two days now, and how I must look to him – just another Western wanker, drunk too much and crashed on the beach.

'She owns it. I mean, she owns this.' I waved my arm at the shacks.

'These are Hotel Janahki beach apartments, sir, just open. You want room? You want beach? Go to Hotel Janahki.'

He pointed along the beach. I just stared at him, as if something in his face might tell me what was going on; but he was either waiting for a tip or for confirmation that he needed to call security from the mobile on his belt. It seemed the hotel was my best chance of finding out what was going on, so I pulled my flimsy wad of soft notes out of my pocket, pushed a couple at him and walked along the beach. There were lots of Europeans lying around and I felt they were all looking at me, at my winter clothes bundled round my waist like I was an umpire. I couldn't get to the hotel fast enough, even though I wasn't sure I'd get more than short shrift there.

The girl on the desk advised me to fuck off and die, more or less, but I wasn't having it. Eventually she said she'd get the duty manager and I almost wept with relief when Charlie, the blonde who used to run bookings for Mum, walked round the screen in a pressed linen suit with a silk scarf tied round her neck. It didn't take much to see she no longer worked for my mother; instead of giving me the fatted-calf treatment, she just filled me in on how Mum had sold up and moved back up the coast.

'It's much easier up there. You pay a bribe to get a hut put up, pay another bribe to get it taken down at the end of the season. No rent, no landlords. Here, the hotels can't ignore the business any longer.'

Mum was okay. She was doing what she did. All the things that had happened off in England were like a rainstorm at the coast underwriting white fluffy clouds inland. And if she was cool, then Tinder was out of the picture.

Mum's guests didn't drink, didn't get rowdy, and that was the kind of business the hotels wanted, so they'd turfed her out, Charlie said. This whole stretch was going upmarket, to resort status. Mum had got sick of the hassle and moved on; Charlie didn't know where to precisely. But she let me change some more money, called a cab on the phone to take me up the coast, no doubt keen to get me out of her lobby. She let me wait in her office until the cab came, and when she asked why I was back so soon, I told her my dad had been on my case. I'm sure she'd been well primed on my father's failings whenever Mum was on the Bailey's, and certainly my laying it on my dad was enough to make her change the subject.

When the cab came I let her instruct the driver and sat back in the seat, working on my attitude. I was still going to get there. The fact that uni was out the window, that I wasn't going to be in a smart flat in London in four years, that I wouldn't see Alita again unless she came out here; all this had diminished behind the immediate objective of finding Mum, warning her what was going on, and going away with her somewhere safe until all this'd been forgotten. That was all I had to do. I was still going to be all right.

When she wasn't at the new place either, I didn't let it blow me out of the water. I made the cab wait this time, and swiftly established that no one doing yoga there had ever heard of her. I almost laughed as they shrugged their shoulders and shook their heads. Here I was, no money, no stuff, three thousand miles from home, and all I was getting was my chain pulled. I paid off the driver, which took most of what I had, but I couldn't even sit down in the sand to cry, since, again, everyone on the beach was looking at me. I started walking along the shoreline, thinking to walk to a town, try and sell my Berghaus and my Swatch in the next open bar I got to.

Walking along the beach by the sea, it chills you out a little. I drifted, staring at the water, and when I looked up and saw that I knew this place, the sun was nodding down to set over the rim of the ocean.

Ranj was where he always was, glass of mango juice collecting condensation on the bar in front of him while he smoked imported cigarettes and glanced suavely round for women he hadn't knocked off yet.

'Ranj, man,' I said. 'Fuck, it's good to see you.'

He turned his head, but the smile died on his face as it came out of profile. I saw him flick a look at his bar guy, who put down the optic he was messing with.

'Whatta you want here, man?' he said, and then, narrowing his eyes, 'Your father with you?'

'You what?'

'You fucking with me?'

'Jesus, Ranj, what's the matter? You remember me?'

'Yeah, I remember you,' he said, and nodded to the barman, who scuttled out round the side onto the beach.

'Bay,' I said, looking quickly between him and the bar guy. 'I came out to see Mum – Cassandra, yeah? But she sold up. I need to find her, I've got nowhere to stay.'

The bar guy came back in and spread his hands. Ranj lit a cigarette and looked at me through the smoke.

'You fucking with me?' he asked again. 'Because you fuck with me, I fuck you. You understand?'

'Ranj, mate, what is the problem? I just need to find my mum.' I tried to do a normal voice. 'She with Tinder?' I asked, my gut tightening.

He gave me a long look, like he was weighing something, then stubbed the long butt in his ashtray.

'You're fucking with me, I'm gonna find out.' He got up, dusted his palms on his thighs. 'Come back here.'

He barked something in Indian to a couple of guys who'd been scratching their bellies at a table, took me round the back of the bar through a beaded curtain into a windowless room, where he left me with some goon with poor muscle tone and a baseball bat. I sat down on the edge of a trestle; the goon brought the bat up and waggled it at me like it was his prong or something. For a moment I was like, ah Jesus; I recognised that look on his face from some of the weirdos at school, the mama's boys who used to whack off under their desks. But then he said:

'You Shana brother?'

'Uh-huh.'

He drew himself up. 'I fuck your sister.'

He clearly regarded this as some kind of feat.

'Yeah, you and the rest of the coast,' I said, trying to look round him through the curtain beads. He pushed my face back towards him with the end of the bat.

'Yeah, I give her what every white bitch wants,' he said.

I sat back. 'You did, huh?'

'Yeah,' he goes. 'Dark meat on the bone.' It was obviously a pretty big line of his, but I couldn't help snorting. The way the arsehole was acting was a reassurance. There wasn't any big deal here; it was just the way these dickheads were. The way they were brought up, the women staying at home while the boys did whatever they liked, made them reckon themselves, think they were big men; then they got the tourist bints slavering all over them, making them think they were catnip, and dickless here was the result. He didn't seem to find it very funny.

'Maybe I fuck you too,' he growled.

'Yeah?' I said. 'Why don't you come and have a go, flip-flop boy?'

I might have been tired, but this loser had never done a pec fly in his life, and I was doing reps of twenty on bar fifteen last time I was in the gym. I could twist the bat out of his hands and stick it up his flabby arse quicker than he could say 'cultural imperialist'. I was sick of this shit now. This was the difference between being squired around by Tinder and having to do things on my own, and I was tired of it. And what was Ranj's crap about my father? I dreaded to think how, but McCormick must've got to him, put the squeeze on, and he must've given them Mum's numbers, the silly sod. He could lead them right to me.

Me and the fat man squared up, but before it could get silly, Ranj came back in.

'Ranj, call off your chav here, eh?' I said. Ranj jerked his head at the door, and the dickhead weighed the bat in his hand a couple of times like he had to have the last word, then flip-flopped out.

'All right, Tjinder'll see you,' Ranj said.

'Is my mum with him?' I asked.

'Yeah,' he said. 'But I'm warning you, guy, you're playing anything, it's not gonna work for you. I'm gonna drive you but you keep your head down. If I think for a second we're being followed, I stop and you're out. You got it?'

If all this had been too weird for words, if Ranj was the kind of guy to be freaked out by a call from a cop on the other side of the planet, then Tinder most assuredly was not. Whatever else he might have been, he was the man on this coast, and everywhere else he'd taken me too; this would just be bullshit to him, a matter of a couple of calls from his cellphone, closing the trail down. Then I could have it out with him, make him take me to my mother, explain what he'd tried to pull with me: make her see what he'd told me, how my father had wrecked my life that sunny morning out by the bypass. I didn't believe the cops for a second now. It was him, not her. She'd freak, but she'd want to help me, help make it up to me; put me back on track, somewhere a long way from those two bozos, somewhere we could come back from when the heat was off.

That was the way it ought to have been. But when I finally got to see Tinder, in an apartment in a city I could only guess was Bombay, after a ridiculous series of cop-video transfers and pickups and await-further-instructions, he was with my mother, and they were both even more freaked than I was.

'If you're pulling any kind of stunt for your father, man, you'd better tell me,' was the first thing he said.

I tried to find some idea of what he was talking about in his face, half-shadowed in the soft lamplight that turned the apartment's white carpet the colour of cappuccino foam. He was sitting on a bamboo-and-chrome chair at a glass-topped dining table in the room Ranj had ushered me into. My mother sat next to him, smoking a cigarette.

'Why would I be trying to pull something for him? I've barely spoken to him in weeks,' I said. 'Tinder, man, you've got to help me.'

'It's Tjinder,' he said, in a tone he'd never used before. 'You're not a kid any more.'

'Mum?' I said.

As I cut through the water in a slow, clean crawl, I turned around for a moment and trod water while I checked to see that Tinder was still there, that I wasn't as alone as I felt. If he was, I couldn't see him. India was a dark thing, humped in silence between the green glow of the ocean and the indigo glow of the sky; the silhouette of the dinghy was lost against it. I turned back round, oriented myself towards the boat at anchor in the bay, itself a dark blob between the sea and the sky, and swam on, the physical facts of chill water and dark sky recalling other nightswims, skinnydips, the easiest way to see girls naked, one they never ever balk at. Seemed like years ago; I went under for a moment, duck-dived a metre or so to shake it, then switched to a slow breaststroke when I came up, spooked out of a crawl by the noise – huge to me, all alone in the night-milky ocean – of resurfacing.

I hadn't swum since the last time I was here and it was harder work than I'd anticipated, trying to keep the splash to zero while correcting my course every thirty seconds or so. It was deep water here, not like swimming off a beach at all, and I spent as much time reorienting myself as I did moving forwards. Still, I was there sooner than I wanted. I did the last ten metres underwater, came up slowly against the hull, below the sight-lines from the windows, handed myself gently around to the anchor chain and hauled up.

'The police weren't looking for you, they were looking for your father,' Mum said.

Whatever she was doing here with him was left behind in the wake of my rush, my swerve, as the gap cracked open again.

'They told me it was you they wanted,' I said weakly. 'They were going to pull me unless I could get you back there.'

Tinder gave me a look like he couldn't believe I was being so thick, like he'd been wasting his time with me.

'It was him, but he was ahead of them,' he said. 'Ahead of you too. He's been here almost a week. Didn't you notice he was gone?'

I used the shaft of the right-hand propeller to give myself purchase – if I'd been a fraction shorter, if I'd been my father's height, I couldn't have done it – and pulled myself up by degrees, a few centimetres at a time, to let the water run off me little by little rather than hauling myself up with one big splash. The textured fibreglass of the boat's sundeck was wonderfully warm and dry as I pulled myself over it, but this was the critical part and there was no time to linger. I padded swiftly around to the rail, then crouched down by the door of the cabin, listening for movement inside.

'You mustn't blame your mother,' Tinder said. 'When they started sponsoring me it was with the best intentions, on her side at least. What I was pushed towards as I grew up was your father's doing. She knew nothing about it until it was too late. I tell her she shouldn't feel sorry for me,' he went on, shooting her a glance. 'I might have drifted towards it anyway. Kids from the street do. But that was why she left your father. When she found out what he'd made me.'

As she covered his hand with hers, I saw how it was between them. How had I missed it before? Because you don't see intimacy between a woman and a man in solicitousness, I saw now, you see it in carelessness; in the way she didn't thank him, didn't even acknowledge him as he held his lighter out now to the tip of her cigarette.

'I didn't know anything until it was too late, sweetheart, you have to believe that,' she said through the smoke from her Marlboro Light. 'I didn't know the truth about your father's business until the money from it was all we had. Christ!' She tossed back her head, blew smoke at the ceiling fan. 'I thought he was making our money from his developments, but they were just to launder it. The capital came from the drugs, and that's all he sees it as: it's money coming into the country to him, nothing more. He doesn't get his hands dirtier than that. He collects investors, wires out a chunk of money a month, divvies the proceeds up, then pisses his share away on his stupid building works. Offices that no one wants to rent. I mean, he's not even rich from it. You can't blame me for not seeing it.'

She dared me to break eye contact, and I couldn't.

'He lost control,' Tinder said. 'That's why I wanted out, that's why I asked you to work for me. It got too big for him to handle. He had too many people working for him, kept too much distance down the chain of command. When he heard about your friends' little factory, he suggested it be sat on. They were making drugs locally; he was spending hundreds of thousands a year importing them. Maybe they were only meant to be frightened, maybe not. The police want him for murder, in the absence of the two heavies who disturbed your friends for long enough for their equipment to overheat and blow up in their faces. Now he's here. He wants to negotiate. He's acting without reason, and he wants your mother to hide him.'

Mum put her face in her hands, ran them back through her hair.

'Now listen,' said Tinder.

I had to do it because Tinder couldn't swim. Where would a street kid have learned to? I, however, had been born in a pool, had swim club since I was old enough to hold a float. Swimming lessons and tennis lessons and membership of the country club, and a swipe-card for the gym that might as well have renewed itself for all the thought I gave it.

My body was pumped with money, but the swim tired me out nonetheless, making withdrawals from muscles that I usually only deposited into. My arm shook as I pushed the cabin door open; I had to look hard inside myself for the resources to do what I was about to.

He drove me to the coast in silence. When we were out of the city the satellite phone rang. Tinder picked it up. It was my mother. He handed it to me. She talked, I listened, thanking fuck the phone wasn't a hands-free. She explained how it had got out of hand. She told me how men let things get out of proportion. She told me what needed to happen next.

When she was done, we were driving along a coast road. As I put the handset back in its cradle, Tinder glanced over at me.

'She told you?'

'She told me what's going to happen,' I said.

'You understand why you have to do this?'

'Because it's the only way.'

'Anything you're not sure on, anything you want to ask me, you go ahead.'

'I'm cool,' I said.

He shrugged. 'Cool.'

We drove in silence for a bit, while I tried to get used to the new arrangement. It was easier than you'd think. I risked a glance at Tinder, but he was staring so pointedly at the road that I could study him for a moment. Thought he'd got everything wrapped up, the bastard.

'There were two Indian kids fell out of a 747 onto my town last year,' I said. This was my last chance to call him out, see where he was really at. 'You hear anything about that?'

He shrugged, kept his eyes fixed on the road.

'Running from something,' I said, waiting for him to go into one. 'Would've thought you'd followed it.'

He shrugged again. 'Happens. Yeah, I may have read something about it.'

'So young,' I said. 'Must've been pretty bad. What were they? Farm kids? Had their inheritance crop-sprayed?'

I waited, but he didn't even look up from the road. He didn't care any more than I did; he'd just listened to too many backpackers, thought they meant what they mouthed off about. He'd thought that was the way to get to me.

'You could've just told me,' I said.

He didn't say anything.

My father'd rented a boat in the marina and was moving it around the coast; but after he'd made contact and demanded a meet, it hadn't taken Tinder long to find out where he was. The boat was top-whack and idiot-proof, with a GPS system on board for when you called for help but couldn't give coordinates, the kind of motor yacht they hired out to rich Westerners who wanted all the fun and none of the work.

Tinder paid the boat-rental guy to track him, and got daily reports of his movements.

I couldn't believe it. 'A *boat*?' I'd said, back at the apartment. 'But he hates the water. He can't even swim.'

'He's got nowhere else to go,' Tinder said. 'He's holed up out there with a hull full of heroin. Looks like he didn't want to change the money he ran with into rupees. Looks like he wanted a more versatile currency.' He lifted a chromed demitasse to his lips and sipped. 'The guy he bought it from in Bombay is one of my suppliers. Your father persuaded him that I'd authorised the deal; he bought a shotgun too. He'd break his shoulder if he tried to use it, but still I wouldn't want to have him point it at me. We can't get close to the boat unless we catch him with his pants down, and I don't see that happening. He's on a knife edge.'

It was him saying 'pants down' that did it.

'He gets up every morning an hour before it's light,' Mum said. 'I still sleep in foam earplugs, even now.'

She was right. The cold-water tank was above my bedroom; the swishing of its refill when he flushed woke me most mornings before dawn, as long as we'd lived there.

It could even look quite natural. Tinder said it was a known cardiac thing. Your heart pounds like a bastard when you get up to piss in the middle of the night. He knew a story about a business tycoon – some guy from the eighties, Mum knew it too – who'd had a heart attack as he pissed over the side of his yacht at dawn, and they never found the body. When the cops got to the end of the trail out here, if they ever did, they'd find the boat back in harbour. The guy who rented it out would tell them how they'd found it at anchor in the bay, the bed slept in, alarm clock ringing weakly, but the Englishman who'd rented it as vanished as if he'd been abducted.

'He'd do it off the back,' Tinder said, spreading the gaudily-printed brochure of the boat out on the table. 'He's been out there five days without getting his toilet pumped. It will be getting somewhat ripe in there. Not what you want to be breathing in the middle of the night.'

He pointed at the picture of the boat, floating white and beautiful on an unreally blue sea.

'Swim out in the dark, climb onto the roof, wait till he comes out, then take him from behind. Tie something heavy to him and down he goes. Then we're set,' he said.

'Set for what?'

'To go north, find a new retail end for our supply. Someone who's not going to lose control.'

He looked at me. I looked at my mother, but there was nothing there.

'You're kidding,' I said.

'Why not?' said Tinder. 'You're white. Like I told you, that's useful in this business. Especially where you come from.'

'You're crazy,' I said. 'If the cops are looking for him, they'll be looking for me.'

'Not in a couple of years they won't,' he said. 'You can learn the ropes here in the meantime. You've already made a start.'

'I have?'

'Sure,' he said. 'What have you been doing all this time? Where did you think I was pointing you?'

My mother glanced away; but Tinder looked at me in the old way then, and it almost beached me. He looked at me not like I was family, but like I was someone he chose. Like what you did in the world was what counted, like blood didn't matter.

* * *

I was to see how it did.

The cabin door was locked; I thought of knocking, but realised I might get a shotgun blast through the door for my politeness. Instead, I crept around towards the prow between the rail and the cabin, keeping low on the non-slip fibreglass in case Tinder was watching me. A row of videotape-sized windows ran along by my feet, set just below the ceiling of the kitchen and then the cabin; I followed them to the front, where the swell of the living quarters was between me and the shore, knelt down and peered. My father was sleeping; foetal, fists up by his face under the pillow. It was the same position I slept in. But there wasn't time to hang around.

I tapped on the window; nothing. I put my face down to the ventilation gap and said, 'Dad?' Then again, louder.

He lifted his head, his hair sticking up like a little kid's. His face registered four swift reversals. I said, 'Quick,' and motioned back towards the cabin door, then made a fast squat-crawl back.

When he opened the door a crack, I pushed against it and slipped inside. He stumbled back against a cupboard, covering his groin with his hands, and I realised that I'd never seen him naked before.

'Wha' fuck?' he mumbled, still thick with sleep.

I looked down at the floor, embarrassed despite everything. I didn't know where to look. His feet had the same long toes as mine, the legs the same scrawny shanks that I'd had to work for years on the calf-press to build over. You'd never have seen it when he was clothed. His trainers, his sportswear, his Nike and Reebok and Adidas had always made him look as sleek and ergonomic as everyone else, as though we were all off the same slick production line, bought in the same store. You use money to hide what you are, hide where you come from, but there was no hiding now.

So I told him the score, need-to-know, four short sentences. His face seemed to expand, his eyes and mouth widening, as though his skull was visibly swelling. I let him get on with it, jerked the window open; then I slipped the handgun Tinder had given me from the groin of my wetshorts, stepped back and levelled it between both hands. When I fired I got a dry click. The safety; Tinder'd made me put it on so I didn't shoot my dingus off. I thumbed it back, squeezed again and this time heard the report echo back from the hills around the bay.

I went back outside. I was supposed to toss the gun over but I slipped it back into my wetshorts and fished out the steel Magiclite to flash my signal, two short one long, back to the Range Rover above the beach. I strained my eyes for the return flash from the headlights that would show the coast was clear, that the shot hadn't attracted any unwelcome attention; but there, closer, fifty metres away, something else drew my focus.

There was a real grace to the brown figure angling towards the boat under the blue, cutting through the water with slow, strong strokes that propelled him almost inhumanly swiftly forwards. I didn't have to look hard to know it was Tinder, and I didn't have to look to know there were no bullets left in the chamber either. But I was ready for him. I was set. He was coming to clean this up, but I was on the boat, he was in the water. Hadn't he taught me that was the way it went?

He burst out of the water like it was vomiting him up, swarmed over the back of the boat and landed on his feet, taut as a kick-boxer, dripping, grin spread from ear to ear. I watched it fade as his eyes shifted focus to where, behind me, the shotgun's big black eye poled dark light into his pupils.

'Down,' my dad said. 'On the fucking floor, shitbag.'

Tinder turned his head to me, bored into my eyes so hard

I could barely see his grin widening below. His head snapped to the left as my father whipped the butt of the shotgun under his jaw, and his body followed. Dad put a foot on the back of his neck, ground it down so Tinder's face was squashed against the hard, white fibreglass.

'Rope,' he said, shotgun in one hand, free arm extended, and I jumped to a coil of blue nylon on one side, slipped its loop from the dolly-hook, handed it to him. He passed me the shotgun as he knelt on Tinder's shoulderblades, wrenched his arms around behind him and commenced winding the rope, cuff-'em style, round Tinder's wrists. I took the shotgun – it was heavier than it looked – and as my dad busied himself connecting Tinder's wrists to his ankles, I sat up in the driver's swivel chair and watched.

When he was done, my father kicked Tinder in the side. It didn't have much effect, in his bare feet; he spat on the back of his neck as if to compensate, ground it in with his foot.

'Like that, eh?' He shifted his whole weight onto Tinder's neck, and he cried out against the deck. 'Know your place now?'

'Dad,' I said. He looked up.

'You're a good lad,' he said, turning to me, but still standing as if he was inflating a lilo with a footpump. 'I'll see you all right for this.'

'Yeah? With what?' It wasn't unreasonable to point this out. 'The police came looking for you. I had to leave everything.'

'I brought my fighting fund,' he said. 'Hundred grand. It's in the cabin. Why don't you give me that?' He gestured at the shotgun, held out his hand.

'Why don't you show me the money?' I said, pointing the barrel at the deck. 'I'll cover him.'

'I had to change it,' he said.

'Yeah?' I said, and raised the barrel.

'Bay,' he said, his arms coming up as his brows went. 'What're you doing? C'mon, give that to me.'

'And what'll you give me?' I said. 'A couple of bags of smack?'

'It'll buy us what we need,' he said, 'buy us a new start.'

I racked it, pumped another round into the chamber. To my astonishment, it made the right noise. I loosened my grip, tried to handle it more gingerly.

'You and me, eh,' I said.

'You don't know,' Dad said. 'It'll be different. Away from all the shit. There'll be time –'

'Oh, you'll have *time* for me, will you? Like you had so much time for me that I didn't even notice you were *gone*, Dad. I thought the cops were looking for *me*.'

He seemed to go slack then, and Tinder saw the opportunity; but all he could do was writhe beneath the foot. 'He's a bastard,' he said, trying to twist his face towards me.

'And you can shut your stinking mouth,' I said. 'What were you gonna do? Go off with her, eh? Don't mind shacking up with a single mother as long as her kid's out the way?'

'Bay,' he said.

'*Shut it!*' my father yelled, stamping down on his neck until he roared.

'Enough, both of you,' I said quietly, and meant it.

'Just give me the gun,' Dad said, taking his foot off Tinder. Tinder looked up.

'So how was it?' he said.

Dad whirled at him, but I motioned to him to stay back.

'How was what?' I said.

'The payoff, man.' Even down on the deck, he grinned.

'What payoff?' I pointed the gun at him. He was trying to get me, like he always did.

'The payoff from the bet we were the stake for,' he said. 'The experiment we were the raw material for.'

'Experiment into what?'

'Into how much pleasure a person can stand. How did you like it, over there in the First World?' His grin widened. 'Pretty good, huh? What do you say? Think it was worth it?'

'No, man,' I said, caught in his eyes. God, he was good at it. My voice sounded far away. 'It wasn't that great. Not unless you were wasted.'

'You fucking –' Dad snarled. I didn't let him finish.

'He knows more than you do,' I cut in. 'If I had to choose between you, I'd go with him. Uh –' I raised the barrel to keep him where he was.

'Do you know what I remember most about you?' I asked him after a moment. 'I was trying to think on the way here. And you know what it was? Your fucking camcorder. Christmases, birthdays; you standing off on the side, with the JVC clamped on your face so you wouldn't have to join in.' My voice cracked. 'Do you know what you've broken?' I asked him. 'Do you *know*? And for what, you stupid sod? For fucking what. You're not even *rich*.'

My father looked thunder and disgust at me a moment, and I raised the barrel again, weakly; it was enough.

'You have to make choices,' he said after a while, his voice pitched like I hadn't heard before. He gestured weakly with his hands. 'You can't tell . . . you have to make them, and there's no one to tell you which is the right one.'

If I'd always thought of him as a kid, no different from me, holed up in his room just as I was in mine, then now he sounded like one.

'Choices, eh? Well, here's a choice for you.' I sounded like a teacher asking a kid to share the joke with the class. 'You can go home and take the rap for what you've done; or you can fight extradition and stay here. And try to explain this boatful of smack.'

I held the shotgun out over the water, let it drop; he lunged towards me.

'Uh-uh,' I warned, unslotting the ignition keys from the dash in front of me with my other hand. He stopped dead.

'Don't be a tit, Bay,' he said. 'Give them to me.'

'You knew what you were doing.' I stood up, the keys hanging from my outstretched finger. 'You knew what you were doing but you shut it out. Turned the CD up so you wouldn't hear the engine.' A sob surprised me, burped up from my throat. 'Can you hear it now? Can you?'

They were both looking at me like I was some kind of freak.

'Can't hear nothing, can you?' I said, looking from one to the other. 'Won't hear nothing till you turn it on. You want these?' I pinched the keyring between thumb and forefinger, shook them in the air weakly. I was breaking up. I hadn't expected it to feel like this. 'You want to hear the engine now? You're not gonna. If you want to get back to shore you'll have to coast there.'

I let the keys hang from my finger a moment longer, light glinting off them. Then I flipped my wrist and watched their eyes follow the high arc, such a simple thing, both eyes narrowing against the blue of the sky and the blue of the ocean, eyes following the arc to its end, widening involuntarily at the splash and the ripples.

'You enjoy this time together,' I said. 'Open up. Make time for each other.' I took one last look at their faces – bad move, but one I couldn't help – and then, before my father could finish the lunge he was starting, I followed the keys and the shotgun into the sea.

I made a fast crawl till I was out of earshot, letting the water in my ears drown out my father. When I was far enough I stopped and trod water a moment while I looked back; he seemed to be kicking furiously at his ex-partner, down on the ground, probably hurting his bare feet more than he was Tinder.

The sun was all the way up over the land behind me, the horizon taut as a bowstring beyond the boat. I turned and began a slow, tutored breaststroke back to shore, pulling hard against the drift that'd helped me on the way out. I could see the four by four on the coast road where we'd left it, but there was no way I was going to make it. Instead I tried to work with the current, heading for the far reach of the bay. I glanced over my shoulder a couple of times when I could, and the third time I looked, the four by four was gone.

It reappeared as I crawled up to the beach, disappearing behind some trees, then rolling out on the deserted sand towards me. Mackey got out.

'No towel?' I said.

He snorted, but I could tell part of him was checking out my torso, even though I hadn't been in a gym since summer. It was still there, though, and tan now too; unlike his miserable calves, shrinkingly hairy below the cuffs of his khaki shorts.

'It worked?' he said.

'You see anyone else in the water?'

'Shit,' he said, looking out to sea. 'Your father's even thicker than you are.'

I made him look back at me. 'Just don't fuck it up, now, okay? I don't want Tjinder getting off.'

'There's a launch on the way,' he said, 'see it any minute. DI McCormick's on board, make sure they hand over your father.'

'And you're sure he'll go with you?'

'We'll give him the option. Fifty years in some shitpit here, or he comes back, gives us what we want to close this little pipeline down for good. He'll get twenty, do twelve.'

'And you'll leave the meth out of it?'

'No point,' he said, 'muddying the water.'

'You're sure they'll let you? The local?'

For once he didn't blow up on me for telling him his business.

'They've got a yachtful of smack,' he said. 'And our friend can take them all over the country, give them a supertanker more; along with the factories, the fields and the foremen. They don't just get kudos for that kind of collar, they get grants. Development money, debt relief, however they want to play it. They're happy.'

'Give me a phone. I want to talk to my mother now.'

'She's got my car. I called her while I drove here. You're a shit swimmer, you know that? Drifted halfway round the bay. She'll be here in a minute.'

'And what about me?'

'You get lucky. Piss off, and we won't come looking for

you. But I can tell you: you *ever* come back, I'll hear about it and I'll open the file. If it costs me my job, I'll find you and I'll do for you. You understand?'

I shrugged, pushing it; I wouldn't have dared before, but he'd never done what I just had. He held eye contact a moment longer, then turned and walked back to the four by four. As he reached it, a white Range Rover strobed through the trees, then jounced down the track to where he was parked. My mother got out; she said a couple of things to him, held out the keys. He took them, gave her hers, said something, then froze a moment, bent forward stiffly and gave her a kiss on the cheek. Then he got up into the cab, started the engine and swung the car in a wide arc over the sand, not looking at me, and back the way he'd come. As I walked up towards my mother, his tail-lights flashed briefly up by the road, and then he was gone.

When I reached Mum's car, she was in the driver's seat, talking fast in Hindi on the satellite phone. She reached into the back seat without slowing her flow and handed me a towel through the open door; listened for a moment, said something else, then hung up the handset.

'Like a native,' I said, drying off my chest.

'You'll pick it up,' she said, looking at me appraisingly. 'Dry your back too. These seats stain.'

I stretched the towel across my shoulders.

'It's not worth starting,' she said.

'I wasn't going to,' I said.

'You were thinking it,' she said, 'I can tell. I couldn't let you know, Bay. I couldn't call you, I couldn't send a message. You have to understand that. I wouldn't be standing here if I had. Neither would you.'

'I went to hell,' I said. I just wanted her to know, that was all.

She took it without flinching. 'Then you're out of it now,' she said. 'All they were interested in was making your father run, and then making you run. You both had to be scared enough to do it. They couldn't let me jeopardise that.'

There wasn't much else to say.

'Won't Tinder try and pay them off?' I asked.

'He can try, but they won't take it,' she said. 'It's too big a score for them. They'll sit on the export, but there'd be a riot if they closed the home market. And though officially they hate the Westerners, the people who come to party, the freeloaders, you know?' She squinted into the sun at me. 'Unofficially, they'll put up with someone selling to them, as long as it isn't locals getting their hands dirty.'

'So we do it,' I said. 'So we work the coast.'

She shrugged. 'We're going to open another yoga place. Find a good beach, get a hut put up. I've still got my mailing list.'

I squinted back at her. 'What about Tinder's suppliers?'

'What about them? His contacts are mine now: the ones he doesn't turn in, at least. But I've got a pretty good idea who the cops'll take, who they'll let carry on. Maybe the ones that're left will be in touch.'

'You'll speak to them?'

'You can't not,' she said, and gave me a moment to let that sink in. 'But as long as it doesn't get too big . . . and I'll make sure it doesn't. Men are always after global domination. They can't see what's under their nose –' she tilted her head towards the ocean – 'or be satisfied with it if they can.'

I resumed drying my hair. 'So where to?'

'South,' she said, turning her head down the coast. 'There're a couple of places I want to look at. And Ranj says your friend Talya's back, looking for something to do. We could pick her up on the way.'

I stopped towelling. Out at sea, the boat looked oddly peaceful; god knew what was going on inside, but floating like that in the dawn-lit bay, it could've been from the cover of a brochure. I had about as much choice as those two out there. Still, I was needed. Time to grow up about it.

My mother's voice brought me back. 'Well?' she asked. 'You set?'

'Yeah,' I said, snapping out of it. I tossed the towel into the back and climbed into the passenger seat. The leather was warm against my shoulders. 'Yes, I think I am.'

'Good boy,' she said, and turned the key in the ignition.

The first chapter of
Matthew Branton's
new killer thriller,

THE HIRED GUN

follows . . .

1

AT MIDNIGHT, EVERYONE IN the sultry city had been level-pegging; two hours later, Decker had joined the wide-eyed crew who were going to have a lousy week.

Searching with his temple for a cool part of the pillow, his pilot-light consciousness pulled compatriots from the shrouded city. A bathrobed father, maybe, sitting up for his daughter, curfewed for eleven but still necking some pimply streak of piss, her cellphone voicemail innocently taunting him every time he hit the speed-dial. A supervisor from an over-stretched office, wakeful after sex while her husband slept and shifted, wondering if this would be the week that the temp would get tired of plugging the dyke and quit, go paint henna tattoos on tourists up in the Castro as she'd let slip she had last summer. A cop, knowing that every minute lost now would come back doubled in tomorrow's sweltering cruiser. A college student, wondering if a love pledged in dorm-room campus certainty would last out the studio-share, blue-collar vacation; a mortuary attendant, thinking how the blue fluid would smell after five hours' sleep, but unable to summon it nonetheless. Decker shifted over to the other side of the bed. Practitioners of his own profession were popularly understood not to sleep, or to do so in straight-backed chairs, four-square with the door; he knew different. Like the cop and the student, the supervisor and the orderly, he knew two missed hours on Sunday night meant a mis-step on Monday, with a nagging sense of catch-up all week; the feeling of having lost a point before play had started was the same for Decker as for anyone else.

The other side of dawn was time to focus and forget about it. There'd been a Decker once who could sleep on the fly, could fire on all cylinders as long as he had to; running on reserve and, when that was drained, running on fumes till the job was done. His body had changed on him somewhere in his thirties. He could still kick it when he had to, but the last few years even missing his window for a crap left him naggingly off-rhythm for days on end. He'd try a hot bath – maybe a herbal gel cap – when this was done, he thought, making the last turn in the labyrinth of Gallops, Drives, Meadows and Paddocks. Thirty yards from the turn he backed the rental into the realtor's drive, killed the engine, turned down the volume and shut it all out.

Two hours ten to go. The house across the street was booting up on schedule. Lights were on in bathrooms and hallways. Figures were discernible through the kitchen window, above the neat shrub border: the Kurtz's wife and daughter, moving between the refrigerator, the tea kettle and the counter. The drapes were still drawn behind the master bedroom's leaded window: textbook Kurtz, thought Decker, shifting his seat back and folding his arms. When they lost the plot, they stopped getting out of bed in the morning. It occurred to him that he should've added the Kurtz to his cadre of wakeful *compadres*, as he'd lain awake earlier; the guy hunched under hi-watt halogen against the dark of his den, plying an Exact-o-Knife under an ID laminate or whatever he did these days. Decker flicked his eyes up and down the suburban street reflexively, saw the same pattern of drapes and lights in every double-garaged, redwood-trimmed, half-mil-plus property. The same striped protective covers on every lawn chair and swing seat, the Kurtz's too. No one planning on going anywhere. He checked the time: two hours and five. It was a drag, but watch-and-wait intel was the only real route into the frame.

The paperboy hove into view down the street: 6.54 by the dash LCD, bang on the button. Little-league suburbs were a good place to work: routine-heavy, no surprises. His clients tended to live there for that reason: each unfamiliar car would catch an idle eye, and a strange pedestrian would have the dispatcher at neighbourhood security working through her break. Decker didn't plan to upset her routine this morning. The driveway he was backed into fronted the four-bed, two-bath estate of a realtor with four full days left on Maui. The rental he sat in was an Acura, blue-gray; same year, model and spec as the realtor drove, along with most people around here. It was a two-piece suit, a collar and rep tie, a pair of black Oxfords on wheels.

It wasn't Decker's choice. They were apt to shed tires when rammed a certain way, and the beverage holder, when he located it, was too small to take the cup from his brushed-steel Thermos. He poured out coffee anyway, balanced the cup on the dash and noted the mailman in the distance making his honeybee progress from one sunflower- or daisy-painted box to the next. As a kid Decker'd loved the mail, the whole round of daily renewables, reassuring you that you were part of something bigger, that there was a game plan in operation, that the machine was doing what it said on the box. The sight now made Decker think, as it always did, of 16 June 1980: *Time* magazine, an auto-insurance coupon and a credit-card statement. He could remember his name buzz-printed on the labels, ripping the wrappers, the different gives and textures, heat-sealed polythene, buff and white paper, not knowing this was the last. As a kid he'd loved the mail: forty years later he had five apartments but not one mailbox that wasn't bolted shut.

Hour and forty. He finished up the coffee. The air-con was too noisy to operate without drawing attention to himself in the quiet, dew-wet street, so he had to crack a window, let the car warm up at the same pace as the late-June morning. The Kurtz's drapes were pulled back now, and his shape occasionally darkened the frosted glass of the en suite. Below it, the kitchen was still now, the women gone to dress. A movement to Decker's left made him take the clipboard from the passenger seat, rest it on the steering wheel, make movements with his right fist over it as though checking off a list. The sound of a car door opening gave him the opportunity to look up, make eye contact with the neighbour who was staring at him with a 'Help you?' look on his face. Decker smiled, motioned to his watch and the clipboard, a nonsense gesture, but one that made the neighbour nod, half-smile, get into his car and back out into the street. It was all in the forehead, the neck and the teeth, a PhD hired by the Kurtz had told Decker two decades before. You bounced them back at themselves, like the burglar at the dressing table closing his eyes as the head lifts from the pillow.

When the daughter's ride arrived Decker was ready to do it again, but it wasn't necessary. The driver stared at the bonnet as her Beetle chugged at the kerb; the daughter came out, greeting the street with the high-eyebrow sweep of a fitness instructor, the kind whose job entails making sure that anyone looking up from spinning gets the eye contact they need. Decker watched her closely for a moment. She was sure of her place in the world, and she was about to find out it was all shit. In twenty years' time she'd be offering what happened today as a credential to strangers at parties. Not unattractive, if you went for that type. The fact that there was a kid here didn't bother Decker, though he wouldn't have said that it was the best thing to see them immediately before. Mistresses say they never think of the wife, not the first few times; and since Decker's were strictly one-shot deals, he was never around to be reminded. As it was, the Beetle pulled away before the passenger door was even shut.

The maid arrived and the wife left with a little under an hour to go. The wife looked every inch the woman who'd been screwing her boss long-term until eight months ago and now wasn't sure where she stood. She carried a purse, a notebook case and an antiqued leather satchel; drove the black Lexus that she'd reversed into the drive the night before. The maid looked like a maid and drove a Honda. Decker slipped the seven-shot .22 from where it had been warmed by his armpit. The bore was flyweight, but a small cartridge meant less trauma in the morgue's ID room. He popped the rounds, ran the action, put them back in the order they came out. Lights came on and off as the maid worked the house. With twenty minutes to go, the drapes opened in the Kurtz's study, and Decker caught a flash of the white hand that had signed the paper that had put him in this car today, a quarter-century later. When the maid left for her next job, he opened the glove compartment, took out the cellphone he'd stolen the night before, slipped it into his pocket and opened the door.

The Kurtz was watching him as he crossed the street and strode briskly up the walk. Decker knew it, but neither man gave any sign. The lock on the front door was considerably better than standard issue, and took Decker four seconds instead of two. Inside, the smell got him, as it always did: not just the blend of floor cleaner, laundry soap and soft-furnishing decay that was unique to every house, but the smell of the two women: their skin, their hair, their cosmetics and their sex, raising Decker's pulse rate a fraction as he crossed the hall. Pre-menopause women who lived together found their cycles swinging into sync, he remembered from somewhere as he took the carpeted stairs soundlessly, two at a time. The weapon remained holstered as he crossed the landing to the Kurtz's study, unbuttoning his suit coat as he went. He was about to push open the dark-wood door when it swung open from inside, and there was Miller, there was the Kurtz, in an open-neck dress shirt and sweatpants, grinning sourly at him.

'Decker,' he said. 'Boy. I must've fucked up good to get you.'

Decker stepped into the tiny office and swept it with his eyes. He hadn't been sure how the room would be: whether the loss of control in Miller's life would be projected in an obsessive neatness of in-tray, or whether it would look as if a first-year drama student had dressed it for sophomore symbolism. Decker had seen a lot of middle-age treehouses – in a dacha on the Black Sea, in a farmhouse outside Lucca, in a Westminster pied-à-terre – and they tended to fall to either extreme. This was somewhere between the two: steel filing cabinets flanking the door, pinboards covering the walls; worktops on three sides of the room piled with paper, toolboxes, technology and bastardized kit. A pre-Celeron PC hummed beside the window opposite the door, monitor on top of the box; fixed just right so Miller's line of sight would never be wide of the street outside.

'Coffee?' Miller asked, settling into his swivel chair and gesturing to a thermal pitcher sharing space on the mouse mat. Decker didn't respond. 'Mind if I do?' He unscrewed the cap a little, poured into an oversize mug with a marlin stencilled on it. '*Salud*,' he said and raised the mug to his lips, holding eye contact over the rim, swallowed. 'Not the time-honoured shrimp platter and pie à la mode,' he said, cupping the mug in both hands, 'but like they say. Good cup of coffee – meal in itself. You sure?'

He took another sip, watching Decker over the rim. Decker shook his head.

'You look like you could use it,' Miller said, setting the mug down on a pile of fading, coffee-ringed faxes. 'You're what, forty-six?'

'Seven,' Decker said.

'You look ten years older,' said Miller, tilting his head. 'That postman of yours must think it every time he sees you.'

Decker kept his neck in line with his spine.

'Yeah, you must think it, huh? Every time you look in a mirror,' Miller went on, settling back in the leather-padded semi-recliner, finding the hollows his shoulders and buttocks had moulded already in the couple of thousand hours since he'd puzzled over the assembly instructions last Christmas. 'Never thought you'd still be working at your age, did you? Bet your postman never did either.' Miller's eyes narrowed. 'Though I bet his idea of where you'd wind up is pretty different to yours. Bet he –'

The phone cut him off. He turned to his desk, checked the caller-ID display and flinched – almost imperceptibly, but Decker saw it. It rang four more times before he picked up the receiver.

'Sweetheart?' He listened for a long moment. 'Daddy's busy, honey. Can't your mom do it?' His eyes relaxed focus to a point in space hanging in the morning air outside the window. 'How about if I call the store, give them my Visa number?' Decker could hear the girl's voice, faint but like a dry blade on a windshield. 'I see. So what's wrong with your debit card?' Miller listened, rolled his eyes. 'Okay, okay. I'll be there in a half-hour,' he said, checking his watch. 'With the money. There's only one of those stores in that mall, right? Okay. I said okay. Don't be that way. I love you.' He hung up, sat looking at the phone a moment, his hands in his lap. Then he swung round till he was almost facing Decker.

'My daughter,' he said, his expression only partially falling into line with his matter-of-fact tone. 'Her period started early, she's spotted the seat of her slacks. When this is done you're to call a cab, give the driver an envelope with seventy bucks in, have him drive it to the mall by exit 34 and deliver it to my daughter, who'll be waiting outside the Foot Locker franchise there. She'll think I'm a jerk for sending a cab, but she thinks I'm a jerk already. You want to ask, don't you.'

It wasn't a question, but Decker responded anyway. 'Ask what?'

'Whether it's been good to have a child,' Miller replied. 'I didn't have to. I could've faked infertility. I could've faked a lot of things.'

Decker held the man's steel-ball stare.

'The answer, anyway, is no,' Miller said, and broke it. 'They expect it of you – one, at least, to help fit your cover – but they give you no fucking backup whatsoever. That's her.' He nodded at a framed snapshot; the girl with the high eyebrows maybe ten years before, arms round her father's neck, grinning over his shoulder. 'But then you know that, don't you?' Miller's voice could've been giving a departmental briefing. 'Despises me. I would, if I were her. Dad who spends fourteen hours a day shut in his office. Running the precious consultancy that never makes any more than it did the year before. Or ten years before.' He took off his half-moon glasses and rubbed his eyes. Then he put them back on, looked up at Decker.

'But then we don't care, do we? We accept from the start that we drink the champagne alone, inside ourselves. It fits with how we think we ought to be. You can't anticipate how much it's gonna hurt, having your kid look at you like you're a loser, but you turn it around. You make it work for you. Up till this morning, I was even counting on it. Her –' he smiled, mouth only – 'how do we put this? Her low regard for me was what was going to take her up through the tax bands. Do better than her old dad to get back at him. But that's busted now, isn't it? You don't need to think about this, Decker, but I'm going to tell you. She's going to spend the next twenty years screwing losers to get what happened today out of her system. And then it'll be too late for her. You want to remember that? If you live that long, which frankly I doubt.'

'You had a choice,' said Decker.

'You still run yourself that line?' said Miller, disgusted. 'You know it like I do. None of us have a choice.'

'You could have chosen to follow orders.'

'I haven't had orders in twenty-five years, soldier, and you know it.' This was the old Miller, the pre-Kurtz Miller, and Decker's back straightened involuntarily.

'You're aware of what I'm referring to, sir.'

'I am, huh? Some careerist fuck calls time out, and I'm supposed to shut down my life's work overnight? Rule fucking one: you become a postman, you're on your own. The Depot wants control back, too bad. Too late. I'm on my rounds. Delivering the fucking mail, Decker. You understand me?'

'Yes, sir. But you know why I'm here.'

'I do. Certainly I do. But tell me something, doughboy. Do you?'

Decker took it, flexing his bicep against the bulge beneath it, feeling the good weapon press into his side.

'Do you, Decker?' Miller continued. 'I think I know better than you. Twenty-five years ago I told you to put a bridle on the bad thing inside you, you remember it? That thing that was fucking up your life. I told you to put it in a harness and make the sonofabitch work for you. And you did it. Yes fucking sir. You remember what it was?' He snarl-grinned. 'I don't think you do, soldier. C'mon, tell me.'

In Decker's experience, it was best to let them take the ball and run with it. They tired eventually.

'Mommy's too busy,' Miller taunted. 'And Daddy's eyes are for Jim and Jack, not Johnny. Johnny wants to play, but Daddy's in the bag . . . you know where they are now?'

'You don't have to do this with me.'

'Oh, but I do. Because you don't feel anything any more, do you? You don't feel for them because I wiped it. *I* did, and now there's just a fucking hole, Decker. And you know what? I'm not going to plug it. I'm not gonna give it back to you. It goes with me. Is that okay with you, Decker? Is that cool? Is that fucking-A, man?'

Decker stood straight and square.

'I took away a part of you and I'm not giving it back,' Miller said, eyes slotted, teeth bared. 'But I wouldn't fret, Decker. What you can't remember, you can't miss. That doesn't change where it'll take you, if you give it time. And you've given it plenty. The question is, how much longer till it's over? Is that what you ask yourself when you lie awake at night?'

'I sleep all right,' Decker said, without inflection. Miller didn't seem to hear it.

'And it isn't even your call, it's your postman's,' he said. 'What's come to me is coming to you, man. And it's coming when he says so. You ever think of that, you self-deluding shit?' Miller's eyes were bright behind his glasses. 'You ever think he might want to get out himself? He's fifty-fucking-six. You think he's going to go on for ever? Because you know they're not going to let him retire. And when they come for him, they'll come for you first.' He ran his tongue over his lower lip as though he were tasting it. 'Man, if you're thinking that having less than me means you'll have less to lose when your time comes, you're wrong,' he went on, shifting pace. 'I'm here and I know. It doesn't matter what you have, it's the same.' His eyes seemed to falter a moment, but Decker saw the man wrench control back. It wasn't good to watch: there was something left in there somewhere, but it had been pushed too far for too long. Miller's voice had dropped to a snarl. 'And it's already happening for you, Decker. The bird is on the wire. I could give you a date and a time, you sorry sack of shit. It's already *started*.' Miller held it a moment, chin down, mouth drawn back; then he laughed. It was the forced laugh of a poorly briefed guest on a shock-jock show, and Decker had to wait, skin pricking, for the silence that followed it.

'Do you have a note, sir?' he asked.

'You'd like it if I did, wouldn't you? Well, maybe I do, maybe I don't. Would you read it if I did? Say it was on this desk. Would you have the respect not to check I didn't say anything I shouldn't?'

'You ought to tell me.'

'If I had, you wouldn't find it,' said Miller, all Kurtz now. 'I watched you for an hour before you came in. I could've sent a little press release down the wire. Set some Bernstein on the start of the trail. Not much of a victory, but you find them where you can.' His voice had lifted, but Decker – whose ear had been tutored for such things – could hear the fight going out of it. The Kurtz seemed to sense it in himself; his teeth glistened. 'Where do you find your victories, Decker?' he spat.

The answer pulsed through twenty years, from one of Miller's own far-off tutorials.

'Where we always did, sir,' Decker answered, taking out the .22. 'In the absence of defeat.' He took two steps towards the seated man and offered him the weapon grip-first. The Kurtz took the little gun, weighed it in his hands a moment. Then he thumbed off the safety and raised his arm.

'You know there's no note,' he said and grinned. Decker ducked his head sharply, turning away. When it was done he reached into his breast pocket for a plain white sachet, tore it open and took out a pre-moistened towelette. He took the gun by the muzzle, finger and thumb, and wiped it down. Then he put it back in Miller's hand, dialed 911 on the stolen cellphone and reported the sound of gunshots at 237 Riverhead Drive. When the operator asked him who he was, he snapped the phone shut. It wasn't until he was out on the freeway and opening the Acura's window to toss it that he remembered the daughter, the seventy dollars, the Foot Locker store. He considered it a moment, then let the lightweight Motorola fall from his hand into the slipstream. Maybe it would do her good. She wasn't going to have the best day, anyway.

Fourth of July. Decker sat in the grey space of his Detroit apartment. A recliner and a TV were the only furniture in the room, positioned in line with the window so that Decker could see the entrance to the building without getting up.

The TV gave off a hot-wire smell. The woman on the screen said 'I need to pee' and moved her hand faster. Decker sat in front of her, sipping a Cuba Libre, his one drink of the year. His eyes focused on a point three feet beyond the screen.

'The wife put the house on the market,' the Postman said. 'Waited three days, then went to Cancun, left the keys with the realtors. Daughter's with her.'

Decker wondered how much the Postman's own house was worth. He'd never seen it, didn't know where it was, but he knew it would be a lot. Postmen's houses were their insurance policies, because if a postman died with his boots on, chances were it'd be suicide. Especially when it wasn't.

'It was a nice place,' Decker said.

'God bless the suburbs,' said the Postman. 'Room to maneuver. You catch that new John Woo tape? Helicopters and gas tanks and office blocks exploding.' He ticked them off on his fingers. 'Somebody should tell Hollywood where the shit of the last forty years really went down. Behind dwarf columns and carriage lamps, on streets called Greenacres and Fairlawne. Save them a lot of dough.'

'You didn't call me out here to debrief me on a Kurtz,' Decker said.

'I didn't,' said the Postman, and signalled through the windshield to the driver of his idling Lincoln, parked nose to nose with Decker's truck. Behind it was a boarded-up diner with 24–7 WE NEVER CLOSE in six-foot neon letters, turned off. The Lincoln reversed slowly, then snuffled away on heavy treads to join the backup car blocking the truck-stop access ramp.

'Did he mention me?' the Postman said. He might have been asking after an ex.

'He made the most of his fifteen minutes,' said Decker.

The Postman looked round sharply. 'What's the thing you have that he doesn't?'

'A heartbeat,' Decker said.

'Don't you forget it.'

'You didn't call me out here to debrief me on a Kurtz.'

The Postman stared straight ahead a moment. Decker followed his line of sight. This was his sixth meeting in two decades with the man who controlled his life, and he was hoping for a reward, a survey-and-set-up, maybe; something to get his teeth into, to take away the taste.

'There's no good way to put this,' the Postman said, and for a second Decker looked to the positioned cars with something worse than panic. No exit, except feet first. But he would have seen that coming; and then he saw what it was.

'A contender?' he said, with something close to wonder. The Postman looked away. 'You got a name?'

The Postman shook his head almost imperceptibly. 'But we wouldn't be here if I wasn't sure.'

'How serious?'

The Postman turned back to face him for a second. 'Did you hear what I just said?'

Decker looked away.

'You want a cigarette?' said the Postman. 'I have a pack in the glovebox out there.'

Decker shook his head, irritated. The Postman twisted his pinkie ring while he waited for the other man to speak, fooling with the weird grey stone set aslant in heavy gold.

'So which?' said Decker. 'Revenge? Pre-emptive? A rival?'

'I bid on a big Miami gun shill last summer; no take-up, and two months later he ODs. Okay. Then February I bid for a Korean trader, washing yen through San Francisco. Guess the rest.'

'What do you think? I mean, really.'

'We don't rule anything out. But get this: I bought the autopsy tapes. They were suicides.'

'Then he's a player,' Decker said. 'So where?'

'Wherever you go.'

'Do I get a team?'

'I'm sorry,' the Postman said. 'I'll do what I can otherwise. But at this stage he could be after closing me down too. I commit men in the field with you, it's making his job easier.'

'You have a lot of faith in me.'

The Postman looked him in the eye. 'John, I have faith in you doing what you do.'

Decker looked down.

'You're welcome,' said the Postman dryly. 'Is there anything else?'

'I guess not. I'll need the usual arrangements.'

'The new drops are as follows.' The Postman reeled off a list of grid references – the location of bridges, trash cans, ducts and culverts in seven North American cities – and Decker jotted them down into the palm of his hand.

'Why don't you take an extra fifty?' the Postman said when he was done.

'I got forty Gs two months ago.'

'I have it here.'

'When I need, I'll ask.'

The Postman looked over sharply. 'For what it's worth, everyone that matters wants to see you come out of this,' he said.

Decker registered that, stored it away. It mattered. For twenty years the Postman's job had been a three-hander: to feed Decker work; to be his eyes and ears so the man could sleep at night; and to persuade all interested parties that Decker was worth more to them alive than dead. If he hadn't done the last, he would have become as dispensable as Decker swiftly after. But that didn't change the way it was between them.

'I think the home stadium,' Decker said.

'Good man.'

'But no cities. The rolling road.'

'Of course.'

'Not till I have the sheet on him that he has on me.'

'You'll be the first. As and when.'

There was an awkward silence that, if they hadn't been in the Life, they might've filled with sports. But once the Life was in you, guy talk could give away where you lived, where you came from. You never did it. Decker searched his mind for something to take it down.

'Tell me,' he asked. 'You know I don't smoke cigarettes. But you always offer me one. You always tell me there's a pack in the glovebox.'

The Postman looked out the windshield. 'I knew a guy on death row once, three-packs-a-day man,' he said. 'You can smoke as much as you want there. You're locked down twenty-three hours a day, there's nothing else to do, but most guys still quit there. As did mine. Everyone knows, the ones who keep smoking don't get the last-minute call from the governor. Deep down, they don't expect to.'

'I never smoked,' said Decker.

The Postman glanced to his own car. 'One thing you learn, you work with people their whole life,' he said, 'is that they change. Even when they think they can't.' He leaned over to the steering column, flashed the headlights once: the Lincoln began rolling towards them almost instantaneously. The Postman looked back over his shoulder at Decker, one hand on the door release.

'I don't change,' said Decker.

'Then let's put the world back how it was,' said the Postman.

And Decker got the full taste of how it was now. 'Yes, sir,' he said.

'You know where I am,' said the Postman and got out.

Decker watched him walk across the hot asphalt to his car, a man in Nikes and a sixty-dollar sports shirt, a man who might once have been an athlete, a man you might mistake for a film-school professor were it not for the set of his shoulders. And that pinkie ring. The Lincoln's rear door was opened from inside, and he got in; one car followed the other, textbook-style, back to the highway; and then there was just Decker, the deserted truck stop and the dead neon, silhouetted against the boundless sky.